DYING
TO MARRY

*Also by Janelle Taylor
in Large Print:*

Don't Go Home
Night Moves
By Candlelight
Love With a Stranger
Not Without You
Savage Ecstasy

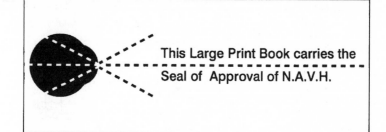

This Large Print Book carries the
Seal of Approval of N.A.V.H.

DYING
TO MARRY

JANELLE
TAYLOR

Thorndike Press • Waterville, Maine

Copyright © 2004 by Janelle Taylor

Published in 2005 by arrangement with Kensington Books, an imprint of Kensington Publishing Corp.

Thorndike Press® Large Print Core.

The tree indicium is a trademark of Thorndike Press.

The text of this Large Print edition is unabridged.
Other aspects of the book may vary from the original edition.

Set in 16 pt. Plantin.

Printed in the United States on permanent paper.

Library of Congress Cataloging-in-Publication Data

Taylor, Janelle.
    Dying to marry / by Janelle Taylor.
      p. cm.
    ISBN 0-7862-7452-2 (lg. print : hc : alk. paper)
    1. Private investigators — Fiction. 2. Rich people —
Fiction. 3. Weddings — Fiction. 4. Cousins — Fiction.
5. Large type books. I. Title.
PS3570.A934D95 2005
  813′.54—dc22   2004030244

Dedicated to
my newest and third grandson,
Ean Michael Joseph MacIntyre

As the Founder/CEO of NAVH, the only national health agency solely devoted to those who, although not totally blind, have an eye disease which could lead to serious visual impairment, I am pleased to recognize Thorndike Press* as one of the leading publishers in the large print field.

Founded in 1954 in San Francisco to prepare large print textbooks for partially seeing children, NAVH became the pioneer and standard setting agency in the preparation of large type.

Today, those publishers who meet our standards carry the prestigious "Seal of Approval" indicating high quality large print. We are delighted that Thorndike Press is one of the publishers whose titles meet these standards. We are also pleased to recognize the significant contribution Thorndike Press is making in this important and growing field.

Lorraine H. Marchi, L.H.D.
Founder/CEO
NAVH

* Thorndike Press encompasses the following imprints: Thorndike, Wheeler, Walker and Large Print Press.

PROLOGUE

Never before had a wedding invitation wreaked so much havoc in a small town. There were gasps. Confusion. Screams.

One elderly woman had to reach for her heart medication.

A young man crumpled up the lovely invitation and burned it on his stove.

A grown woman threw a temper tantrum and ripped it up into tiny pieces.

Two hundred and twenty-five invitations had been sent out. And there were two hundred and twenty-five similar reactions. Scorn. Ridicule. Disbelief, mostly. All around town, people were having the same conversation.

"There's no way it's a real invitation."

"Maybe it's one of those joke events where you bring the ugliest girl or biggest loser to the dance!"

"It's an awfully expensive joke — the paper and vellum and gold embossing must have cost a fortune."

"Please — those two engaged to be married? No way."

"Omigod — now I know why he's been so unavailable — he's been with *her!*"

"I'll bet she's pregnant!"

"His mother must be hyperventilating!"

"His father must be turning over in his grave."

"You go, girl!" (There was only one of those.)

In another house, there was anger. Red-hot anger. "Engaged?" seethed its occupant, stabbing at the invitation over and over on the kitchen table with a steak knife. "One of you will be dead before you're ever wed. I'll see to that."

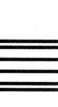

BUSINESS REPLY MAIL

FIRST-CLASS MAIL   PERMIT NO. 184   APPLETON, WI

POSTAGE WILL BE PAID BY ADDRESSEE

ATTN: CUSTOMER RESPONSE CENTER
THRIVENT
4321 N BALLARD RD
APPLETON WI 54913-9850

26062 R5-21

Getting your 2022 Thrivent calendar is easy

People like you have shared images and reflections on what helps them bring their purpose into focus. Now this unique calendar is available to pre-order for a limited time.

Visit thrivent.com/calendar or mail this reply card by **July 31, 2021**. We'll mail your calendar in late September.

thrivent

THE TRIPLETT HOUSEHOLD
240 OLD ADOBE RD
LOS GATOS CA 95032-1653

CHAPTER ONE

An elderly woman wearing pink sweats and white satin shoes with three-inch heels was practicing her dance moves on the sidewalk in front of her house. A shimmy. A shallow dip, despite the fact that no one was dipping her. A twirl. And then her own version of the classic John Travolta move from *Saturday Night Fever*. Ellie Finnaman pointed her right arm high in the air, then reached it down to her hip and laughed.

"That was great, Miss Ellie!" Holly Morrow called from her seat on the top step of her house, next door to Ellie's.

Miss Ellie Finnaman, seventy-six-year-old bride-to-be, was breaking in her shoes for her wedding tomorrow, and a small crowd of neighbors and the postman had stopped to cheer her on. Some joined her in the Seventies-era moves; others started singing "Night Fever."

"See, Holly, dear, I told you I'd show these shoes how to boogie up," Ellie called, twirling around, her hands high in the air.

"That's 'boogie *down*,' Miss Ellie," Holly

called back. She laughed. Holly was Ellie's self-appointed worrywart. The elderly woman refused to worry about tripping or breaking a leg. Ellie insisted that her groom, eighty-year-old Herbert Walker, would catch her if she fell. "And you were right. I worried for nothing. Those heels are high, but you're as steady on your feet as you were yesterday in your pink sneakers. You'd think you wore three-inch-high heels every day."

Ellie laughed and began shimmying up the street. The neighbors cheered as she twirled and then grabbed the handsome mail carrier for a partner.

"Miss Ellie, if you'll dance me to Holly," the mail carrier said, a few pieces of mail in hand, "I can get in a dance and do my job at the same time."

Miss Ellie grinned and tangoed the man up the walkway to Holly. "Ooh, Holly, that big envelope in Michael's hand looks like an invitation to something fancy, like a wedding!"

The mail carrier handed Holly a catalog and two envelopes, one of which was a bill and the other of which was indeed some kind of invitation; then he tipped his hat at Miss Ellie and headed back to his cart. Ellie continued her tango, solo, along the grass between her and Holly's houses, but she was headed straight for her own prized azalea patch.

Please don't fall. Please don't fall. Please don't fall, Holly prayed to the fates of the universe. "Eyes on the ground, Miss Ellie!" Holly called.

"And miss the world going round?" Ellie shouted back with a grin as she barely missed decapitating a beautiful flower. "No, thanks." She twirled back over to Holly and eyed the outsized envelope in Holly's hand. "Yes, that is definitely a wedding invitation, dear. My, what lovely calligraphy — in gold, no less! And what heavyweight paper this is. Friend of yours?"

Holly glanced at the envelope and shook her head. "You're the only bride-to-be I know, Miss Ellie." As the woman practiced a curtsy, her foot slipping perilously close to Holly's thorny roses, Holly slipped the envelope into her purse. "Careful, Miss Ellie!"

The woman smiled and waved dismissively. "Not to worry, dear. Besides, the wedding isn't in our yards or on the sidewalk — it's at the boring senior center. You couldn't slip and fall in that place if you tried."

Holly laughed. "You've got me there."

Still, the formal dining room at the town senior center, despite all its wall railings and soft surfaces, did not have a rubber floor. And with all the tables, chairs, and dancing people to bump into, Miss Ellie couldn't be too careful. Especially in those ridiculous heels.

Holly was so excited about the wedding tomorrow. The staff at the center — where Ellie's fiancé Herbert lived, and Ellie volunteered (that was how they met) — was decking the halls for the nuptials. Holly was so happy for Ellie and Herbert, both of whom she adored. Miss Ellie, who'd been Holly's neighbor since Holly had moved to the large town ten years ago, was very much a mother figure, which Holly welcomed as her own mother lived so far away in Florida. And Herbert — smart, kind, gallant Herbert — was very much like Holly's own father and reminded her every day of the qualities she wanted in her own husband . . . if she ever had a husband, that was.

A boyfriend, even.

Holly sighed. *When was my last* date? she asked herself.

Two months ago. And it had been a disaster. Miss Ellie and Herbert had fixed

12

her up with the grandson of a man in Herbert's bridge circle. The grandson had reported back that Holly couldn't have seemed less interested in him.

That wasn't entirely true. Not false, but not true. Okay, she hadn't been attracted to her date from the get-go, but he'd talked nonstop — about himself — and buzzed in her ear during the movie they'd seen, a violent action film Holly couldn't even bear to watch. And he looked at her lasciviously, his eyes lingering on her breasts as though he wanted her to know he found her sexually appealing from the moment she opened her front door. She'd felt uncomfortable in his presence their entire date.

She's too proper for me, the guy had reported to his grandfather, who'd shared it with the entire bridge group. *Cares too much about manners and what people think of her. So what if I belched at dinner and knocked over my water glass? She was so embarrassed! Holly really needs to loosen up.*

Loosen up. Holly knew she couldn't be classified as uptight — well, maybe on dates with guys who thought belching on a first date was hilarious — but no one would ever call her a free spirit, either.

And she did care what people thought of her. She always had and she always would.

13

She had her own mind, of course, and she was no one's pushover or fool, but she did take care to project a certain image, and she supposed that *prim,* unfortunately, did seem an apt word to describe that image.

A familiar tightening in her chest forced her eyes closed. She willed away the memories of Troutville, New Jersey, where she'd grown up. *I'm far, far away from there,* she told herself. *Far away from that place and people's opinions of me.*

In Troutville, you were what people said you were.

"Ooh, it's almost five o'clock!" Ellie said. She was working on her John Travolta moves by the rosebush. "I don't want to miss the early bird special at the Rosebud Grill. Herbert's taking me there for our last dinner as a courting couple."

"Miss Ellie, I thought the groom wasn't supposed to see the bride before the wedding," Holly said teasingly.

Ellie wagged her finger. "Dear, Herbert and I are a bit too old to wait for *anything.*"

Holly burst out laughing. "That's all right, Miss Ellie. Anyway, I think it's only before the ceremony *tomorrow* that Herbert isn't supposed to see you."

"Oh, too bad," Ellie said. "I love to break traditions. I've already broken the big one of waiting for the wedding night!"

Holly burst out laughing again and shook her head. Miss Ellie was absolutely wonderful. She was also a little hard of hearing and tended to shout, which meant everyone on the block now knew that Miss Ellie, confirmed bachelorette for sixty years, was no virgin.

As their neighbors cheered and clapped and laid hands over their hearts and went on their way, Holly watched Ellie walk a la the "Wedding March" to her own house. "Have a good time, Miss Ellie. I'll see you bright and early tomorrow to help you dress."

"Thank you, dear. Will you come by at seven? The gang should all be over by nine, and I'd love to have some time to get ready with just the two of us."

"Seven, it is," Holly called.

Miss Ellie, with no children, grandchildren, nieces or nephews, managed to have quite a network of friends of all ages. Neighbors and people from the various places at which she volunteered loved her dearly. Miss Ellie attended more family functions than just about anyone Holly knew.

It was very comforting for Holly to see that one could be single their entire life,

15

never have children, and live a very happy and fulfilling life. Miss Ellie had so many interests and she was so happy and she had wonderful friends. Holly was very single and had been for a long time. She was twenty-eight and had never been married, never even been close.

As the tiny, elderly woman climbed the two steps up to the porch and then headed inside her house, Holly's own feet hurt just watching her walk in those heels. She kicked off her pumps to massage her insteps.

Holly took the invitation out of her purse and studied the envelope. It was addressed in beautiful dark gold calligraphy. She slit open the heavyweight envelope, lined with gold foil. *Who do I know who's getting married?* she wondered. None of her relatives or girlfriends were engaged. The invitation must be for something else.

Oh, Lord — please tell me it's not to my ten-year high school reunion, Holly thought, now eyeing the envelope with dread. A couple of weeks ago, her cousin Lizzie, who still lived in Troutville, had mentioned seeing posters all over town for the reunion.

Holly would not be attending.

Despite the warm August weather, she shivered at even the thought of Troutville High School.

16

None too gently, she pulled out the contents of the envelope. Inside was another envelope, inside which was a very fancy invitation. It was a wedding invitation. Curious, Holly read the first line — and burst out laughing.

A belly laugh sent long distance from her cousin Lizzie was just what Holly needed after the long, hard day she'd had at work and the long, hard night she faced ahead of baking and decorating Ellie's wedding cake.

As Holly read the first line of the invitation again, she had to slap her hand over her mouth to suppress another round of giggles.

You are cordially invited to witness the wedding of Lizbeth Morrow and Dylan Dunhill III . . .

Holly chuckled as she read the rest of the invitation, then ran inside to call "Lizbeth," aka Lizzie Morrow. Lizzie, her twenty-eight-year-old cousin (the daughter of Holly's father's only brother), was the funniest person Holly had ever known. Creating a phony invitation to her wedding to the last man on earth Lizzie would ever marry was up there with her cousin's best jokes.

It had been two weeks since the cousins

17

had last spoken, and Holly was hungry for Lizzie's voice, exuberance and comical stories about what was going on in Troutville, where they'd grown up together. Holly wasn't fond of the small, gossipy town; to say that she hated even the thought of Troutville wasn't overstating her feelings, but her cousin and aunt lived there, as did Holly's oldest and dearest girlfriends, and a small part of Holly's heart was still untouched by all the pain she associated with the town. A very small part, but a part, nonetheless.

Holly couldn't wait to hear what was going on in Lizzie's life, who she was dating, what was happening with their friends Gayle and Flea, how Lizzie's mother was doing, how business was at the bar that her mother owned (and where Lizzie was a waitress). Holly and Lizzie hadn't been able to talk much or for long during the past few months. Holly's job as a high school English teacher kept her away from a telephone all day, and her hobby — which was turning into a true side job — of making specialty cakes for weddings and catered parties was keeping her too covered in flour and icing to get to the telephone at night. And Lizzie, serial dater, barmaid and budding photographer for the *Troutville Gazette*, had a full plate herself.

A long, much-needed conversation with her terrific cousin was just what the doctor ordered, and luckily, Lizzie was home. She answered on the first ring.

"Lizbeth, dear," Holly intoned in an upper-crust accent, "I simply wouldn't miss your wedding to Mr. Dunhill for the *world*. Tell me, dear, will you be wearing a Vera Wang custom gown or a Chanel?" She laughed. "Oh, Lizzie, you don't know how badly I needed a good joke. Today was one of those days. My boss, Principal Eggers, has been so —"

"Holly, honey, it isn't a joke," Lizzie interrupted. "I *am* getting married."

"Of course you are, *Lizbeth*," Holly droned, still in her lofty accent. "To Mr. Dylan Dunhill, who wouldn't deign to speak to a Morrow if he ran over one with his Mercedes!"

No, that wasn't quite accurate — the Dunhills *had* spoken to a few Morrows in their long history of living in the same small town; after all, the matriarch of Dunhill Mansion had to give orders to her maids, and two Morrows had worked in that stately colonial up on Dunhill Place.

Holly tossed the invitation on the

kitchen table, shook her head and smiled. "Lizzie, you are too funny! So what's going on? How's your mom? And Gayle and Flea?"

There was dead silence on the other end. "Lizzie?"

"Holly, the invitation isn't a joke," Lizzie said. "I really am marrying Dylan."

Now there was silence on Holly's end. Lizzie sounded very serious. Holly waited a moment for Lizzie's *Ha, Gotcha!*

But it never came.

"Holly, things have changed," Lizzie said. "Big time. I know the invitation must come as a major shock, but it's true. I'm getting married. To Dylan."

Okay, wait a minute. Lizzie wasn't kidding? This invitation wasn't a joke that Lizzie had made on her computer in the back office at the bar?

"Oh, Holly-Molly," Lizzie continued, using the pet name she'd given Holly when they were five. "Me, Lizzie Morrow, a bride-to-be! A big church wedding and a fancy reception hall and everything! It's just like I always dreamed — like *we* always dreamed!"

As Lizzie went on without a breath about gowns and floral arrangements and caterers, and whether or not a local

Troutville band could do justice to Céline Dion, her favorite singer, Holly sank back into the chair, unable to process the very simple information she was receiving. Her cousin was getting married? And to a Dunhill?

Okay, I'm Holly van Winkle, and I've been asleep for twenty years, and things in Troutville, New Jersey, have changed. Morrows aren't dirt poor and looked down upon. Dunhills aren't wealthy beyond belief and downright mean. Lizzie and Dylan have been dating for a couple of years and he proposed and she accepted and they're getting married, in the wedding that Lizzie has always dreamed of.

Only it wasn't possible. Troutville would never change. Dunhills would never change. And Lizzie couldn't have changed so much in the month since Holly had last seen her that she was suddenly a completely different person, a person who mingled with the Dunhill crowd and had fallen in love with one.

The last time Holly had spoken to Lizzie, her cousin wasn't even *dating* anyone. In fact, Lizzie, who usually dated a different guy every weekend, had said she'd taken herself off the market and that she was concentrating on her photography.

And that was only two weeks ago! Granted, Lizzie was spontaneous and impulsive, but she wasn't crazy. Nor was she one to take love lightly.

Yet somehow, as evidenced by the wedding invitation in Holly's hand, Lizzie and Dylan had fallen madly in love in a few weeks' time, he'd proposed, she'd accepted, and she was now planning a wedding — three weeks from this Saturday.

Three weeks. Who got married after dating someone for two weeks and then rushed into marrying him? Who got married after five weeks? Celebrities, maybe. Then again, Lizzie's husband-to-be *was* something of a celebrity, in Troutville, New Jersey, at least.

"*Mrs. Lizbeth Dunhill,*" Lizzie breathed into the phone on a sigh. "Oh, Holly, doesn't that sound so fancy? Me, a Dunhill! Can you believe it?"

No, I can't. I really can't. This makes no sense!

Holly glanced down at the invitation, at the flowery gold type on the cream paper. *You are cordially invited to witness the marriage* . . . She wasn't surprised that the parents of the bride and groom were not mentioned on the invitation.

As Lizzie continued on about the particular shade of dark blue of Dylan's eyes, the cleft in his chin and his "adorable toes," Holly shot up from the chair.

"You're pregnant," Holly blurted out. "That's what this is about."

There was silence on the other end for a few moments. "Holly, I expect that kind of talk from just about everyone," Lizzie said quietly, "but not from you. Never from you."

Guilt hit Holly in the stomach. "I'm sorry, honey," she said. "I'm just shocked, that's all." *Are you pregnant?* Holly wondered. *And would Dylan really marry you because you were? Doubtful.*

I don't get any of this! Holly thought crazily. *The world was perfectly normal the second before I opened the invitation!*

"I am so happy!" Lizzie exclaimed with her characteristic inability to remain angry with anyone — especially her cousin — for longer than ten seconds. "So, so happy. I've never felt this way before, Holly. Like my heart could just burst with how in love I am, how happy I am."

Holly took a deep breath. Lizzie deserved to be happy; she'd never had it easy.

But a marriage to Dylan Dunhill was absurd.

"Holly, I'm sorry I didn't mention that

23

Dylan and I were dating, let alone that we'd gotten so serious about each other, but I guess I wanted to keep the relationship to myself since I knew how everyone would react."

"How long were you dating before he proposed?" Holly asked. "And how *did* everyone react? What did your mom say?"

"Ooh, there's the doorbell," Lizzie said. "It's the florist with samples."

Convenient, Holly thought. *What does Aunt Louise think of the relationship? Of having Dylan Dunhill as a son-in-law? Of having Victoria Dunhill as an in-law? The very idea was preposterous!*

"Oh, and Hol, the bridal party is going to meet next weekend to shop for my gown and bridesmaids dresses," Lizzie said. "Do you believe we have an appointment at Bettina's Bridal salon? Only the most expensive dress shop in town! Dylan told me to spare no expense for our wedding. Holly, you can come dress shopping, can't you? I especially made our appointment for next weekend because I know summer school will be over for you by then and maybe you could even stay with me until the wedding. Oh, Holly, that would mean the world to me. There's so much to do and hardly any time! And you will be my maid of honor, won't you? I didn't even think to ask — I just assumed!"

Holly took a deep breath. "Of course, I'll be your maid on honor, Lizzie. I'd do anything for you. You know that." *But stay in Troutville for three weeks? Could I do that?* Holly wasn't sure she could stomach Troutville for a half hour, let alone three weeks.

"I do know that," Lizzie said. "And the most important thing you can do for me is be happy for me. I know the sudden marriage must be quite a surprise, but Dylan and I are so happy together and we want to be married. We want to spend the rest of our lives together. He is so wonderful, Holly! I can't wait for you to get to know him."

I could, Holly thought, then chastised herself. She owed Lizzie respect.

"Did you get an invitation to the class reunion the weekend after next?" Lizzie asked. "I was, um, thinking of maybe going."

O-kay, Holly thought. *Now I know I'm hearing things. My cousin couldn't have possibly said she was actually going to our ten-year high school reunion. Voluntarily.*

"And since you'll be in town," Lizzie continued, "we could all go. The whole

25

gang — me, you, Gayle, Flea. And Dylan, too, of course."

Of course. Because Dylan Dunhill always accompanied our gang, Holly thought sarcastically.

"Lizzie, I don't know about the reunion . . ."

"Well, we'll see, then," Lizzie said. "I'm just so excited you're coming! I can't wait to see you, Holly-Molly. It's been way too long and there's so much I have to tell you."

Such as how you and Dylan ever got to talking, let alone dating or marrying.

"Oh, Holly," Lizzie said, "I know it all must sound so strange to you, but love is love. It's about caring and sharing and happiness — it's not about who your family is or where you grew up."

It was in Troutville.

"I can't wait to tell the gang you're coming!" Lizzie exclaimed. "Flea asks after you all the time, Holly. She's missed you so much. Gayle, too. They're going to be so excited!"

Holly smiled as the image of Gayle, with her long red hair and movie-star smile, and Flea, with her pretty blue eyes and trademark black silk scarf around her neck, came to mind. "It'll be great to see them,"

Holly said, and she meant it. She hadn't seen her old friends in way too long. "And it'll be great to see you, too, Lizzie. No one's missed anyone as much as I've missed you."

After promises to arrive promptly on the ten a.m. train next Saturday, Holly and Lizzie said their good-byes, Holly clamping her mouth around the many questions she had. And with a shake of her head to clear her mind of Troutville and Dylan and Lizzie's impending marriage, Holly headed into the kitchen to start baking a masterpiece for the one wedding in her future that did make perfect sense.

"You have a safe trip now, Holly-girl."

Holly set down her suitcase on the train platform and gave Ellie and her new husband of one week a kiss each on the cheek. "Thanks for seeing me off, you two."

Herbert wrapped Holly in a hug. "There's nothing like going home for a visit," he said. "Nothing like it at all."

Unless you're me and headed to Troutville, Holly thought. *And Troutville isn't home.*

"Then again, home for me for the past few years was the senior center, and I much prefer my new home at Miss Ellie's," Herbert added. "She's a much better cook

— and much better-looking — than those busybodies at the center."

Ellie playfully swatted at Herbert. "Look, dear, your train is coming."

The train rumbled into the station, and Holly took a deep breath. This was one time she wouldn't have minded if the train had been late.

"Well, you two just behave yourselves while I'm away," Holly told them with a smile.

Herbert swept Ellie up in his arms and very slowly spun her around. "Oh, we will, Holly, dear," he said. "Behave like twenty-one-year-old newlyweds!"

Holly laughed, hugged and kissed the couple, then boarded the train. She settled herself into a window seat, then turned to wave good-bye to Ellie and Herbert, but the sweet, elderly duo were doing a little slow dance on the platform. As Holly watched Herbert dip Ellie — as he'd done at least twenty times at their reception last weekend, she wondered about Lizzie and Dylan Dunhill — as she'd done at least a hundred times since Lizzie's bombshell. She could not imagine the two of them talking, let alone dancing. Kissing. Doing anything, for that matter. Lizzie and Dylan.

She had so many questions, questions that had been bouncing in her mind all week long. She'd been tempted to call Lizzie for answers, but Lizzie did sound happy, very happy, and Holly could not and would not give her cousin the third degree. Lizzie had always been very open with Holly, and she'd chosen to keep her relationship and engagement to Dylan a secret for a reason.

Because I reacted exactly the way she feared, Holly thought.

She owed Lizzie better than that, but the idea of Lizzie and Dylan engaged, planning a wedding, planning a *life,* was simply unbelievable. When did they start dating? How did his parents feel about the relationship? About the marriage? And what did Lizzie's mother think of all this? Louise Morrow couldn't possibly be pleased.

Then again, perhaps Holly was being silly. Perhaps no one blinked an eye over the romance, over the announcement of the engagement. Perhaps Holly had been away from Troutville for so long that things *had* changed. Perhaps "Down Hill" now simply referred to the area of Troutville behind the railroad tracks, down the enormous hill from "Troutville proper" as the residents liked to refer to it. The railroad station, two bars, including one that hid a strip club in a back room, a truck stop, and an all-night grocery, made up Down Hill, which was populated by the folks who either owned or operated the businesses (though the strip club was patronized by the folks who lived up the hill). When Holly was growing up, Down Hill had been synonymous with downtrodden. With seedy. With less than. Up Hill, as the residents of Down Hill called it, was full of bank presidents and Fortune 500 chairmen and PTA leaders and debutantes. The difference between Up Hill and Down Hill was night and day. Money and none.

Here comes Holly the Whore and Lay Me Lizzie and Good Time Gayle and Filthy Flea, the other kids would whisper — or shout — when the girls ventured Up Hill. And venture Up Hill they had to, since school and church and the shopping district were there.

Holly hadn't stepped foot in Troutville in ten years, since she graduated from high school and earned enough money by the end of that summer to help her parents afford a condo in Florida, where they'd always dreamed of living. Their branch of the Morrow family had finally bid

Troutville good-bye. But Lizzie and her mother, like Gayle and Flea, had inexplicably stayed. *We won't be chased out of our home, our town, by people we don't care a hoot about,* Lizzie's mother and father would say.

But they had to care. How could they not? How did stares and leers and jeers and rumors and stories ever roll off your back?

Holly the Whore. The first time Holly had heard herself called that, by a boy in Dylan Dunhill's crowd, it hadn't registered. She hadn't understood. But by the tenth time, she'd understood that she'd gone from ignored thirteen-year-old to infamous thirteen-year-old. At thirteen and never-been-kissed, Holly Morrow had been called a whore — for what she hadn't done — and the label had stuck, despite the fact that she'd graduated from high school a virgin.

Jake Boone's sweet seventeen-year-old face came into mind. *"It doesn't matter what people say you are, Holly. It only matters who you know you are,"* Jake would say over and over. *"Screw them!"* he'd add vehemently, slamming a fist down on the table or the ground. "One day, when I'm a cop, I'm going to catch one of them spitting on the sidewalk or tossing a gum wrapper into

31

the street or jaywalking, and I'm going to arrest them and throw them in jail!"

Jake Boone. It had been ten long years since she'd seen him, but not since she'd thought about him. What she'd said the last night she saw him, prom night, still shamed her, still caused her to suck in her breath at how misguided she'd been. She wondered where he was now, what he was doing. If he still had to constantly push his thick dark hair out of his eyes. He'd had aspirations of being a cop like his father and grandfather, and Holly wondered if that dream had come true.

As the train began to pull away, Holly waved good-bye to Ellie and Herbert, who stood with one arm around each other and one arm waving at Holly. At times like this, crazy times, when the world didn't seem to make sense, Holly would long for her own partner, a husband. But in the past ten years, since living on her own, Holly hadn't really connected with anyone, even though she'd met much nicer men than the belcher. Once, she'd overheard a few teachers talking about her in the teachers' lounge at school; they were surprised that "such a pretty woman" had no life to speak of or that the male teachers weren't beating down her classroom door for a date. One of the women sitting at the table had said it was because Holly was *prickly* — that was the exact word she'd used — a little standoffish; not so much with women, but with men, as though she didn't trust them. *She must have gotten hurt real bad once,* added the woman. *More than once,* probably, said another. *And that'll do it,* the third woman had put in.

Yes, that'll do it, Holly thought. What she wouldn't give to feel someone's strong arm around her shoulder. Someone to share things with, be with. Someone who'd see through the prickly attitude, the false primness, the veneer of tailored, conservative clothes.

The way Jake Boone used to, she thought, leaning back against the headrest. For a few minutes, Holly let herself think of Jake, those dark blue eyes framed by dark, dark lashes, his voice, deep for a boy of seventeen, his muscular arm slung over her shoulder in friendship.

At least Jake Boone won't be in Troutville this weekend, Holly thought. She had no doubt that he'd hightailed it out of town the moment he could, just as she'd had, and that he'd never looked back, just as she hadn't.

You are *looking back, Holly,* she realized.

CHAPTER TWO

The cloying scent of whatever awful perfumes Pru Dunhill and Arianna Miller wore hit Jake Boone full in the face as he stepped onto the outdoor platform at the Troutville train station. *Stop. Turn back. Run!* he warned himself, but it was no use. A client's train was due in at nine-thirty, and Jake had promised to meet the man on the platform. Besides, it was too late; Pru and Arianna had spotted him.

"Why, if it isn't Jake Boone in the flesh," Pru said, her thin, pink-glossed lips stretched into a smile.

Why Pru Dunhill couldn't speak like a normal person was beyond Jake. She was always saying things like, *Why, Jake Boone, I do declare that you're looking very handsome today.* Her brother Dylan, who had become one of Jake's best friends after graduation, had told Jake that their mother had encouraged Pru from birth to conduct all conversations as though she were being interviewed on stage for the Miss America pageant. Pru had clearly listened to her mother. And decided that she was representing a southern state rather than New Jersey.

She smoothed her long, wavy blond hair. "Arianna and I are waiting for the train from New York City. We have a girlfriend coming in for the weekend." She suddenly dropped the stack of magazines in her arms. "Oops. Arianna, didn't I say I shouldn't try to carry so many magazines? But that's me, always striving to do more than I possibly can."

Jake had to restrain himself from bursting out laughing at the absurdity of that. Pru went from the beauty salon to the movies to a friend's house to a restaurant, and that was about the extent of her daily achievements.

Arianna nodded at Pru and toyed with one of her light brown ringlets. "Jake, I always tell Pru she has way too much on her plate, but will she listen? No, no, no, she just keeps on, helping, helping, helping. She absolutely insisted on meeting the train this morning to collect our friends herself instead of sending her family's driver. I tell you, Pru is going to make someone an incredible wife, Jake. Why, she's willing to do absolutely anything to make the world a better place. Imagine what she'd do for her own husband!"

Jake would really rather not. With a silent sigh, he bent down to pick up the magazines for Pru, as he always did. Whenever they ran into each other, Pru dropped whatever she was carrying, Arianna went on and on about her attributes, and both women waited for Jake to kneel before Pru and admire her legs, her body, her femininity.

And granted, she had a body to admire. Slender, yet curvy, with long legs always enhanced by heels and a dress that whished around just above her knees, Pru Dunhill was considered a hot babe by most of the men Jake knew. A hot babe no one — especially he — could tolerate for longer than five seconds, but a hot babe nonetheless. That she had a crush on him wasn't lost on anyone. *You are one lucky dude — sort of,* his friends said often, running an eye up and down her lovely form, and probably thinking about her trust fund bank account.

He felt anything but lucky at the moment. Jake was a polite man, an adjective that hadn't always described him, and escaping Pru wasn't as easy as nodding a hello and continuing on his way. She wasn't the nicest person in the world — far from it — but she did have strong romantic feelings for him, and that was something that Jake would never handle carelessly, despite his complete lack of interest in her as a woman and a person. Personally, he found her detestable. She'd been cruel to people he cared about, one person in particular. It might have been a long time ago, but Pru was still as disdainful as ever of people she considered beneath her. Back in high school, Jake had been one of those people, and her feelings for him had driven her crazy. She hadn't been just physically attracted to him, the bad boy. She'd liked him, really liked him, and it had tormented her. Prudence Dunhill, one of the wealthiest girls in Troutville, with Jake Boone, Down Hiller and son of a police officer who'd been on disability for years?

That coupling would have been as scandalous then as Dylan Dunhill with Lizzie Morrow was now.

Jake hadn't known about Pru's crush back then. Pru herself had told him on their one and only date a few months ago, when she'd had too much to drink and had draped herself over him during the car ride home. "But you only had eyes for trashy Holly Morrow,"she'd slurred, both literally and figuratively. "I don't know what you saw in that skinny, shy girl in the raggedy hand-me-downs. Yeah, she put out. But I would have, too. A choice between her or me? I mean, *c'mon*."

Jake knew what he saw in Holly Morrow. And it hadn't taken the mention of her name, the memory of his feelings for her, his love for her, to peel Pru off him and deposit her just inside her front door; Jake would have politely rebuffed her, regardless. The next morning, Pru had called him, giggling about his "taking advantage" of her "low tolerance" for alcohol by making love to her right there in her car, which apparently was what she'd told her friends. Jake had told her five times that nothing had happened, that they hadn't even so much as kissed, but Pru had decided to believe, or decided to pretend, that they had slept together.

That was how easy it was to make up a lie. To make up a lie and share it. And suddenly, something that had never happened *had* happened. Jake knew about the power of lies all too well.

"Thank you soooo much, Jake," Pru gushed as he handed her the magazines. "I'm planning on bringing these old magazines to the free clinic Down Hill that the less-than-fortunate in Troutville utilize. Even if those folks can't afford the fashions in *Vogue*, they still like to dream," she added, patting the glossy cover of a beauty magazine.

Jake responded the way he often did to the unbelievable things that came out of Pru Dunhill's shiny pink mouth — by just looking at her in disbelief and wondering, somewhat vaguely, if there was anything inside her resembling a decent human being.

"My goodness, Arianna," Pru said, staring from the magazine cover to her friend, "You could so easily be a supermodel if you chose to be."

But Arianna *chose* to do absolutely nothing, other than live off her trust fund and occasionally offer decorating tips to her parents' friends. "Interior decorator" was Arianna's and Pru's supposed profession, but in reality, both women dined, shopped, gossiped all day, and paraded themselves in front of Jake and Dylan Dunhill.

Pru Dunhill was constantly talking up Arianna to Jake. Pru wanted Jake to convince Dylan that Arianna was the woman for him. Pru had been trying to do just that for years with no success. Dylan had dated

Arianna in high school and a few times over the years because it was expected by both their families, but he'd never been able to summon any real romantic interest in her. Pru was forever pushing Arianna on Dylan, at family functions, at the mansion, on the streets, everywhere. Even now, when Dylan was spoken for, an engaged man, Pru hadn't stopped. In fact, she seemed to be working double-time to make Dylan see that he'd overlooked Arianna. Which meant that Arianna walked around in very revealing outfits and Pru spent a lot of time making thinly veiled nasty comments about Lizzie Morrow, Dylan's fiancée.

"You are one impossible man to find, Jake Boone," Pru tsk-tsked with a seductive shake of her head as she stood straight up and turned slightly sideways as she always did to accentuate her chest. She smoothed her hair and twisted a bit on her heels. "Haven't you gotten my messages about the reunion next weekend? I've been calling you all week long."

"Pru, I have no interest in attending our class reunion. If you're forgetting, we had two very different high school experiences. And besides, I work on the weekends. In fact, I'm working now and I'm late for a meeting, so —"

"Oh, silly Jake," Pru interrupted, ignoring his need to move along. "You were an entirely different person back then! You would be the *hit* of the reunion. When everyone sees how you've changed, they'll be positively shocked. I mean, no one else in our class went from complete and utter ruffian to a successful Mr. GQ. Everyone from the wrong side of the tracks stayed there. But you showed everyone what a little polish can do. Do try to attend, Jake. I'll save you a dance."

If that was a promise, he most certainly would not try to attend. Not that he would try, period. He'd already "tried" once with Pru, and that had been more than enough. Why he let Dylan talk him into finally asking out his sister was beyond him. Dylan insisted his sister had some good qualities and that maybe she'd become a normal person if she was happily ensconced in a relationship with the guy she'd loved for twenty years. Their one and only date hadn't been an out-and-out disaster, but Jake didn't like Pru and he never would.

"Dylan's going to the reunion, isn't he?" Arianna asked hopefully. "He's on the list."

"Yes, he mentioned he's planning to go," Jake responded, eyeing his watch — a

41

pointless gesture, since the two women had no interest in others' social cues. Such as the fact that Jake was desperate to escape them.

"I suppose he'll be going with Lizzie Morrow," Arianna said, venom dripping onto the name.

"Well, she is his fiancée, so I imagine so," Jake said, mentally shaking his head in wonder. Dylan and Lizzie were getting married in three weeks whether Pru or Arianna liked it or not.

Pru mock-shivered. "I will never understand that match. My brother with Lizzie Morrow! My gorgeous, successful brother with that lowlife bimbo. Ick — what he sees in her is beyond me. I mean, the woman is so beneath him!"

"She's totally bottom of the barrel," Arianna added, tossing her long blond hair behind her shoulder.

Pru leaned in close as if sharing a confidence. "When my mother told me that my brother — the most eligible bachelor in town, in the state, probably — had been carrying on some kind of secret affair with Lay Me Lizzie, I almost dropped dead."

"Of course he kept it a secret," Arianna said. "He was obviously *way* too embarrassed to let anyone know he was dating her."

"Trust me, for Dylan to be engaged to her, she must have something on him," Pru insisted. "He can tell me he's in love till he's blue in the face, but I know she has something on him. Something really bad. There's no other reason he'd marry her."

Jake had had more than enough. "Not that I want to dignify any of your sickening conversation with my own two cents," he said, his stomach turning, "but just what terrible deed do you think Dylan has committed that would be worthy of such blackmail? Did either of you ever stop to think that he simply loves Lizzie? You two should know better than anyone that Dylan Dunhill defers to no one. He's his own man. If he didn't love Lizzie, very much, I might add, he would not be marrying her."

"Give me a break," Pru said, rolling her eyes.

"I agree with Pru one hundred percent," Arianna said. "She is *very* smart. I mean, c'mon, Jake. Why would a man like Dylan want Lizzie? Did you *see* Lizzie today? She's wearing the tackiest outfit I've ever seen — I spotted her a half mile away this morning. First of all, I don't think I've ever seen a skirt that short, that bright, or that cheap-looking. I swear it's made out of a plastic garbage bag or something!"

43

The two women shared a laugh. "And c'mon, that hair?" Pru said. "How bleached can it get before it all falls out?"

"Lizzie's hair is so big, it'll take forever to all fall out!" Arianna added.

As the women laughed, Jake felt his stomach turn over, as it had been doing since they began their verbal attack on Lizzie Morrow.

"I'm not going to waste my time correcting you both," Jake said, "But I happen to like Lizzie a lot. And your brother happens to love her," he added with a sharp glance at Pru. "So why don't you keep your vicious comments to yourselves."

"Jeez, Jake," Arianna muttered. "A little harsh."

"No," Jake corrected as a train rumbled into the station. "It's the two of you who are harsh — and that's about the weakest word I can think of to describe you both."

"Whatever," Arianna snapped. She said something under her breath, but with the roar of the train slowing to a stop, Jake couldn't hear her. His lucky day.

"Oh, come on, Jake," Pru exclaimed. "Don't be such a fuddy-duddy! C'mon, give us that famous Jake Boone smile. C'mon, let's see it." She leaned against him and ran a hand along his stomach to tickle him, just above his belt buckle, and pressed her body hard against his. He felt her breasts crush against his chest, and she spread her legs against his leg and leaned even closer against him. "Smile for me, Jake," she whispered huskily in his ear as she ran a finger along his neck. "C'mon, honey."

"Get a room!" Arianna shouted with a giggle.

Embarrassed and repulsed, Jake stepped back, but Pru stepped forward and almost stumbled. He reached out to steady her, and she fell into his arms. "There's so much more where that came from, Jake," she whispered. "You know where I live."

In a dungeon? he wanted to say, but held his tongue.

"Oh, look, there's the bimbo bride-to-be now," Pru said, nodding her chin way up the platform.

Out of the corner of his eye, Jake saw Lizzie Morrow and her friends Gayle and Felicia come through the station's double doors onto the platform. They stood close to the wall and seemed to be in animated conversation. For a second he imagined they were waiting for Holly Morrow. The four had been best friends their entire lives until Holly had moved away after high school, and whenever he saw the three women, he always felt Holly's absence the strongest, as though something were definitely wrong with this picture.

Holly would have a good laugh over that. What was wrong with this picture, according to Holly, was anyone living in Troutville a second longer than they had to.

He shook thoughts of Holly from his mind. The last place he'd ever see her was in Troutville.

"I can't believe Lizzie's walking around in public in that outfit!" Arianna exclaimed, loudly, of course. "And look at those tacky friends of hers. They make me so sick."

"I happen to like Lizzie's friends, too," Jake snapped. "So I'd appreciate it if you kept your comments about them to yourselves."

Arianna smiled. "Jake, you don't need to be so charitable. Just because you're friends with Dylan doesn't mean you have to like his so-called fiancée's friends."

"Ugh — don't even call her his fiancée," Pru said. "That's way too official. I doubt they'll ever make it to the altar."

Jake eyed Pru and mentally filed away that last comment. "There's my client now,

46

so good-bye, ladies." As he stepped away, he heard Arianna say to Pru, "He *so* wants you."

Of all the false statements that came rushing out of Pru and Arianna's mouths, that one could easily take first place as the least true.

As the train slowed to a stop at the Troutville station, Holly spotted her cousin immediately, despite how crowded the platform was. Lizzie's long platinum curls, fuchsia top and ruffly skirt stood out against the gray, soggy August morning. Holly's heart leapt at the sight of Lizzie, who as usual was in the middle of an animated conversation, talking with her hands and throwing her head back in laughter.

Oh, how good it was to see Lizzie! Holly saw Lizzie so infrequently, which was Holly's own fault. Several times a year, Lizzie would take the two-hour train ride to Hoboken, where Holly lived, and sometimes, Lizzie's mom and Gayle and Flea would come, too. And every time the train took them all away, back where Holly couldn't bear to go, couldn't even bear to think about, her heart would close up just a little bit more.

When the train doors opened, Holly saw

Lizzie stop in mid-sentence and jump up and down, trying to see over heads through the windows. Holly laughed. Standing next to Lizzie was the old gang, Gayle Green and Flea Harvey, whose real name was Felicia. The four of them had been best friends through grade school and middle school and high school, and whenever Holly talked to Lizzie, Lizzie's conversation was peppered with who Gayle was dating and what exquisite dress Flea had made, and for just a moment, Holly was almost nostalgic for the old days, the friendship, the insular world they'd created in the face of exclusion and derision.

The four girls had spent their after-school hours in an abandoned playground near the railroad tracks that separated their Troutville from the Dunhills' Troutville. There, they dreamed for the present, for the future. They talked about boys they liked, clothes they wanted, teachers they liked, what they wanted to do after high school. And every so often, when it hurt so bad it couldn't be ignored or forgotten, they'd talk about how they were treated in Troutville. The rumors. The stories. The lies. And they'd soothe themselves with dreams of leaving town after high school. But only Holly had left. Lizzie had become a barmaid at Morrow's Pub. Gayle was a secretary and had recently enrolled at the local college. And Flea, an exceptional seamstress, now owned the small dress shop she used to work in.

When Holly used to bring up plans for after graduation, the girls would talk big, about heading to sleepy southern towns or for the big city lights, but Lizzie's mom had broken her leg at the graduation ceremony itself and Lizzie felt she should stick around until her mom's leg healed. But it never did heal properly and Lizzie stayed on at the bar — waitressing until she came of legal age to bartend. By then, Lizzie had said, she had put down some new roots, some different roots, made some new friends at the bar. She liked her job and she liked her cozy little bungalow.

Gayle had stayed for a man. A boy she'd been crazy about in high school had gone to law school and come back and opened his own practice, and when Gayle saw his advertisement for a receptionist, that was that. After a few of her hints about dinner or a drink, he'd told her he thought it best not to mix business and pleasure. So Gayle took pleasure in just continuing her crush and had decided to pursue becoming a paralegal or even a lawyer herself.

Then there was Flea, who'd dreamed of making dresses for a major designer in New York City and opening her own business, but had instead taken a job sewing dresses in a claustrophobic back room of a dress shop Down Hill, which at least she now owned. Word-of-mouth of Flea's amazing handiwork had spread, and Up Hill women sometimes ventured down to her shop or had her come to their homes with fabrics and a sketch pad.

Their lives were full and busy, and after a while, Holly had stopped asking when they were going to leave town. And her friends had stopped asking her to come visit, since she always made excuses. They enjoyed coming to Hoboken, a fun town just across the river from New York City. And when she'd drive them to the train, that tiny part of her wished she could go back with them, to find the peace with Troutville that they'd found. The peace with themselves.

As Holly looked out the window, she noticed that Flea was arranging her hair back around her face, taking care to cover the patches of scars on her neck. *Oh, Flea,* Holly thought, her heart squeezing. Flea had barely escaped a fire when she was fourteen, but she hadn't escaped the nasty rumors that her own father had set the fire for the insurance money. Flea had just added those mean lies to all the others that people liked to tell about the four friends.

It's because you're all so pretty and smart and kind, Holly's mother always said whenever Holly came running home with tears in her eyes. *You may not be rich, but you and your friends have character — and that'll end up buying you everything you need.*

Before Holly had left for Troutville this morning, she'd called her mother in Florida, and let her know the big news that Lizzie was getting married — to a Dunhill. And that Holly would be spending the weekend — and possibly the next three weeks — in Troutville.

"You just forget the past, honey," her mother had advised. *"And don't you worry about Lizzie. She's a flamboyant girl, but she's got a good head on her shoulders. If she's marrying a Dunhill, then he must be all right. Who knows, maybe things have changed at last."*

But Dylan Dunhill wasn't all right. How could he be? And what could have possibly changed in Troutville, ten years or not? Nothing had changed during the eighteen years Holly had lived there. Perhaps the sunny warmth and swaying palm trees of

Florida had worked their magic on her mom, making her forget just how awful they'd all been treated in Troutville. Then again, her mom had always been a turn-the-other-cheek type of person. *"We know who we are and what we're made of,"* her mom had often said, *"so who cares what some people think of us?"*

Holly cared. She'd always cared. She'd tried so hard not to, just as Lizzie, Gayle, and Flea had tried. But they'd all failed. They'd cared plenty.

Holly sighed. Heavy-hearted, she stood and collected her suitcase from the overhead rack and waited to exit the busy train. She glanced out the window as another flash of blond hair caught her attention.

Holly stiffened.

It was Prudence Dunhill.

Pru stood in the center of the platform, unmistakable despite the decade that had passed since Holly had seen her. Voted "Best Looking" by their class, Pru had saucer-wide blue eyes, long blond hair, and a fantastic figure. On prom night, just before Holly's argument with Jake, Holly had run into Pru and her friend Arianna having their own argument in the school gymnasium's courtyard; apparently, Arianna, who'd been crowned prom queen, was upset that Pru had been voted Best Looking. Arianna felt that she should have taken that honor (she'd come in second) as her boyfriend at the time, Dylan, had won Best Looking and prom king. Holly had been shocked by their conversation; the two girls had been friends forever, but there was nothing friendly about their fight.

"Well, *I* won, Arianna," Pru had snapped. "What do you want me to do about it? If everyone thinks I'm the best-looking girl of our class, I must *be*."

Arianna had fumed. "I'm more classically beautiful than you are, Pru. I'm the one who finaled in the beauty pageant. Not you."

The beauty of the courtyard, with its manicured grass plots and low stone wall, just the right height for jumping up onto it for a seat, and the rows of blooming flowers and tall trees, seemed marred by the ugliness Pru and Arianna brought to it. Back and forth, they'd snipped and snapped, until they noticed Holly.

"Hey, look, Arianna," Pru had shouted. "It's the winner of Biggest Slut!"

"And Trashiest," Arianna added.

"Where'd you get your prom dress?" Pru asked. "The Dumpster? Hey, Arianna,

Dumpster chic — maybe it'll be the next big thing."

"I'll bet Scar Girl made it," Arianna put in. "Fleabag's always walking around with her needle and thread and pathetic little pieces of cheap fabric!"

"How dare you," Holly bit out. "How dare you refer to my friend that way!"

"Well, you knew who we were talking about, didn't you?" Pru asked, examining her nails.

They were so mean, so unbelievably mean, that Holly was always too shocked to defend herself, defend her friends. It infuriated her that she could only think of blistering responses later, when it was too late.

"Look at Holly the Whore, standing there with her mouth open," Pru said. "There's no guy around here, Holly, so you might as well close it."

"Actually, there is," said a deep male voice. "And if there were a prize for Most Vile Human Beings On the Planet, you two would win."

The three girls whirled around, and there stood Jake Boone, scowling fiercely in his tuxedo.

Pru stared at him, and for a moment, Holly thought the girl might burst into

54

tears, but Arianna put her arm around her and muttered, "Like your opinion means anything, Jake." Then the girls walked away.

Jake glared after them and shook his head. "If there was a prize for Most Everything, Holly Morrow, you'd win," he said. "You're the most beautiful, most intelligent, most creative, most interesting, most everything girl in this stupid school."

Holly had burst into tears, and Jake wrapped his arms around her. "Don't listen to those witches, Holly!" he said fiercely. "Don't let them get to you. They're nothing. *They're* the trash!"

"I can't wait to get out of this town!" Holly muttered, tears running down her cheeks. She'd secured a summer job as a day camp counselor and then she was headed to a good college an hour away on a scholarship. "Once I leave I'm never coming back."

"So, they win?" Jake asked.

"I'm not like you, Jake," she said. "What they say doesn't roll off my back like it does yours."

"Well, how about I convince you to stay here for the five minutes it'll take me to go get us two cups of punch?"

Holly had smiled. That was Jake, able to

change a heated subject and draw a smile at the same time.

"And by the way," he added, turning around. "I think your dress is beautiful."

With a wink, he disappeared into the gym, and Holly leaned against the stone wall. She wouldn't let Pru and Arianna get to her. She would enjoy this night, her last in Troutville, and spend it with her friends. She hopped up onto the stone wall and gazed at the stars.

And then Pru had come back. If only she hadn't.

"Where's Jake?" Pru demanded, hands on her hips, and Holly wondered how someone so angelic-looking could be such a monster. Pru wore one of the prettiest dresses Holly had ever seen, pink and floaty and feminine, with pink strappy sandals.

"He went inside to get us punch," Holly answered.

"You're a slut!" Pru hissed. "The only reason Jake trails after you like a puppy is because you have sex with him. You're nothing but a trashy whore! No wonder he chose you over me as his prom da—"

"You shut up, Pru Dunhill!" came Flea's voice. Half visible in the dim light from the windows of the gym, Flea stood in her lovely black dress, which she'd made herself, clutching the beaded purse she'd also sewed herself. Flea, like Gayle, didn't have a date to the prom, so they'd come together. "You just shut up."

Pru smiled. "Oh, look, it's the Fleabag. The only reason you're not a slut is because no guy will even *touch* you."

Holly had sucked in her breath in shock at Pru's viciousness. Flea's lower lip was trembling, but she neither cried nor spoke, just stared at the ground.

"Pru, c'mon, they're playing our favorite song," called a girl's voice from the gym's doorway.

"You both make me sick!" Pru snapped to Holly and Flea, and then stormed away.

Holly let out the breath she'd been holding. "I know I'm not supposed to hate anyone. I know it does no good. But I hate her. I really hate her."

"She's not worth it," Flea said, adjusting the black scarf around her neck.

"Jake and I haven't so much as kissed," Holly said. "How dare she! How dare she!"

Flea put her arm around Holly's shoulder. "Forget it, Holly. She's in love with Jake, that's why she's always picking on you. She's crazy about him and she hates that she can't have him and you can."

"Jake and I are just friends!" Holly said. "Just friends, and that's all we'll ever be."

"I've never understood that," Flea responded. "He's so good-looking and kind and he adores you. And you're best friends. Your best friend is who you're supposed to *marry*, Holly!"

"Marry Jake Boone? Don't be stupid Flea," Holly snapped. "I'll probably never see him again after I leave Troutville and that's fine by me. He represents everything I'm leaving . . . everything I hate here. He's the last man on earth I'd ever marry!" Her voice broke with emotion.

She didn't really mean it, but the whole evening was just too much.

Holly's response had ended her friendship with Jake. If only she'd turned around, if only she'd known he was behind her, holding two cups of punch in his trembling hands.

She would never forget the look on his face, what he'd said to her, how he'd put down the cups and turned and walked away.

She never saw Jake Boone again. He'd skipped the graduation ceremony the next day. And all calls and visits to his house had gone unanswered. She'd tried his and their favorite places to hang out, but she never found him. A few months later, when she'd worked up the courage to try calling again, she'd choked up at the sound of his voice when he picked up. *Hello? Hello?* he'd said, and Holly had broken down into sobs. A few weeks later, she'd tried again, but when she said, *Jake, it's me, Holly,* he'd hung up on her.

She hadn't tried again.

"Final call for Troutville station," called the conductor, jolting Holly out of her memories. "Doors will close in exactly thirty seconds."

Holly started and realized there was fifty feet between her and the passenger who'd been ahead of her. She hurried up to the doors. A glance out revealed Pru Dunhill pressing provocatively against a very good-looking man, one of her legs kicked coyly up behind her. Arianna Miller stood beside them, and she yanked on Pru's hair with the same supposedly playful passive-aggressiveness that had always under-scored their relationship. The man stepped away from Pru and then headed down the platform, and Pru and Arianna seemed to engage in their usual whisper-fight.

So much for thinking that they might have changed, Holly thought, shaking her head.

With a deep breath, Holly stepped off the train.

CHAPTER THREE

The platform was very crowded. Home-coming and the class reunion was next weekend, Holly realized. During the hot, lazy days of August, people tended to take vacations, and it seemed everyone who'd ever lived in Troutville had returned for homecoming and the reunion. Her chin raised, Holly clutched her bag as she weaved her way through the crowd. As she neared her friends, she noticed the way women stared at them, up and down, with disgust. And men leered, as they always did. Ten years or not, nothing had changed.

"I'll bet she's blackmailing him into marrying her," said a female voice behind Holly.

"She has to be," another voice said. "There's no way Dylan Dunhill would go for someone like Lizzie Morrow unless she was holding something over him."

"Ten to one she's pregnant," the first woman said.

Holly stiffened, then turned around. "Sorry, but you lose," she said to the women. "She's *not* pregnant. And even if she were, it would be none of your business."

"We were having a *private* conversation," one of the women replied. "So I suggest you mind *your* business."

"I am," Holly said. "That's my cousin you're gossiping about."

The women peered closely at Holly. "Omigod, it's Holly the Whore!" exclaimed the other woman.

Holly was too stunned to speak for a moment. She'd been in Troutville for exactly one minute, and already it was high school all over again.

As the two women continued walking as though nothing out of the ordinary had just happened, Holly heard one say, "She looks good. Very elegant. Maybe she's a high-priced prostitute now."

Unbelievable.

"Holly-Molly!"

Holly whirled around at the sound of Lizzie's voice. Her cousin grinned from ear to ear and held out her arms. Holly dropped her suitcase and grabbed her cousin tight against her.

"Oh, Lizzie, it is so good to see you," Holly said, breathing in Lizzie's familiar rose-scented perfume. She pulled back and looked into Lizzie's hazel eyes, tucking a stray blond curl behind her ear. Lizzie's trademark huge, dangling earrings hit her finger.

When the train had first pulled into the Troutville station, a blond woman in a dressy black pantsuit, her hair twisted up into a neat chignon, had caught Holly's eye, and for a split second she wondered if the woman were Lizzie, made over to fit in with the Dunhills and their crowd. And then Holly had spotted her cousin, unmistakable in her short, flouncy colorful skirt and giant dangly flower earrings, and she'd breathed a sigh of relief. Lizzie was still Lizzie.

And Troutville was still Troutville.

"You look great, Holly," Lizzie exclaimed. "Your hair looks real pretty that way."

Holly had her curly hair professionally straightened at a salon every six months; though she loved Lizzie's wild curls, Holly couldn't stand her own.

"Sickening — hardly a stitch of makeup and absolutely beautiful!" mock-complained Gayle as she squeezed Holly into a hug. Gayle's side job was selling cosmetics door to door, and she loved testing on herself. "C'mere, you, and give me a big hug."

Holly laughed and complied.

"You do look terrific, Holly," said Flea. "It's so good to see you!"

Holly squeezed her oldest and dearest friends into at least three hugs.

"Hey, let's go to the diner for lunch," Lizzie suggested. "I'm dying for a bacon double cheeseburger and fries buried in barbecue sauce."

Holly laughed and breathed another sigh of relief. If that was still Lizzie's lunch of choice, her cousin definitely hadn't changed a bit.

As the group headed the half block to the Troutville diner, the stares and leers continued.

"Just ignore it, Holly-Molly," Lizzie whispered. "If you pay it no mind, it can't bother you."

Why are you all still living in this town! Holly wanted to shout. Why should they have to be treated this way?

"Could her skirt be any shorter?" Holly heard a woman sneer.

"She must have a pound of makeup on her face."

"Well, she should share it with whatshername — the little one with the black scarf around her neck. She could use some makeup."

"Is that Holly Morrow? She looks good."

"Yeah, good for trash."

Laughter.

The laughter was always followed by a change of subject, about the weather or a television show, and Holly was always amazed that people could verbally attack someone so viciously, so openly, then just discuss the particular hue of blue of the sky, or a movie, as though they hadn't just done serious damage.

Holly glanced at Lizzie; she was deep in animated conversation with Gayle and Flea about the wedding dress she favored at Bettina's Bridal. Did they not hear it? she wondered. Did they block it out? Were they treated like this on a daily basis?

"Here we are," Lizzie said, opening the door to the Troutville Café, a glorified diner that they had never entered as teenagers. They wouldn't have been welcome.

When the hostess led them to a small table near the kitchen, despite two empty tables for four near windows, Holly coughed loudly. "Excuse me, but we'd prefer one of those tables." She gestured to the empty tables.

The hostess glanced at Holly, then slid her snotty gaze up and down the length of Lizzie. "We have a dress code — no shorts.

64

And your skirt" — she gave Lizzie's micromini a dirty look — "is so short that it could be counted as shorts."

"Does your dress code note hem lengths?" Holly asked the hostess.

"Well, no, but —" the hostess began.

"And is she wearing shorts?" Holly interrupted.

"No, but —" the hostess began again.

"Holly," Lizzie said, gently touching her arm. "It's not worth it. Let's just go somewhere else."

"No," Flea said. "Holly's absolutely right. We would like one of those tables," she added. "The dress code says nothing about hem lengths."

The hostess snatched the menus off the small table and led the way to one of the empty tables. "Enjoy your lunch," she snapped.

"Oh, we will," Gayle said, flashing her a megawatt smile.

Before they'd walked into the restaurant, Holly had been starving. Now her appetite was all but gone. She'd been in Troutville for six minutes and had been insulted countless times. How did Lizzie, Gayle and Flea live with this every day? *Why* did they?

"Maybe we should have the fries

checked for poison," Gayle said with a chuckle as they sat and perused their menus.

"And the chair cushions for tacks," Flea added.

"Guys . . ." Lizzie warned, shooting a *shut up* look at Gayle and Flea.

"What?" Holly asked. She'd assumed Gayle and Flea were joking about the hostess's attitude, but now she had the feeling they were talking about something else entirely.

"Nothing," Lizzie said, closing her menu. "They're just joking. I'm going to have the chicken salad. Holly, have you decided?"

All right — something was definitely going on here. "There's something funny about poisoned fries and tacks on chairs?" Holly asked.

"It's no big deal," Lizzie said, "Nothing to worry about. We've been the target of a few incidents. Stupid pranks."

"Incidents?" Holly repeated. "Lizzie, what are you talking about?"

Lizzie gnawed her lower lip and remained silent. "It's nothing, really, Holly. Nothing at all. Let's just forget it and enjoy our lunch. I say we order onion rings *and* fries!"

"If I were the one getting married in three weeks," Gayle said, flipping her long red hair behind her shoulder, "I'd have to forgo *all* food. Lizzie, you're so lucky that you can eat whatever you want and not gain an ounce."

As Lizzie, Gayle and Flea began discussing diets, workouts, the reunion, and then moved on to what Lizzie and Dylan planned to serve for dinner at the wedding reception, Holly felt like she'd fallen into the Twilight Zone. How could her friends so blithely — so happily! — chatter on about color schemes and party favors while enduring the hatred and cruelty of most of the town? Luckily, their waitress came over at just that moment to take their order.

"Guys, I don't mean to harp," Holly said once their waitress had come and gone. "I really don't. But can someone please tell me what's going on in this godforsaken town?"

"I gained four pounds even though —" Gayle began.

Holly had to smile — Gayle was obsessed with dieting. "No, sweetie — the *pranks*. The *incidents*."

"Oh, just the usual jealousy," Gayle put in. "We could either let it get to us, or we can ignore it. And if we ignore it, I'm sure whoever's behind it will get bored and quit. So we don't want to even waste time discussing it."

"Quit *what?*" Holly asked. "Exactly what has been happening?"

No one said anything. Holly looked at Lizzie, but her cousin was busy biting her lower lip and glancing away. Flea was staring down at the napkin on her lap. And Gayle was twirling a tendril of hair around her finger, which she always did when she was uncomfortable.

"Okay, someone tell me what's going on here," Holly insisted, "or I'll — I don't know what I'll do, but I'll do something."

Gayle looked at Lizzie, and Lizzie nodded. "Okay, Hol," Gayle said, "but it's not pretty. In the past week, someone locked Flea in the back room of her dress shop, someone keyed up my car door, someone threw a stink bomb in Lizzie's bedroom window and left a couple of nasty notes in her mailbox."

A chill ran up Holly's spine. "What kind of nasty notes?"

"Look, let's just forget it," Lizzie said. "Hol, you didn't come all this way to Troutville for the first time in ten years to hear about some silly pranks. Let's change the subject."

68

Flea sipped her water. "I don't think they *are* silly pranks, Liz. And I think you need to take them more seriously than you've been."

"Oh, hell," Gayle said. "Flea's right. It's been bothering me more than I've been letting on."

"Seems to me that someone's trying to scare Lizzie into canceling the wedding," Flea said. "One of the notes she got said that the wedding would never happen."

"What!" Holly shouted, alarm coursing through her. Diners around their table glanced at her, and she lowered her voice. "That sounds like a threat to me."

"Not a threat, just someone being mean," Lizzie said. "It's just the same old crap, nothing to take seriously."

"Have you told Dylan about these incidents?" Holly asked.

The waitress returned with their lunch, and silence settled over the table.

Lizzie popped a fry into her mouth. "Yes," she finally responded. "I did tell Dylan. And he dismissed them, too. Someone's just being immature. That's all."

Flea put down her turkey sandwich. "But it didn't start until you and Dylan announced your engagement," she pointed out. "It sounds to me like someone isn't

69

too happy you're engaged."

Holly could imagine more than a few people who weren't too happy about the engagement.

"Well, the Dunhills have been quite civil to me lately," Lizzie whispered. "They're making an effort. And once they're on board, the entire town will be on board."

But it shouldn't have to be like that in the first place! Holly wanted to scream.

"How's my bride-to-be?"

Holly whipped her head around and there was Dylan Dunhill. Tall and muscular with thick blond hair, dark blue eyes and dimples, Dylan truly looked like a movie star. He pulled over a chair from the next table, sat down next to Lizzie and kissed her on the cheek, then held her hand on top of the table.

"Holly!" Dylan exclaimed. "How nice to see you! Lizzie, you didn't mention Holly was coming home."

There it was again: *home*. She couldn't be farther from home.

"I wanted to surprise everyone," Lizzie explained. "And you know what a gossipy town this is — if I told one person, it would have been all over Troutville, and I wanted to surprise Gayle and Flea and my mother."

"No one's as surprised as I am," said a deep male voice from behind Holly.

Jake Boone!

Holly whirled around again. Jake Boone, ten years older, more handsome than ever, and tall and strong, stood before her, very little expression on his face. His green eyes gave nothing away.

No, it can't be, she thought. *The same man Pru Dunhill was all over at the train station.*

Jake Boone and Pru Dunhill? she thought wildly, her stomach lurching.

"Hello, Jake," she said.

She half expected him to say, *Who's Jake? I'm so-and-so.* But no, there was no mistaking Jake Boone close up. And close up, she could understand why she'd been unable to recognize him at the train station. The Jake she'd known had run around in jeans and T-shirts with his mop of thick dark hair in his eyes. The one suit she'd seen him in, on prom night, had come from the thrift store, where she'd bought her prom dress. This Jake wore a very fine suit and tie, and his silky hair was expensively cut. The ten years from teenager to man had done him very well.

"Jake's my best man," Dylan said, standing up and slinging an arm over Jake's shoulder.

Holly's mouth dropped open and she quickly shut it. *What?* Jake Boone was Dylan Dunhill's best man? Jake had grown up next door to Holly and was treated just as she was, worse maybe. He *hated* Dylan's crowd in high school.

And eventually he'd hated Holly, too.

From the look in his eyes before he muttered quick good-byes and walked away, it was clear that hadn't changed.

Between the "little pranks," the knowledge that Jake Boone was in town, and the sight of Lizzie and Dylan sitting thigh to thigh with their arms around each other and occasionally nuzzling each other's necks, Holly's head was spinning and her appetite had completely vanished. In the half hour they'd been in the Troutville Café, Holly could plainly see that Dylan and Lizzie were absolutely madly in love. They gazed into each other's eyes, played absently with each other's hair, told cute story after cute story about the other, tapped each other's noses and said "I love you." When Dylan had left a few minutes ago, they'd hugged as though they were parting for months.

"Wow, Lizzie," Holly said as the foursome headed outside.

"Oh, Holly," Lizzie breathed. "I love him so much!"

Holly smiled. "I saw. And he clearly loves you so much, too."

"I could do without the PDA, though," Flea said with a grin.

"Yeah," Gayle agreed. "You two could go into the *Guinness Book of World Records* for Public Display of Affection and the Loviest-Doviest Couple."

"And this is during the day," Flea added, elbowing Lizzie in the ribs with a wink. "You should see her and Dylan when they're out on the town at night."

"I swear, people shout 'Get a room!' to them," Gayle said, laughing. "You'll see next weekend, Holly, if not before then."

"Next weekend?" Holly repeated. Then she remembered all too well what next weekend was.

"The reunion," Lizzie said. "We're all going. Oh, Holly, you have to come! It'll be fun, I promise."

The Troutville Senior High School reunion, fun? I don't think so.

"I don't know," Holly said. "I'm not too interested in reliving high school."

Especially with Jake.

"I'll second that," Flea put in. "But it won't be like that. It'll be just us, enjoying

73

ourselves, celebrating a milestone."

"Flea's exactly right," Gayle said.

"So which dress did you decide to wear to the reunion?" Flea asked Gayle. "The red one I made you for your company Christmas party last year?"

Holly looked from Gayle to Flea to Lizzie as though they were all crazy. First of all, they seemed to have forgotten all about the so-called pranks and incidents. Second, they were actually looking forward to the reunion? Holly had no doubt the "threats" were the handiwork of a former classmate, someone who enjoyed throwing around names like Lay Me Lizzie and Holly the Whore.

I don't get it, Holly thought.

"Oh, I forgot to tell you — I bought a new dress at the mall," Gayle told Flea. "Greg's already seen me in the red one, and he's the only one I want to impress, so I bought something new. Very slinky, very gold lamé."

"Gayle!" Flea scolded. "I told you that you should just bring me any dress you want and I'll copy it for you. Why pay good money for a dress when I could make you the same thing for free?"

"Flea, you're so sweet," Gayle said, squeezing her hand. "I appreciate you so much. But you've been working yourself to the bone lately. You have the big order for dresses from Clark's Department Store, and your private clients. Your friends are supposed to give you a break, not beg you for favors."

Flea adjusted her scarf. "Trust me, I'd rather make free dresses for my friends than expensive ones for those snotty Up Hillers any day."

"What are you wearing to the reunion, Flea?" Lizzie asked. "That gorgeous black dress you made a few weeks ago?"

"I don't know," Flea said, "That one's a little showy for me. Something a little more simple."

"I'm wearing a royal blue matte jersey dress with a plunging neckline," Lizzie said. "Dylan loves me in royal blue. But I'm sure the town snobs will have a lot to say about the dress's 'inappropriateness.' "

"Who cares what they think!" Holly snapped.

"Actually, we've turned what they think into a game," Gayle said. "Sometimes we show up in really wild clothes just to give 'em something to talk about. Like my orange spandex, leopard-print jumpsuit that I wore to the mall last week. You should have seen the look on some of the faces!"

Holly sat back, impressed. This new attitude was a long way from the tears and insecurity they'd experienced as teenagers.

"You are going to the reunion, aren't you, Holly?" Gayle asked. "I know it must seem crazy, given how miserable we all were back in high school, but now we just have fun as a group and say the hell with everyone else."

"Yeah," Lizzie said. "And there are a whole bunch of people from Down Hill who are going. It'll be a blast! Plus, it'll be a nice way for you to get to know Dylan."

The thought of going to the reunion filled Holly with dread. But for Lizzie, she'd go. "All right. I guess it doesn't sound too bad."

Lizzie clapped. "All right! Serious progress has been made!"

After making plans for the foursome to meet at Bettina's Bridal salon the next morning to shop for dresses, Gayle and Flea headed their separate ways to work, and Holly and Lizzie headed Down Hill toward Lizzie's house.

"Why didn't you tell me Jake was friends with Dylan?" Holly asked Lizzie.

Lizzie glanced at Holly. "Honestly, Holly, I didn't realize I should have. I mean, you haven't spoken to him in ten years, since prom night, right?"

Holly nodded around the lump in her throat.

"Hol, are you okay?" Lizzie asked.

"I'm just surprised," Holly finally said. "I didn't expect to see him. Didn't expect him to be Dylan Dunhill's best man. How did that happen?"

"They've been best friends for years," Lizzie explained. "They're so close now that it's hard to remember they were once in very different crowds."

Different worlds *was more like it,* Holly thought.

"When did he and Dylan become friends?" Holly asked, trying to appear nonchalant. Best friends? How was that even possible?

"Seven, eight years back maybe," Lizzie responded. "Jake's very close to the entire Dunhill family. He helped them out with something, some sort of scandal, and he's been practically a family member ever since."

"Scandal?" Holly asked. "What kind of scandal?"

Lizzie shook her head. "I don't know. I asked Dylan how he and Jake became friends, how Jake became so close with the Dunhills, but he said the scandal was something he'd rather not talk about, that it was all water under the bridge. Jake was a cop then, and apparently, one of the Dunhills was in some kind of trouble and Jake sorted the mess out."

"*Was* a cop then?" Holly asked. "Isn't he still?"

Lizzie shook her head. "He left the force a few years ago to start his own private investigation firm. He's very in-demand. A few months ago, he tracked down the Cardwells' kidnapped daughter."

"A private investigator," Holly repeated.

"Hol, I would have told you all about these things and others," Lizzie said. "but you were adamant that you didn't want to hear anything about what was going on in Troutville, that you wanted to put your life and the people here behind you, so I respected your wishes. But I can see you're interested in what happened to Jake Boone," she added with a wink.

"Lizzie, don't you go matchmaking. Jake Boone and I aren't exactly friends anymore."

"Oh, Holly, that was so long ago," Lizzie said.

So long ago, Holly echoed in her mind.

As the two cousins walked down the slope, Holly noticed that Down Hill was in much better condition than it had been when she'd left. There were new stores, including a cozy coffee bar with some overstuffed couches and brightly painted walls. A few establishments and homes that Holly remembered as rundown or boarded up were now well maintained and beautifully painted; lawns that had been brown and uncared for were now shimmering green.

"Down Hill looks great," Holly said in wonderment, taking in the small house next to the gas station that she'd grown up in; her father had managed the station for years. The house, which her parents had taken great care of, was now even nicer, with a bigger porch and a swing. A new playground and an enclosed dog run had been built in the square next to the small park; children played and dogs frolicked, chasing Frisbees and balls. "I can hardly believe it."

"I told you things have changed, Hol," Lizzie said, smiling. "There's my house," she added, pointing at a cheerful yellow bungalow at the end of the road.

"I always loved that bungalow," Holly said.

"Wait till you see all my photographs on the walls," Lizzie said. "I've been making great progress, Holly. I've even had a bunch of photos published in the *Troutville Gazette*."

"That's great, Lizzie!" Holly said.

"I mean, my photography isn't generating enough income for me to give up my job at the bar," Lizzie said, "but at least I've got a portfolio started. Maybe next year."

"But —"

"What?" Lizzie asked. "You think just because I'm marrying Dylan Dunhill I'm not going to work anymore?"

"Well, yes," Holly admitted. "Unless that's one of the things in Troutville that's changed — the Dunhills are now poor?"

Lizzie laughed. "Nope, they're richer than ever. I'd never stop working, Holly. Being a barmaid at Morrow's has been good to me. I've met a lot of people, including the editor at the *Gazette*, who loves the pub, and it's not as mindless a job as people think. I like working with people. Plus, I like working with my mom and chowing down on her home cooking."

"And Dylan doesn't have a problem with you working as a barmaid?"

"Dylan doesn't have a problem with anything about me, Holly," Lizzie said.

Holly glanced at Lizzie and saw that her

cousin was quite serious. "So I'm dying to know how you and Dylan got together. Tell me the whole story."

They sat on a park bench across from the seesaws, and Lizzie's launch into Boy Talk reminded Holly of the old days when the cousins would discuss their crushes for hours in this very spot.

"He and Jake came into Morrow's one night about a year ago to watch the Yankees," Lizzie explained. "They ordered a platter of wings and a pitcher of beer, but instead of watching the game, Dylan kept asking me for things — another napkin, an extra plate. At first I thought he was making fun of me, enjoying ordering me around, waving around his money, but he kept engaging me in conversation, asking me cute questions, complimenting me on this or that."

"Did he remember you from high school?" Holly asked.

"Yup. He said he always thought I was beautiful and vibrant and he always noticed me, but he had a steady girlfriend, Arianna, the quote unquote *right* girlfriend, and back then he'd been so under his father's thumb that he hadn't thought to do anything but toe the line. And then something terrible happened in his family several years ago — I still don't know quite what — and Dylan said it changed him, he broke free of who he thought he was supposed to be and started being who he *was,* who he wanted to be. His own person. So he started doing pro bono work, which enraged his mother, he moved out of Dunhill Mansion, and a few months ago, he started dating me."

Holly let everything sink in. "So what's he like?" she asked, and Lizzie's eyes lit up.

"Oh, Holly, he's everything I've ever dreamed of. Romantic. Kind. Sweet. He calls me five times a day for no reason, just to hear my voice. He brings me little gifts — wildflowers that he picked in the woods, a book of photography that he thought I'd like. He makes me feel like the most special person in the world."

"Oh, Lizzie, I'm so happy for you," Holly said, and meant every word. "You deserve this."

Lizzie squeezed Holly into a hug. "He proposed last month, and we decided to do it as fast as we could. In just a few days, we had the invitations printed. It was the happiest day of my life."

"Well, I'm honored to be your maid of honor, Lizzie. Is the bridal party just the four of us?"

"Well, it would have been five," Lizzie said, frowning, but —"

"But what?" Holly asked.

Lizzie stared down at the ground and didn't answer.

"Lizzie?"

"I asked Dylan's sister to be a bridesmaid. But Pru declined," Lizzie explained. "I asked her in person, too. I told her I'd be honored if she'd stand up for me as one of my bridesmaids, and —" Lizzie took a deep breath.

Holly let her cousin take her time. Clearly, this was painful for her.

"Pru just stared at me for a moment, and then she laughed. She actually laughed, right in my face. 'You're not serious,' Pru said. 'You can't possibly be serious.' And then she walked away."

Holly's mouth hung open. "That bitch."

"Holly . . ."

"How dare she!" Holly growled. "Did you tell Dylan?"

"I prettied it up for him," Lizzie said, "but he got the idea. He was upset about it and said he was going to have a word with her. I told him it was okay, that we might never be friends, and he said that Pru and I were going to be family and that his sister had better start showing me respect."

"Has she?" Holly asked.

"If dirty looks and innuendos could be construed as respect," Lizzie said, then giggled. Clearly nothing could sink her buoyant mood.

Holly shook her head. "Well, you don't need Pru Dunhill. You've got your three best friends as your bridal party."

Lizzie hugged Holly. "C'mon. Let's go. I can't wait to show you my house!"

They hopscotched to the end of the walk as they always did as girls and teenagers, then crossed the street and walked down Piper Lane to Lizzie's house.

The moment Lizzie opened the front door, she broke into a huge smile. "Dylan is so sweet! He left a trail of rose petals!"

Holly followed Lizzie inside the cozy home, and there, indeed, was a line of rose petals leading to a door at the end of the hall. She felt so happy for her cousin. "Lizzie, you've got one romantic guy." She glanced around the bungalow. "Your home is so cozy and wonderful. I love how you decorated the place." Lizzie's favorite color, fuchsia, was everywhere, in accent pillows and rugs and even on the walls.

"Thanks, honey," Lizzie said, picking up a rose petal and bringing it to her nose. "Ahhh, I could smell roses all day." She gestured toward the end of the trail of rose petals. "That's my bedroom," Lizzie said, grinning. "I'll bet Dylan's covered my bed with dozens and dozens of roses! Oh, Holly, he is so romantic."

Lizzie ran down the hall and threw open the door. But there were no roses on the bed. Only a pile of dirt, on which was a note:

You're nothing but dirt.

Lizzie gasped, then dropped to her knees. In an instant, Holly was beside her.

"Come on," Holly said gently. "Let's get out of here."

Lizzie let Holly lead her into the living room. She fell back against the couch. "I can't take this!" She covered her face with her hands. "Who's doing this?"

"I don't know, honey," Holly said. "But whoever it is is very jealous. And very immature."

Lizzie nodded. "Maybe I should just cancel the wedding. Who knows what this person is capable of doing? Whoever it is is going to a lot of trouble to make my life miserable."

"So you *are* worried," Holly said. "The way you sounded in the diner, I didn't think you were taking any of it seriously."

Lizzie took a deep breath. "I really wanted to believe everything that's happened was just coincidence. Just silly stuff. The usual crap. But I can't deny it any longer. This is the first time someone's come inside my *home*. Notes in my mailbox are one thing, but someone came into my bedroom. Whoever's behind this is serious. I don't want my friends or family to get hurt. I'm canceling the wedding."

"You are doing no such thing," Holly said, surprising herself with her vehemence. "You have every right to marry the man you love, and no one's going to stop you! Not some jealous lunatic. Whoever's behind these incidents isn't going to win the way those who treated us like trash in school won."

Tears welled in Lizzie's eyes. "I am trash and I'm always going to be trash."

"Lizzie Morrow," Holly scolded gently, "you are not trash! People treated us that way and we were too young and too confused and too insecure to know how to handle it. But we knew who we were then and we know who we are now. You are a beautiful, intelligent, wonderful person, Lizzie. Whoever's behind this is the one who's trash!"

Lizzie took a deep breath. "I'm just so overwhelmed, Hol. Ever since Dylan and I announced our engagement, I've been besieged by hatred. Everything from terrible stares and comments on the streets to hateful notes."

"Oh, Lizzie, you made everything sound so nice on the phone," Holly said. "Why didn't you tell me how bad it was? I could have helped."

"How?" Lizzie asked, tears falling down her cheeks. "You're so far away. So removed from all this."

"But not from you, Liz," Holly said. "I love you so much. You're my family. My blood. My best friend, no matter how far away I am."

Lizzie flew into Holly's arms, her chest heaving. And as her cousin slumped against her, Holly vowed to get to the bottom of what was going on in this rotten town.

CHAPTER FOUR

Hey, Jake, here's a joke for you: How many private investigators does it take to figure out that Holly Morrow would come home for her own cousin's wedding — even if that wedding was in Troutville, where Holly had vowed never to step foot in again?

Ba-dum-pa. If Jake had been willing to think of Holly, willing to let his mind conjure up her face, her body, his memories of her, perhaps it would have occurred to him that of course she'd come. But the sight of her sitting in the Troutville Café a few hours ago had come as a complete shock. When he'd walked into the restaurant behind Dylan and realized that the elegant brunette with her back to him was Holly Morrow, he felt as though he'd been punched hard in the stomach. For a moment he'd been unable to form a thought, a word, a sentence. He's used what few wits he had left to force all expression from his face. He had thought of Holly over the past decade; his heart had won the battle over his mind many times, yet he never expected to see her again, especially not here in Troutville. He knew that Lizzie and her friends went to visit Holly in Hoboken, where she'd moved after high school and become a teacher. Those first couple of years, when the wounds were so fresh, when his love for her was still burning in his gut, he'd hang around Morrow's Pub, where Lizzie and her mom worked, having two or three helpings of whatever just so he could listen to their conversation while pretending to be absorbed in the ball game playing on the overhead television.

But he'd paid very close attention. Sometimes he wondered if Lizzie were giving so much detail for his benefit because she knew how he felt about Holly. Jake wasn't sure, but it was more likely because Lizzie adored her cousin and missed her so much.

He'd listen as Lizzie and her mother — or Felicia and Gayle, too, if they stopped in for lunch — talked about how nice Holly's apartment was, *where* it was (as if he'd ever visit her), how lovely she looked, how she wasn't dating anyone or anyone special, how she'd put herself through college and become a teacher like she always wanted. How she baked amazing cakes and was thinking of trying to start a side business of baking for restaurants or special events.

As the women talked, he'd feel as though he'd been there, too, and he'd leave satisfied instead of conflicted. He supposed that was because he had loved her so much, and regardless of how she'd treated him in the end, her happiness was important to him.

Holly Morrow in the flesh. Back home in Troutville. Jake shook his head. If he hadn't seen her with his own eyes, he might not have believed it if someone said she was in town. He'd been honestly shocked.

But he hadn't been shocked by how beautiful she was. Holly Morrow had been a very pretty teenager, fine-boned with wildly curly light brown hair she was always trying to control into a ponytail, and those dark blue eyes that mesmerized him. Yet now, as a woman, she was stunning. Truth be told, he preferred the wild, curly, messy hair to the pin-straight style she wore now, but she was absolutely beautiful no matter what her hair was like.

He leaned back in his chair, ignoring the case file on his desk and the two new messages from Pru Dunhill "regarding the reunion" and stared out the window of his third-floor office.

Perhaps it's a good thing that she's in town, Jake thought. *I can finally get her out of my system. I'll be able to see that she's just a woman, just a snob-in-reverse. Not the goddess of my fantasies that she'd been for the first eighteen years of my life.*

The intercom on his desk beeped. "Jake, there's a Holly Morrow to see you," came the voice of Jake's secretary.

He immediately straightened, smoothing his tie and his hair as though he was a teenager about to see the girl he worshipped, instead of the woman who'd broken his heart. He leaned back in his chair, adopting a more carefree position, and forced himself to remember what she'd said that terrible night ten years before. He needed his heart and mind on red alert against her, or he could get himself into very big trouble.

His intercom beeped again. "Jake? Shall I have her wait?"

"Yes, Sally," he responded. "For just a moment. I'm just finishing up some paperwork."

Holly Morrow was here to see him.

Surprise, surprise, he thought. She'd managed to shock him twice in one day. He hadn't expected her to come seek him out.

"Sally, send Miss Morrow in, please," he

said, then took a deep breath.

Holly's perfume, a light, clean floral scent that she'd worn since she was fifteen, preceded her into the room. He breathed it in, and for a moment, he was his fifteen-year-old self again. His sixteen-year-old self. His seventeen-year-old self. A boy deeply in love. With a girl who had no interest in the likes of him. Only he hadn't realized it was disdain that had kept Holly from him.

His entire body jerked in response to seeing her. There was no hiding her curves, despite the conservative beige jacket and matching pants she wore. Tasteful was the second word that popped into Jake's head. That was what Holly had always wanted to be. Tasteful. Her family had been too poor to afford stylish clothes, let alone new ones, so Holly had done her best at sales with her baby-sitting money and thrift shops and dressed as well but plainly as she could.

As she sat down in the guest chair opposite his desk and looked everywhere but at him, Jake studied her. *She's still living in the past,* he realized, his investigative instincts kicking in. He could see it in how guarded she was, how carefully dressed she was, how "proper" she looked. She was trying to overcome who she used to be.

But who she used to be was absolutely wonderful. Until Jake realized he'd been wrong about her.

"I heard from Lizzie that you're a private investigator," she said. "And I'm here about a case."

He nodded. "I assume it's about Lizzie and what's been happening to her and her friends lately."

Her eyes widened. "You know about that?"

"I've been on the case since Dylan told me about the first of the anonymous notes in Lizzie's mailbox," Jake explained.

She nodded again. "Did you find out anything?"

He shook his head. "It was impossible to know if the so-called pranks were connected to the notes or just a coincidence. Felicia being locked in the back room of her shop, the stink bomb thrown into Lizzie's bedroom window, Gayle's car being keyed. I couldn't ascertain whether those incidents were connected to the threatening notes in Lizzie's mailbox."

"There were two, right?" she asked.

"Yes. Computer typed and printed and impossible to trace."

"Do you *think* the incidents and the

notes are linked?" she asked. "Do you think the same person is responsible?"

"My gut says yes," Jake responded. "The timing gives it away. The first incident and the first note happened on the same day — Flea being locked in her shop and the note in Lizzie's mailbox saying: Lay Me Lizzie will never marry Dylan. It's possible it was coincidence — someone playing a mean trick on Felicia and someone being spiteful to Lizzie, but both happened the day the wedding invitations were received. The next day, Gayle's car was keyed. The third day, there was the stink bomb and the second note."

"Gayle and Flea are in Lizzie's wedding — they're going to be bridesmaids," Holly said. "Do you think whoever is behind all this is after them because they're part of the wedding?"

"Yes," he said. "Whoever wants to stop the wedding knows that Lizzie cares more for the safety of her friends than her own. Which is why I have to caution you to be very careful while you're in town. I assume you're in the wedding, too."

"Maid of honor."

"Just make sure you're with someone at all times," Jake said.

"I hear you're the best man?" The way

she said it registered her disbelief.

I thought I was the best man for you at one time, he thought out of nowhere. Get a grip, Boone!

"Yup, the best man," he said. "Although Dylan and the groomsmen have been spared such petty immaturity."

She stared at him. "So it's just Lizzie and her friends, her bridal party, who are being hurt. That seems a clue in itself. Whoever is behind this is not a fan of Lizzie's but has no problem with Dylan or his buddies."

"I've thought of that, too," he said. "Although, it's only been a week since the invitations went out. No one's gone after Dylan or me, and his two other groomsmen live out of state. They're his close friends from college."

"I'm surprised he doesn't have ten of his high school best friends standing up for him," Holly said, her tone icy.

"Actually," Jake responded, "Dylan didn't have many close friends in high school. He was very popular and had a ton of acquaintances and everyone wanted to be his friend, but he never really clicked with any of the guys in his crowd."

"Didn't click with them? I don't understand. A crowd is made up of people you click with."

"Not always," he told her.

She glanced at him, and he could see she didn't understand what he was talking about, but she didn't press him. Dylan wasn't who she thought he was, a snot-nosed rich kid who ran with a mean, reckless bunch who got away with everything. Dylan was a smart, sensitive person who'd been under his father's thumb for too long. Rather than risk his dad's wrath, Dylan had done what was expected of him — was at the center of the popular crowd, was captain of the football team, dated the right girls, got into every Ivy League school he wanted, and came back home after college to one day take over the family empire. Dylan might have revolted on his own eventually, but the truth about Dylan's father's own way of living had made itself uncomfortably clear one fateful day, and Dylan had become his own man. He might have left Troutville years ago if he weren't so involved with the Boys' Center that he and Jake both volunteered a lot of time to.

"Well," Holly said, "I imagine it'll be tough to figure out who's behind these 'incidents' and the notes. There are a lot of people in this no-good town who'd like to see Lizzie hurt rather than marry a Dunhill."

"No-good town?" Jake repeated. So he was right. She was still living in the past.

"You know what I mean, Jake," Holly said.

He stared at her. "It's been a long time since you've been in Troutville, Holly."

"I was in Troutville for one minute when I was called Holly the Whore. Five minutes before my cousin was insulted in a restaurant."

He winced. "I understand all that. I know that Lizzie and her friends are still picked on for absolutely no reason at all. What I'm saying is that they don't let it affect them anymore. They took the power back."

Sparks flew in her blue eyes. "Excuse me?" she asked, incredulous. "Are you saying we had the power back then to change how we were treated?"

"Not how we were treated," he said. "How we *responded* to it."

Holly shook her head. "That's very healthy, Jake. And very difficult to do when you're thirteen years old."

"I'm not talking about then. I'm talking about now. If someone called you Holly the —" He stopped. "If someone called you a name, would it hurt? Or would you think the person was an immature loser with nothing better to do?"

"The latter," she said.

"Exactly my point."

The sparks were back in her eyes. "Well *my* point is that Lizzie and I arrived back at her house an hour ago to find a mound of dirt on her bed with a note atop it that read: You're nothing but dirt. How do you propose she *respond* to that?"

He let out a deep breath and shook his head. "Dammit. How's she doing?"

"As expected," Holly said, the angry sparks changing to concern. "She's very upset, scared. It took me a half hour just to calm her down."

Jake slammed his fist down on his desk. "I will find out who's behind this. You can count on that."

She seemed relieved. "So you are officially working on the case?"

"Yes. I officially am."

She nodded. "Who are your suspects?"

"You're not my client, Holly."

"Excuse me?" she asked, eyeing him.

"You're not my client. I've hired myself here. I don't discuss a case with anyone."

"Fine. I'll discuss *my* thoughts of the case, then," Holly said, the sparks returning. "Lizzie told me that Pru Dunhill declined her invitation to be in the bridal party. In fact, Pru was downright mean about it. I'll assume she's number one on your list."

Jake leaned back in his chair. "She's not, actually."

"Because you're involved with her?" Holly asked.

Jake almost spit out his mouthful of coffee. "So now *you're* listening to gossip?"

"I saw the two of you in a heated embrace with my own eyes this morning at the train station," Holly explained flatly.

"Well, you're wrong," Jake said. "On both counts. We're neither involved nor was I in a heated embrace, as you put it."

"Then why isn't she number one on your list?" she asked.

"Because someone else is," he said.

"Who?"

"I repeat: you're not my client. I initiated this case. I don't share information on an ongoing case."

"We're talking about my cousin!" Holly snapped.

"Well, rest assured that I'm on it," he responded calmly.

"Fine. I assume the other Dunhills are on your list. Dylan's mother and father?"

"You're assuming that they're unhappy about the wedding?"

"Aren't they?" Holly asked.

"That, you can discuss with your cousin," Jake said. "But I'm sure Lizzie or Dylan won't mind my alerting you that Dylan's father passed away several years ago." Memories of that strange night passed through his mind. It was a night that had set off a chain of events that had changed his perceptions, perhaps even his life.

"Oh," she said. "I didn't know."

"There's a lot you don't know, Holly. Like I said, you've been away from Troutville for a long time."

She crossed her arms over her chest. "And like *I* said, I was in Troutville for one minute when I witnessed firsthand how *little* has changed. My friends and I were subjected to the same treatment as always. Comments about the way we look, about Dylan and Lizzie —" She stopped and bit her lip.

"What is it?" Jake asked.

"When I stepped off the train this morning," she said, "two women in front of me were gossiping about how Lizzie must have blackmailed Dylan into marriage. I was just realizing that the list of suspects is going to be *very* long. I didn't even recognize those two women. And

100

with a town full of people in for home-coming and the reunion" — she leaned back in her chair — "It could be anyone."

"Yes, but the incidents started before this weekend," Jake pointed out. "So it's most likely not an out-of-towner."

Holly shot up. "I can think of another person who'd like to see Lizzie out of the picture. Arianna Miller. Lizzie says she's still in love with Dylan and has been since they were the king and queen of the Troutville High prom."

Jake's mind went back ten years to senior prom night, to when Dylan Dunhill and Arianna Miller, who'd long been a couple and king and queen of the school, were officially crowned at the prom. Jake's own date had been Holly. They'd gone as friends, and Jake had been about to declare his love for her when he overheard her telling Felicia how she really felt about him.

Nothing Jake had ever been through had cut him the way that what Holly had said that night had done. Nothing had ever hurt that bad, and nothing had since.

Jake had loved Holly his entire life, since first grade, when the Boones had moved into the house next to the Morrows, but childhood sweethearts and soul mates had given way to super-sensitive puberty: Holly had realized how the Down Hillers, including herself, were perceived, and she'd taken it very hard. Perhaps harder than anyone.

What makes us so different? she'd asked over and over. Just because they have money and we don't? Nice clothes and big houses and we don't?

It wasn't that she wanted to be an Up Hiller, he knew; she was proud of who she was, even if she didn't always know it. She was proud of her family and her friends. But Jake always knew that he was out of the running because she dreamed of something else, something Up Hill-esque for herself. He'd understood her so well, then.

Just once, after their terrible argument, he'd wondered if her bad reputation had been deserved. If perhaps she had given herself to the Up Hill boys, trying to make them like her, hoping one would fall for her and take her away into their world. He'd immediately cursed himself for going there. He'd been hurt was all, terribly hurt, and he'd wanted to hurt her back by thinking something awful about her.

Only once, when they were fifteen, Holly had told him that none of it was true, that she'd never slept with any of those boys,

that her reputation was completely undeserved, and he believed her. She'd never
had to tell him again. He knew the stories
and lies floating around school and in the
boys' bathrooms were all lies. About Holly,
Gayle, Lizzie, and Felicia. And a few other
Down Hill girls. When he was sixteen and
seventeen, and desperately in love with
Holly, he'd wanted to tell her how he felt
about her, but he'd been afraid. He'd
known she wanted more for herself than
just a Down Hill boy, even though she'd
never said such a thing, and he hadn't
wanted to take her dreams away from her.
She deserved more than him. And so he'd
loved her silently. But on prom night, when
she was leaving the day after next — after
graduation — when he couldn't keep it inside any longer, when he planned to ask if
he could come with her, he overheard her
telling Felicia at the senior prom that he
wasn't good enough.

It had been one thing for him to think
himself not good enough for her. It was another to hear Holly say aloud that she
thought so, too.

"Marry Jake Boone?" Holly had said as
she'd leaned against the low stone wall in
the gym's courtyard. "Don't be stupid
Flea. He represents everything I'm leaving.

He's the last man on earth I'd ever marry!"

"Well I'll be sure to never propose to you, Holly," he'd said flatly.

Holly and Felicia had whirled around, shock on their faces. Holly's mouth opened to speak, but he put the punch cups down and then walked away into the night.

"Jake, wait!" Holly had screamed. "Stop, please!"

But he hadn't stopped. And he'd never seen Holly again.

He represents everything I'm leaving . . . the last man on earth I'd ever marry.

"Jake?" Holly said, jolting him out of his memories. "Did you hear me? You look like you're a million miles away."

"Not a million. Not even a mile," he said with a wistful grin.

She stared at him, and he wondered if she thought he was referring to prom night.

"Arianna Miller is a lot of things," Jake began, getting back to their conversation, "but underhanded has never been one of them. She's made it very clear that she wants Dylan for herself. I think she'd go after him straight up — not try to hurt Lizzie or break up the engagement. Pru is similar."

She regarded him for a moment, then

slung her purse over her shoulder. "Look, Jake, I don't know what your relationship is to Pru Dunhill — or the Dunhills, for that matter. Lizzie did tell me that you've become very close to the entire family. So perhaps I should work with someone more *impartial*."

"I didn't realize we *were* working together, Holly," he said without expression.

"Jake, I'm really worried. I don't know what to do. Maybe I should just go to the police."

"You'd be wasting your time," he told her. "I've already discussed the case with the police. They're only too happy to have me working on it so they don't have to."

"Fine," she said. "Then I'll investigate on my own."

He sat straight up in his chair and looked her in the eye. "Holly, I have a bad feeling about these incidents and notes. Someone's seriously bent out of shape about this wedding, and I don't want you investigating on your own."

"You just said you wouldn't work with me. I don't think we'd make a very good team, anyway," Holly said.

"I agree with you there. So why don't you just leave it to me."

She looked as though she wanted to

argue, but decided against it. "Thank you for your time."

And with that, she stood and left, leaving behind the faint scent of her perfume and too many memories.

"Holly Morrow, stop thinking about the dirt this minute," Lizzie gently scolded as she led the way into Morrow's Pub. "It happened three hours ago and I forgot about it two hours ago."

"But —" Holly began. She couldn't get the dirt mound or the note or anything Lizzie had told her out of her mind. Nor could she get Jake Boone out of her mind. For the past hour, she'd tried to concentrate on Lizzie's well-being, but Jake's face kept intruding.

"But nothing, Hol," Lizzie said, taking Holly's chin in her hand. "It won't do me any good to dwell on it or try to figure out who did it. So why should I let the person victimize me twice by making me all upset when I'm happier than I've ever been?"

Holly squeezed Lizzie's hand. Her cousin never ceased to amaze Holly with her positive outlook. *I could learn a lot from Lizzie,* she thought.

"Now, you just forget all about it, which you will anyway because once you taste

Mama's famous macaroni and cheese, you'll forget everything but your taste buds."

"She's not kidding," said a familiar female voice.

Holly turned to find her beloved Aunt Louise smiling at her, a tray laden with two heaping, hot plates of macaroni and cheese, and two tall lemonades.

"Lizzie, baby, come take this so I can hug the dickens out of my favorite niece!"

Lizzie took the tray and set it down at a table near the picture window, and Holly flew into her aunt's arms. Louise Morrow smelled heavenly, of comfort food and her trademark White Shoulders perfume. Fifty-five with short, graying blond hair and a voice husky from cigarette smoking — both hers and her customers' — Louise squeezed Holly close.

"You look absolutely beautiful, Holly," Aunt Louise said, tucking a strand of Holly's brown hair behind her ear. "Like the city gal you always wanted to be."

"Thanks, Aunt Louise," Holly said. "You look wonderful, too. It's so good to see you!"

"Okay, you two," Louise said. "Sit down and enjoy. Holler if you need anything."

Lizzie and Holly sat and dug into their

feast. It was Morrow family tradition to have Louise's famous macaroni and cheese at homecomings, and Louise made the best mac and cheese — Holly's favorite — in the world.

"Oh, Holly, wait until you see the wedding gown I have in mind," Lizzie said around a mouthful. "I saw it in the window of Bettina's Bridal a few months ago and fell madly in love. I still can't believe it — me, Lizzie Morrow, shopping in Bettina's for my wedding gown, marrying the most gorgeous, most sweetest man there ever was. It's like a dream — well, except for the few stupid incidents lately." She took a long sip of her lemonade. "I'm not going to let it get to me, Holly. You were absolutely right earlier — no one is going to stop me from marrying the man I love."

Holly smiled. Lizzie had her there. She had said those words to Lizzie. She might not like what was going on in Troutville, but Lizzie had the right to love the man of her choice, no matter who didn't like it. "That's the spirit, Liz. You're absolutely right. All right — I'm dying to hear about the gown."

Lizzie grinned. "It's totally different than the one I always thought I'd want. Remember how we'd spend hours talking about the wedding gowns of our dreams, and Flea would sketch them?"

Holly smiled at the memory. The four friends had whiled away many afternoons discussing in detail the style, shape, length and material of their dream gowns. Lizzie had always described a low-cut, sparkly number that an A-list actress might wear to the Academy Awards. Holly had envisioned lace, lots of lace, and a long train.

"Bettina described it as a Victorian style," Lizzie continued. "It's very high-necked, with long sleeves with little puffs at the shoulders. Very simple. It's really lovely."

Holly glanced at Lizzie. *Victorian? High-necked? Puffs?*

Simple?

And nothing Lizzie loved could usually be called *lovely*. Elaborate, yes. Fun. High-style. Fabulous. *Lovely* wasn't even a word Holly had ever heard come out of her cousin's mouth.

"The moment I saw it in the window," Lizzie said, "I knew it was the dress I would marry Dylan in. I walked right into Bettina's and asked to try it on — two months before we even got engaged. But I knew I'd marry him, Holly. I knew it the way they say you'll know."

Holly smiled. "I'm so happy for you, Liz. You're so in love. I can just imagine Bettina Tutweller demanding to see an engagement ring before she'd allow you to try on one of her gowns."

"Oh, she was much worse than that," Lizzie said. " *'I'm sure you'd prefer the selections at Mary Lou's Down Hill,'* Bettina said to me in that snooty tone of hers. *'They have a couple of wedding gowns there — more in your price range, too, I'm sure.'* "

"That witch!" Holly said, outraged. "How dare she!"

"I told her I preferred the dress in her window," Lizzie said, "and repeated that I wanted to try it on. Bettina told me I'd need an appointment — and that it was customary for only brides-to-be to try on her gowns."

Holly's mouth fell open to the table.

"And then she said, *'And I don't see a diamond ring on any of your fingers, Lizzie.'* "

Holly gasped. "And we're going there tomorrow morning to shop for dresses?"

"It's where my dream dress is, Holly," Lizzie explained. "Believe me, if Flea's shop sold wedding gowns or bridesmaids dresses, I'd only shop there. But Flea doesn't do bridal, so I'm going with my dream dress at Bettina's."

"That witch doesn't deserve your patronage!" Holly complained.

"Am I supposed to cut off my nose to spite my face?" Lizzie responded. "Not go to the best shop in the county because the woman who owns it is a jerk? Or am I supposed to get the dress of my dreams, which is in that shop, and the hell with Bettina?"

Holly had to ponder that one.

"Do I let Bettina win by not buying the dress I really want?" Lizzie asked. "No way."

"I don't know, Lizzie. I guess when you put it like that, you do lose by not going to Bettina's. I never thought of it that way."

"Oh, Holly," Lizzie said, "there are a lot of ways to think about these things. If I reacted to every slight, I'd never be able to leave my house or Down Hill."

Every slight? Bettina had done more than slight Lizzie. And in any case, was this a way to live, to put up with "slights"?

"Hol, Bettina's comeuppance is being forced to fuss and fawn and wait on us hand and foot," Lizzie said with a smile. "So eat up, Cousin. You'll need your strength for trying on bridesmaid dresses tomorrow morning."

Holly wasn't so sure it was comeuppance enough for Bettina, but it was something.

"Let's drive Bettina crazy," Holly suggested. "Constantly change our minds and demand different sizes!"

Lizzie cracked up. "Definitely." She clinked her lemonade glass against Holly's.

"You two stop chattering and eat!" Lizzie's mom scolded. "I have two more helpings for each of you waiting to get in your tummies."

Holly laughed and dug in, the delicious comfort food doing its job.

I can learn a lot from Lizzie, Holly thought again. *If only I could brush things off,* she thought. *If only I could stop worrying!*

But she couldn't. After she'd stormed out of Jake Boone's office an hour ago, she'd walked back to Lizzie's, determined to find the person responsible for the "incidents" and the pile of dirt. With or without Jake's help.

Probably without, she thought, absently pushing around macaroni and cheese on her plate.

Why does it have to be so complicated? she wondered. *He was once my dearest friend, for so many years, and then one misconstrued comment and —*

Had he misconstrued what she'd said? Or had she said exactly what she meant, exactly what he'd heard?

He represents everything I'm leaving. He's the last man on earth I'd ever marry!

She hadn't meant it. Not a word of it. She'd simply been determined to ignore her feelings for him.

Because I did love you, Jake Boone. Oh, how I loved you. But you were set on staying in Troutville, proving yourself, not letting anyone dictate how you felt or where you lived, and I wanted to hightail it away the moment I could.

"Will you excuse me for a moment, Lizzie?" Holly asked. Lizzie nodded and began chatting animatedly with several of the regulars she knew well, as Holly walked as normally as she could to the ladies' restroom, where she slid down on the cool tile, covered her face with her hands and cried.

CHAPTER FIVE

"I'm nothing and I'm never gonna be nothing else, so what's the point, Jake?"

As sixteen-year-old Jimmy Morgan crossed his arms against his chest and kicked at the curb in front of Dunhill Mansion, Jake glanced at his watch and hoped Dylan would make an appearance soon. Jake and Dylan had promised to take Jimmy to a free rock concert in a neighboring town, and if Dylan didn't show up in one minute, they'd have to leave without him. Despite his excitement for the concert, Jimmy was down on himself again, and Jake could use Dylan's help in boosting him up.

It had been Dylan who'd suggested several years ago that he and Jake donate their time to the River County Boys' Club, which had been founded fifty years ago by Dylan's grandfather, who'd been rebellious and surly and about to run away from home until he'd discovered an informal basketball "team" that showed up to play every Saturday, all players welcome. The team and the mix of adults and teens from all walks of life whose seemingly only common thread was a love of basketball, had changed Rockwell Dunhill's life, and he'd opened the free club so that all teens would have somewhere to turn. Jimmy, who'd done time in a juvenile center for property damage and fighting, had begun turning up a few months ago, and Jake and Dylan, who volunteered at the center on Wednesday nights, had slowly befriended the teenager, mostly through their basketball playing ability. Dylan was the better player, and when Jimmy found out that Dylan was a Dunhill, he'd been enamored of him ever since. That a Dunhill could be "so cool" and speak to him like he was a person had made quite an impact on Jimmy. With Jimmy's single mother's permission, Jake and Dylan took Jimmy to special events a couple times a month, and his attitude had begun improving immensely.

"Jimmy, you can do anything you want," Jake told the boy. "I'm proof of that. It's all up to you — not the amount of money you have — or don't have. Not your past. Not anything. You always have the power to change your future. Your present."

"Jenny Johnson doesn't think so," Jimmy said.

"Who's Jenny Johnson?" Jake asked, suddenly understanding where Jimmy was coming from. There was a girl involved.

"She's only the prettiest, nicest, smartest girl in school," Jimmy said. "But she'd never go out with me. She's Up Hill, and I'm not, and that's that."

"Bull," Jake said. "How do you know all this if you haven't asked her out?"

"Like I need to?" Jimmy said. "She'd never go for me. She never talks to me."

"Let me ask you something," Jake said. "Do you catch her looking at you a lot?"

Jimmy nodded. "All the time. Because she thinks I'm scum."

Jake smiled. "No, Jimmy. Because she likes you. A woman can say or do anything she wants, but if you find her looking at you a lot, you can count on the fact that she's very interested in you."

"Really?" Jimmy asked, his face brightening.

Jake nodded, and Jimmy bit his lip and dropped his arms. The boy hopped onto the hood of Jake's car and leaned back, his arms behind his head on the windshield. "She's really something. Really smart."

"Smart is good," Jake agreed.

"When she answers questions in English class," Jimmy said, "you can tell she's

116

really read the book, really cared, you know?"

"I know what you mean," Jake said, suddenly thinking back ten years before to Holly in English class, passionately discussing *Romeo and Juliet* and how unfair it all was that two people who loved each other should be kept apart because of reasons that had nothing to do with them.

He also remembered the way he'd catch Holly looking at him. He'd glance up — in class, in the park, at their houses, wherever — and he'd be surprised to find her staring at him. Sometimes, they would be staring at each other and it would take a few seconds before one of them realized it and glanced away uncomfortably. She had to know how much he loved her; it was in everything he said and did. But he didn't know if she loved him, so he was never sure how to express his feelings.

He shook his head at how silly he'd been then; he should have just walked right up to her and told her how he felt, but back then, he couldn't.

And for good reason, he thought. Because it turned out she hadn't loved him, not at all.

So who was he to tell Jimmy Morgan that this Jenny girl was interested just because she checked him out a lot? If Jimmy accepted what Jake had to say and declared his feelings to the girl and she rejected him, it could do serious damage to Jimmy's shaky self-confidence.

A girl liking you or not liking you has nothing to do with self-confidence, he amended. You accepted that she didn't, and you hurt and you moved on.

The way you moved on, Boone? he asked himself. In ten years he hadn't felt about a woman the way he'd felt about Holly. He'd dated, he'd had lovers, he'd had some short-term relationships. But no one had ever captured his heart the way Holly had.

It was strange that she still had the power to affect him so strongly. This afternoon, in his office, it was all he could do to keep from reaching across his desk to touch her silky hair, to feel her hand in his, to come up with some excuse to hug her just so he could be that close to her.

But there was no excuse to hug her and he was sure there never would be.

He'd dropped by Lizzie's a couple of hours ago to make sure she was all right and to have a look at the dirt and the note. And to make sure that Holly wasn't off investigating on her own, not that there was much to go on. Lizzie had assured him that Holly was safe and sound upstairs, taking a nap, and then she'd told him the same thing Holly had about coming home to find the dirt pile.

The note was typed — computer printed like the others. Nothing special, nothing out of the ordinary, nothing that indicated the computer was a special kind or the printer had some quirk that might lead to the culprit. He'd questioned the neighbors, hoping someone had spotted the person going in or out of Lizzie's house, but no one had.

Dammit, who was it? He'd made a wild list of suspects, anyone who disliked Lizzie Morrow or the idea of the Dunhill-Morrow union. The list was long.

"Someone's waving at you," Jimmy said, jerking up his chin toward Dunhill Mansion's stately porch.

Jake glanced up at the house to find Dylan's mother, Victoria Dunhill, with gardening shears in one hand and her Boston terrier in the other.

"Is she going to kill the dog with the shears?" Jimmy asked.

Jake swatted the boy's shoulder with the *Troutville Gazette*, but couldn't hide his smile. "My guess is that she's going to trim the hedges."

Jimmy was incredulous. "Herself?"

"Yes, herself."

"But doesn't she have a gardener?" Jimmy asked. "She could pay someone to do it."

"She could pay someone to do it, but she enjoys gardening."

Jimmy glanced around the manicured grounds. "I'd like to be rich enough someday to do things I like even though I could pay someone to do them for me."

"Like what?" Jake asked.

"Like wash my Harley-Davidson motorcycle," Jimmy said. "I'm gonna have one someday, and I'm going to take care of it myself."

"Sounds good to me," Jake responded, waving at Victoria Dunhill as she started down the walkway, the dog trailing after her. "Hello, Mrs. Dunhill," he called out. "Have you seen Dylan?"

"No," she said, her silver bob not moving as she shook her head. "But then again, he's not exactly pleased with me today, so he might be keeping his distance."

Jake had learned a long time ago that you never had to pry for more information; if you just listened, people generally told you everything you wanted to know. And, he'd gotten to know Victoria Dunhill pretty well over recent years. She was a talker. It was one of the reasons she was so far down his list of suspects of who was trying to scare Lizzie out of the marriage. If Victoria had paid someone to scare Lizzie's bridal party or dump a pile of dirt on her bed, the woman would surely discuss it at length to anyone who would listen.

"I made one small comment about Lizbeth," Victoria went on, as Jake knew she would, "and Dylan got all upset. He's so touchy these days."

Victoria refused to refer to Lizzie as Lizzie, which bothered Dylan enough as it was.

Mrs. Dunhill let out a harrumph. "All I said was that I hoped she'd take me up on my offer to treat for a makeover for her wedding and get rid of that garish makeup and big hair. And he insisted he liked Lizzie exactly as she was and huffed and puffed as though I insulted the girl!"

"Well, you did," Jimmy muttered under his breath.

"Come, Louis," she cooed to her dog. "Let's go trim the rosebushes." She turned to Jake. "Bye, dear. If you do see Dylan, please talk some sense into him about his moodiness lately. It's really unbecoming. If he acts that way at the engagement party, perhaps he should rethink his choice in his bride. She's clearly not making him happy. Come, Louis. Stop dawdling!"

As Mrs. Dunhill walked around the lawn to the backyard, Louis scampering after her, Jimmy jumped off the car with a grin. "It's most unbecoming, Louis!" Jimmy repeated in an upper-crust accent before doubling over with laughter. "Stop dawdling this minute, Louis!"

Jake couldn't help but laugh, too. "She treats that dog like he's one of her children."

Jimmy snorted. "More like she treats her children like *they're* dogs instead of people with minds of their own. I would've liked to have been a fly on the wall when Dylan told Mother Dearest he was marrying Lizzie."

Jake glanced at Jimmy; he was often surprised at how perceptive the teenager was, how much he took in, how much he understood about the people around him. "I'm sure she was delighted that her son is in love and found the woman he wants to spend the rest of his life with," Jake said, shooting Jimmy a gently disapproving look.

"Ha. Like Queen Dunhill wants a Down

Hill daughter-in-law," Jimmy said.

Jimmy was right on the mark about that, but Jake wasn't about to get into the Dunhills' private affairs with the boy. Jake had been there when Dylan told his mother that he and Lizzie were marrying. Not in the same room, but just outside. The night before Dylan and Lizzie planned to tell Mrs. Dunhill of the engagement, Dylan had asked Jake if he'd mind feigning some reason to meet with his mother around noon. Dylan figured that if his mother flipped out about the engagement, Jake, who Mrs. Dunhill adored and trusted, would be there to calm her down, talk some sense into her.

She *had* flipped.

While Jake did some paperwork in the library just outside Mrs. Dunhill's office, Dylan and Lizzie sat across from Mrs. Dunhill and told her the news.

First, though, he'd had to introduce Lizzie. It was the first time the two women had met.

"You're introducing me to your *intended?*" Mrs. Dunhill had asked, rising from her imperial desk chair behind her huge mahogany desk. "You are planning to marry a woman in three weeks whom you have never introduced to your own family?"

123

"I would —" Dylan started to say.

"Dylan," his mother interrupted, "for a young man with a good head on his shoulders, you clearly haven't thought this through. If I didn't even know you were dating this . . . young woman, how is it possible you've been dating long enough to *marry?*"

"Mrs. Dunhill," Lizzie said, her voice warm and strong, "first let me say that it is so nice to meet you. I've heard —"

"I'm sure you're a very nice person, Elizabeth," Mrs. Dunhill interrupted. "However —"

"Actually, my real name is Lizbeth, not Elizabeth," Lizzie said cheerfully. "No one's ever called me Lizbeth, though. I go by Lizzie."

Mrs. Dunhill eyed Lizzie. "Well, Lizbeth, as I was saying, I'm sure you're a lovely girl, but what could you possibly have in common with Dylan? You're from two different worlds. Why not continue dating, if you enjoy each other's company, but leave marriage to the right people for you. I'm sure there's a wonderful young man waiting for you. Why, just the other day, when my car broke down on Troutville Plaza, a very handsome mechanic came to help. He wasn't wearing a ring and —"

Dylan stood up. "Mother! That's enough."

Lizzie hadn't said anything.

"I just meant —" Mrs. Dunhill said, affecting innocence.

"We know what you 'just meant,' " Dylan snapped. "And I'm going to tell you right now that I will not stand for it. I love Lizzie, she loves me, and we're getting married. We kept our relationship a secret to avoid everyone's comments and opinions — we didn't want the negativity we knew would come our way to have any effect on us, on how we feel about each other."

"Clearly, Dylan, you expected negativity," said Mrs. Dunhill. "So I don't see why you're getting so annoyed by my . . . surprise at your announcement."

Dylan shook his head, but sat back down. "I want you to be happy for me, Mother. I love Lizzie so much. For the first time in my life, I know what it means to be in love."

"Oh, Dylan," Mrs. Dunhill tsk-tsked as though her son were a teenager. "Don't confuse being in love with enduring love. Of course you're in love. She's" — she glanced at Lizzie — "very attractive." Mrs. Dunhill ran her nose up and down the length of Lizzie, from her wild blond curls

125

to her high-heeled hot-pink pumps.

"Mother," Dylan said. "Lizzie and I came here to tell you in person that we're in love and we're getting married in three weeks. I wanted to tell you before you heard it elsewhere. I wanted to tell you before you received the invitation."

Mrs. Dunhill froze. "*Invitation?* What?"

"You should receive it tomorrow or the next day," Lizzie said. "They're really lovely. Gold embossing —"

"Invitations have gone out?" Mrs. Dunhill interrupted, the color draining from her face.

"Yes, Mother," Dylan said.

"So you're serious," she returned.

"Very serious," Dylan responded.

Mrs. Dunhill looked from Dylan to Lizzie and then rang her little silver bell that she took everywhere. Walker, her butler, hurried into the room. "Walker, I'm feeling a bit faint. Will you help me upstairs?"

"Of course, madam," Walker said. "Shall I reschedule Mr. Boone's visit?"

"Jake is here?" she asked, visibly relaxing. "No, no, Walker. I'll see him. In fact, send him in." The butler stepped out. "If you're finished," she said to Dylan and Lizzie, "I have some important business to discuss with Jake."

Dylan smiled. "That's fine, Mother. Perhaps you'll invite Lizzie and me over for dinner so you can get to know her."

Mrs. Dunhill smiled nervously, then shot up when Jake came into the room. "Ah, Jake. Do come in. Bye, now, Dylan. Lizbeth."

Lizzie smiled warmly. "Please, call me Lizzie. I'm really looking forward to getting to know —"

"That's fine, dear. Close the door on your way out, will you, Dylan?"

Dylan shook his head and Lizzie bit her lip, and Jake dropped down in the chair Dylan vacated, knowing he had a long afternoon ahead of him.

The sound of an approaching car shook Jake out of the memory. Jimmy jumped off the hood of Jake's car and then kicked at the tire.

"It's not Dylan," Jimmy grumbled as the car continued past. "Where *is* he? He's twenty minutes late!"

Jake slung an arm over Jimmy's shoulder. "Looks like Dylan got tied up at the office, Jim. C'mon, it'll be you and me."

Jimmy's face crumpled. "This is, like, the fifth time he's blown me off. He's probably having sex with *Lizbeth* somewhere."

"Hey," Jake scolded. "Watch it."

"Ever since he started seeing her, he's been too busy to hang out with me," Jimmy complained. "I once had a friend like that — blew me off whenever he got a girlfriend. It really sucks." He picked up a rock and threw it hard against a tree in the yard. "Whatever."

Jake eyed the teenager. Jimmy was angry and hurt and sulking.

Enough to try to scare Lizzie out of marrying Jake?

As the boy slumped into Jake's car, he very reluctantly added Jimmy to his very long list of suspects.

"Good morning, Lizzie and party! Welcome to Bettina's Bridal!"

Bettina Tutweller, proprietor and snob, held open the door to her tony salon on Troutville's most exclusive shopping street. She wore a tight smile. Two assistants flanked her on either side, each with a tape measure around her neck.

As Lizzie, Holly, Gayle, and Flea entered the shop, the assistants swooped, handing out delicate china cups of tea and water with lemons floating.

"I'm simply delighted that you've chosen my shop for your wedding gown and your bridesmaids dresses," Bettina gushed, her curly blond bob shaking wildly.

Of course you are, Holly thought, mentally shaking her head at the woman. *Now that Lizzie is going to be a Dunhill and is spending Dunhill money, she's welcome.*

And you are going to work for every penny! Holly silently promised Bettina.

"Thank you so much, Bettina," Lizzie replied. "You know Flea, of course. She's done some work for you, and this is Gayle and my cousin, Holly. My bridal party."

"Isn't Prudence coming?" Bettina asked, looking out the windows. "She has such wonderful taste."

Lizzie's face fell. "Pru isn't in the bridal party."

"Isn't in the bridal party?" Bettina repeated. "But she's the groom's *sister.* Usually —"

"Lizzie introduced you to the bridal party," Holly interrupted. "The three of us."

Bettina eyed Holly, then slid her beady gaze back to Lizzie. "I see." She clapped her hands loudly. Her two assistants flew to her side. "Why don't you four gals start looking around," Bettina said. "If you need anything, Jenny and Mary here will help you. I've closed the shop so that you and your party will have our complete attention." She and her assistants smiled and flitted away, but Holly noticed that Bettina stood behind her tiny marble desk, watching the group like a hawk.

"Don't let her comment about Pru bother you," Holly whispered.

"I've already forgotten it," Lizzie said. "I'm too excited to let anything bother me this morning." Lizzie could barely contain her enthusiasm. "I feel like a kid in a candy store! You don't know how much it means to me that the three of you are my bridal party, standing up with me, sharing it all with me. I love you all so much!" Lizzie's eyes filled with happy tears.

Holly laughed and threw her arms around her cousin. "Oh, Lizzie. We love you, too."

"We sure do," Gayle said.

Flea nodded. "I especially love you since for the first time in forever, I don't have to make my own dress!"

Lizzie laughed. "All right, let's get started. Since the three of you have such different taste, why don't each of you individually pick dresses you like for yourselves. And then we'll see if everyone can agree on just one."

Gayle nodded and winked at Lizzie.

"Oh, miss," she called to Bettina. "I'd like to see your sexy red bridesmaid dresses in size eight and ten."

"And I'd like to see your more conservative black dresses in petite sixes," Flea called out.

Holly smiled at Lizzie. Apparently, Lizzie had shared with Gayle and Flea her prior experience with Bettina. "I'll just look around and let you know when I'll require your help," she said to Bettina.

The woman smiled tightly, then clapped twice, and her automaton assistants flew around the store, collecting dresses.

"Ooh, look at this one," Gayle exclaimed, ogling a bright red, low-cut, drapey number. "Hot, hot, hot!"

Holly's own gaze landed on a pale pink gown with an empire waist and delicate beading. "Wow — that dress sure is pretty."

"Ooh, I love it," Flea agreed, her expert gaze admiring the craftsmanship. "And pink would suit all of our coloring."

"It's just the right pink for my red hair, too," Gayle said, caressing the silky material. "Holly, I think you've found our dress in less than one minute!"

Bettina's curiosity and business instinct won out and she scurried over. "That dress is pure silk and hand-beaded. A lovely choice."

There was that word again. *Lovely.* Holly glanced at Lizzie, who was ogling a wedding gown on one of the few mannequins. It matched the description of Lizzie's Victorian gown — but it didn't match Lizzie one bit. There was absolutely nothing about the dress that said Lizzie. *If she likes it, she likes it,* Holly scolded herself.

"Isn't it beautiful?" Lizzie breathed. "It's so elegant! It's definitely the one."

Gayle stared at the gown. "It's very pretty, Lizzie. But not what I would have thought you'd go for."

"Yeah, Liz. It's not your style at all," Flea agreed. "I'm surprised you even like it."

"I know," Lizzie said, caressing the lace on the high neck, which reminded Holly of a mock turtleneck. "I surprised myself, too! But when I saw it in the window, I knew it was the one."

"The lace is exquisite," Holly said.

"And you'll look amazing in it," Gayle added.

"The puffing at the shoulders is a beautiful old-fashioned detail," Flea said. "This dress is very difficult to make. It must cost a small fortune!"

Lizzie smiled and shook her head. "No

looking at price tags. That's a direct order from Dylan himself."

"It'll look just lovely on you, Lizzie," Bettina rushed to say. "Why don't I put it in the dressing room for you."

"Before you do that, Bettina," Gayle said, "be a dear and return all these others to the racks." She dumped a pile of slinky red dresses in the woman's arms.

Holly smiled.

"These, too," Flea said, piling Bettina's other arm with a collection of black dresses. "But maybe not this one," she said, removing the top one. "It's so well made, I'd love to try it just to examine the cut."

Bettina harrumped, then clapped and filled her assistants' arms with the dresses. "I'll go get your dress for you, Lizzie," she said. "Size fourteen?"

"Eight," Lizzie corrected.

"Sometimes you can't tell with very busty women," Bettina said coolly. "I'll need to go into our stockroom. I only have a four and six on the display racks."

Holly rolled her eyes, and Lizzie laughed.

"I'm going to try this one on before the pink one," Flea said. "Be back in a jif." She headed back into the dressing room.

Lizzie fingered the pink silk dress draped

over Holly's arm. "You have great taste, Hol. You always did. I wish I had your taste, but even when I try to dress 'appropriately,' I always go back to my wild clothes. They're me, I guess."

"Lizzie, I love the way you dress," Holly said. "You dress like you. Wonderful, colorful you."

"She's gotten a few comments from the Dunhills about the 'inappropriateness' of some of her outfits," Gayle said, rolling her own eyes. "A few days ago, we ran into Victoria Dunhill and a snooty friend of hers on the street, and as we passed, Victoria very loudly commented that Lizzie's dress was 'most unbecoming and inappropriate for an engaged woman!' " Gayle shook her head. "And Lizzie was wearing one of her tamest outfits!"

Lizzie smiled, then bit her lip. "Dylan says he likes me just as I am and that if I changed one single thing about me, he'd cancel the wedding. But maybe I should try to fit in with the Dunhills. Dress differently. More like them."

"But then you'd find yourself without a groom," Holly pointed out with a smile.

"Yeah," Gayle agreed. "So I guess you'll just have to keep being you!"

Lizzie laughed. "Thanks, guys. I don't

know what I'd do without you."

"I have to say, Lizzie," Holly said, "sounds to me like Dylan's doing a very good job."

"Told you so," Lizzie said, tapping Holly on the nose.

Holly smiled. "I'd really like to get to know him better."

"That makes me so happy, Holly. You're gonna love —"

Suddenly, glass shattered and a scream came from the back area where the dressing rooms were.

"Flea!" Holly called. She ran to the dressing rooms, Lizzie, Gayle and the shop staff racing behind her.

Flea was slumped against the wall across from the floor-to-ceiling three-way mirror, a jagged cut bleeding on her forehead.

"Oh, my God, Flea!" Lizzie screamed. "Call 911," she said to the assistants, racing over to Flea and kneeling down beside her. "What happened?"

Flea opened her mouth, but no words came out and she pointed to a stone that was half concealed by her body.

Holly gasped and immediately looked at the bay window behind the mirror. She ran over and parted the curtains to find a stone-sized hole.

"Flea, are you all right?" Holly asked, kneeling beside her. "That cut looks pretty deep."

"I'm f-fine — I think," Flea said, gingerly touching her finger to the cut on her forehead. She tried to sit up straight, but slumped back against the wall. "A little dizzy."

Holly grabbed the rock. "There's paper rubber-banded around it." She pulled off the rubber band; it was a half sheet of loose-leaf paper with a message.

Holly gasped when she read the two lines, then folded the paper.

"Holly?" Lizzie said. "What did it say?"

Now it was Holly who couldn't speak.

"Holly?" Lizzie repeated.

When Holly didn't speak or move, Lizzie gently took the paper from Holly.

"*Whores don't wear white,*" Lizzie read. Her eyes filling with tears. "*Cancel the wedding, or I'll cancel you and your friends.*" Lizzie crumpled up the paper and threw it against the wall, angrily wiping at her eyes. Then she fell on her knees next to Flea. "I'm so sorry, Flea. It's all my fault you got hurt. I'm so sorry." Tears streamed down Lizzie's cheeks.

Bettina rushed into the dressing room. "I knew I should have listened to my friends and the other proprietors on Troutville Plaza! They told me I'd have nothing but trouble if I welcomed you and your party in here!"

Lizzie stared at her, a stunned expression on her face.

"I want you all out of here!" Bettina screamed. "Out! I should have listened!"

"We'll gladly leave when the ambulance and police arrive," Holly snapped.

Bettina harrumphed and stalked out of the dressing room, then stalked back in. "That's blood on my new beige carpeting! I'll be sending you the cleaning bill, Lizzie Morrow!"

"You'll have to try to collect in court," Gayle said. "My boss will fight you on it. Trust me."

"I want all of you out the moment the police and ambulance arrive," Bettina shouted. "You're not welcome in my store."

"Lizzie will be very happy to spend her tens of thousands of dollars in another store, Bettina," Holly gritted out.

The woman turned up her nose and left.

"I'm so sorry, Lizzie," Flea said, wincing as she touched the area around her cut. "I've ruined everything for you. Your gown . . . and these pretty pink dresses —"

"We'll find pretty pink dresses and my gown somewhere else," Lizzie said. "And you ruined nothing — Flea, you got hurt, for God's sake. This is all my fault!"

"I'll make that dress for you myself," Flea said. "I don't care if I have to work twenty-four hours a day for the next two weeks!"

"Flea, sweetie, you don't have to do that," Lizzie said. "You're going to need to rest up and recuperate, not work even harder than you do already."

"I'm making that dress for you," Flea insisted. "And I'm going to rub Bettina's face in it!"

"I'll help," Gayle said. "With the dress *and* the face rubbing."

Flea laughed.

Lizzie let out a very deep breath. "Thank God, you're laughing. Oh, Flea, I'm just so sorry."

"I think I hear sirens," Holly said.

"Ambulance and police are here," Bettina called coldly. "I'll be sure to alert the police that I heard laughter in there. So if you try to sue me for the insurance, I'll see that *you're* all fought on that!"

Gayle shook her head. "She is some piece of work."

"I can't get the note out of my head,"

Lizzie said. "And that stone. Why is someone doing this? Why would they resort to this kind of violence? Flea could have been killed!"

Whores don't wear white. Cancel the wedding, or I'll cancel you and your friends . . .

The vicious words repeated over and over in Holly's mind.

What the hell is going on here? Holly wondered wildly. *Who is behind this?*

"I'm calling Dylan right now," Lizzie said, pulling her cell phone out of her purse. "The engagement party is off. There's no way I'm risking the lives of my friends and family. It's off! And forget about the reunion. I don't think any of us should leave our homes." Clutching the phone, she dissolved into tears on the floor next to Flea.

I will find out who's doing this, Holly vowed. *I'll find you and I'll see justice served.*

CHAPTER SIX

Jake had spent three hours turning over every rock, leaf, and stick in the back alley of Bettina's Bridal salon. Nothing. Whoever had thrown the stone had been careful.

And, apparently, lucky. The window in the dressing room was covered by a sheer drape; it was possible to see a figure in front of the mirror. Had Lizzie been the intended target?

Given that Lizzie and her bridal party had made an appointment at Bettina's, an appointment that had made the society page of the *Troutville Gazette* — and no, it hadn't been a slow news day — where and when the party would be was right there in black and white. Perhaps the culprit hadn't cared *which* member of the wedding he or she struck as long as one of them got hit. Was the shop owner or one of her assistants involved? Had they alerted someone that one of the party was in the dressing room? Had the culprit been hanging around in front of the store, seen one of the four friends go into the dressing room, and then scurried to the back alley to throw the stone?

He pushed through the double doors of Troutville General Hospital with a lot of questions and no answers. The police had dismissed the entire incident as petty vandalism; they'd conducted a brief investigation, had turned up nothing, and asked that Jake keep them informed of any new developments. The police regarded the case as they would a bunch of feuding high schoolers.

He stopped by the information desk for Felicia's room, then rode up in the elevator to the third floor.

"Jake!"

The moment the elevator doors pinged open, Holly was running toward him. He saw Lizzie and Gayle in the waiting area, wearing worried expressions, shaking their heads and pacing.

"How's Felicia?" he asked.

"She's going to be all right," Holly said. "She needed stitches — the cut was so deep it'll scar, unfortunately, but the doctors said she was very lucky the rock missed her eye."

There was that word, again: *lucky*. But Jake didn't think luck was involved here. The culprit had known when and where to throw that stone. And he had a feeling he or she had aimed it for the face so that whoever was hit would be a walking reminder to Lizzie of what would happen if she went ahead with the wedding.

"Is someone with Felicia now?" he asked. "I'd like to ask her some questions if she's up to it."

"The police were here to take her statement but they're long gone. She's alone, but she's resting now."

Jake nodded.

"They're going to send her home in an hour," Holly added. "She'll stay with me and Lizzie for a couple of days. You can come by Lizzie's later today or tomorrow."

"Thanks, I will," he said. "Felicia's been through quite a lot."

Holly smiled gently. "You were always the only person to call her Felicia."

"It's a nice name," Jake said. "I don't know why she prefers to be called Flea. I've never understood that."

"Her father always pronounced her name as though it was two syllables — Flea-sha," Holly explained. "So when she learned her name, she would refer to herself as Flea."

"Ah, put that way, it's a very sweet nickname," Jake said. He remembered the first day of middle school, when they were thirteen, and the teacher called roll. When she came to Felicia Harvey, some of the Down Hillers spoke up and said everyone called her Flea for short. Pru Dunhill snorted and said, "You can borrow my dog's collar, if you need to." The room had erupted with laughter, and Pru had been sent off to the principal's office. But the damage had been done.

"I assume you investigated the bridal salon and the property?" Holly asked.

"I did," he said. "And I also told you that I don't discuss an ongoing case."

"Jake, Flea could have been killed," Holly said, crossing her arms over her chest. "We're not talking notes and scratched cars anymore. We're talking about life and death."

"I'm aware of that, Holly."

She stared at him, taking measure of him. Jake was aware of how well she still knew him. She would get no further information out of him. He saw her process that. He also saw she was angry about it.

She sat on a hard plastic chair, and he sat down across from her. "Lizzie wants to cancel the engagement party," she said. "Dylan was here a couple of hours ago, but he had an emergency with a client and had to go. He also thinks they should cancel it." She buried her face in her hands, and he was tempted to put his arm around her. He braced his hands on his thighs to keep them from touching her, from tucking aside the heavy strand of brown hair that always fell in her face when she hung her head. From comforting her. Soothing her worries. From telling her everything would be okay.

God, how he wanted to do all that.

"I've spoken to Dylan by phone," Jake said. "And I've talked him out of canceling the party."

"What?" Holly said, jumping up. "You can't be serious!"

"Holly, the engagement party is in two weeks. Hopefully, I'll catch the jerk long before then, but if I don't, I can count on him or her being at the engagement party. Practically every one of my suspects is on the guest list. That means they'll all be in one room at the same time. Any suspicious behavior will be noticed. It'll also allow me to question people surreptitiously. Besides, if they cancel the party they might as well call off the wedding."

She seemed to be taking that all in. "But it also tells the person that Lizzie and Dylan won't be scared off. What if they resort to more violence? What if instead of a rock, the next weapon is a knife or a gun or —" She stopped and shook her head, closing her eyes. "I'm just so scared for Lizzie. For all of us, now. I don't know what to think, who to talk to."

"Holly, just be assured that I'm on the case. Dylan has hired discreet bodyguards to trail the four of you at all times. In fact, if you look to your right, there's a rather muscular man supposedly reading the paper." She glanced over. "But he's watching the area very carefully."

"I need to do more," she said. "I need to work with you on this case."

"No."

"Give me one good reason," she said.

"I'll give you three. One, you're not a detective. Two, you could get hurt. And three, I don't want to work with you."

"Because of what happened between us?" she asked softly.

"Nothing happened between us."

"You know what I'm referring to," she said.

"In any case, that's not the reason I don't want us to work together."

"Then why?" she asked.

"I gave you three reasons, Holly. That's all you're getting."

"The police are acting as though what's happening is high school hijinks," Holly said. "Flea might as well have been hit by a water balloon."

"They did conduct an investigation and found nothing," Jake explained. "Not just from what happened at Bettina's, but every incident. They know I'm working on the case and that I'll keep them apprized of all developments."

"Well, I'll be sure to do the same," she said, standing.

He stood, too. "What are you talking about?"

"I'm going to conduct my own investigation," she said. "And I'll keep you informed."

She stared at him, waiting, he knew, for him to tell her she would do no such thing, that she could get hurt, killed, and that, all right, they could work together, but he was the boss and she'd better remember that.

"You will do no such thing," he began.

A hint of a smile crossed her red lips.

"We'll begin Saturday night at the reunion," he said, hoping he wasn't making a huge mistake. At least by working with her, he could keep tabs on her. She was absolutely right about how serious their culprit was. "Similar to the engagement party, a good majority of the suspects will be there."

"And we'll all be safe," she asked, "at the reunion?"

"I'll have excellent security stationed," he responded.

She nodded. "Thank you, Jake. I mean, for agreeing to let me work with you. I need to do something. I need to help."

"I understand." He glanced at his watch. He had an appointment to interview Bettina Tutweller in ten minutes. "Till the reunion, then. I'll see you there."

He froze for a moment; those were his exact words the night of the prom. He'd wanted to pick her up at her house; he'd spent the afternoon polishing his beat-up car, but Holly had wanted to meet at the school gym, where the prom would be held. He'd been disappointed; he'd wanted to do the entire night right — pick her up, knock on the door, be greeted by her parents, wait for her to come downstairs in her beautiful dress, pin on her corsage, his hands sure to tremble.

But she'd wanted to meet at the prom, and so he'd said, "I'll see you there."

If she remembered, she showed no sign. Then again, why would she remember? He'd been just a friend to her then, not the love of her life.

As she'd been his.

★ ★ ★

Holly had been in Troutville for two entire weeks. She couldn't quite believe it. A week and a day ago, she hadn't thought she'd last a weekend. Yet here she was, staying at Lizzie's in her old family neighborhood, spending time with her friends and her aunt Louise and Lizzie, and with Jake Boone, of course.

Not of course. During the past two weeks, she'd seen him a few times. He came by to visit with Flea those first few days after the accident, and once Holly had run into him at Morrow's Pub. He'd been cordial, nothing more, nothing less. She'd asked if there were any new developments in the case — there weren't — and that had been that.

Actually, there had been more, unless she was imagining it. It was in the way he looked at her, with those intelligent, knowing eyes. It wasn't a look of anger or resentment or long-simmering bitterness.

It was a look of . . . desire.

Perhaps she was crazy. Perhaps she'd been without male companionship for too long. But the way he looked at her was the way a man looked at a woman he was very, very attracted to. There was nothing overtly sexual about it; the look in his eyes,

148

his body language, came from somewhere deep inside.

And tonight, they would meet where they had left off ten years ago. With their classmates. At their reunion.

I can't believe I'm really going, Holly thought, glancing at herself in the mirror over Lizzie's bureau. She, Lizzie, Gayle, and Flea were all in Lizzie's bedroom. Lizzie sat at her vanity table, halfheartedly applying cosmetics while glancing sadly at Flea, who lay on Holly's bed with a tray of cookies, a pot of tea, and a thick paperback romance novel. Gayle was rummaging through Lizzie's closet for sexy shoes with which to impress her boss, who would also be attending the reunion. Luckily she and Lizzie wore the same size.

"I really don't feel right about going to a stupid high school reunion while Flea is still recuperating," Lizzie said, absently stroking a blush brush over her cheeks. "Why don't we all just skip the reunion and stay here and have a slumber party. Like old times."

No one jumped at the idea. For one thing, old times might have been not so perfect, but at least no one was hurling heavy stones at them or leaving mounds of dirt on beds back then. Now, their huddling together was necessary for them to feel safe. It was almost too much a reminder of all that was going on.

A week had passed since Flea had been hurt in Bettina's salon — a week without further incident or notes — or clues, for that matter — and Flea was recovering well. The emergency room doctor had encouraged her to stay quiet for two weeks, and though she wanted to get back to work, Lizzie insisted she follow the doctor's orders. Flea was sleeping over at Lizzie's tonight since Lizzie had cable television and a movie Flea wanted to see was on at nine, and a security guard was posted outside the house.

"Lizzie Morrow, if you stay home on my account, you'll make me feel terrible," Flea said. "I've got goodies, a great book, and cable. I'm very comfy. Besides, you know I'm happier being a homebody than going out."

Lizzie swiped a cookie from the tray next to Flea. "I know, but this is our reunion. What's a reunion without the four of us? Especially because Holly's back in town. I never thought I'd see the day."

Holly smiled. "Me, either."

"Lizzie, sweetie," Flea said. "You guys go and have a good time. I'm much happier here, believe me. Plus, I've been dying to see the movie that's on tonight. And anyway, you heard what Jake said last week — the person responsible for all this trouble could very well be there. Maybe someone will slip up or try something and be caught."

"But —" Lizzie began.

"Are you going to argue with an injured person?" Flea asked, grinning. "Look, the reunion is a perfect place to find a whole bunch of people who don't like the fact that our Lizzie is marrying Dylan Dunhill."

"Great," Lizzie said, flopping down on her bed. "All the more reason to go. I can't wait to walk into a room with a group of people who hate me and wish me a lifetime of unhappiness."

"Screw 'em," Gayle said. "And it's not a group of people, it's just one loser."

"Actually," Holly said, "we don't know that. It could be more than one person. Two, or even a group."

"Even better!" Lizzie said, slapping her hand over her forehead.

Holly sat down next to Lizzie and held her hand. "Honey, the last thing I want is for you to be in danger's way. But with Dylan and Jake and the security team watching, I'm comfortable with the safety factor."

"And what more likely place for the culprit to strike," Gayle put in, "than at the high school reunion."

"And when they do," Flea said, "Dylan and Jake will be there to catch them."

Lizzie shot up. "Oh, God. What if Dylan or Jake gets hurt?" She dropped back down and covered her hands with her face. "This is too much. There's too much danger. Too much at stake."

"The only way to catch this . . . this person or people," Flea said, "is to hunt them down. I think Jake's right — he's going to find this monster among us. Whether it's at the reunion, the engagement party, or walking down the street."

"That's so scary," Holly said.

"We'll get him. Her. Them. Whoever," Gayle put in. "Jake is a great private investigator."

"That's true," Lizzie said. "With Jake on the case, I do feel a lot better. Safer."

"He's such a good person, too," Flea said. "It was so nice of him to come by the hospital and see how I was doing. And he stopped by my house twice in the past week. If anyone can find out who's behind what's been happening, it's Jake Boone."

I hope so, Holly thought. *Because I sure don't know how to go about this.* She stood and walked over to the window. Was the culprit out there right now? Watching? Listening?

Holly shivered and closed the window.

"I still can't understand how it's possible that our psycho left no clues any of the times he or she has struck," Holly said, sitting down next to Flea. "In movies, even the most careful criminals mess up and leave clues."

"Perhaps tonight," Lizzie said, "at the reunion, he or she will do or say something that will incriminate them. We all have to be on high alert."

"It's like, on one hand, you want them to do something so that we can catch them," Holly said. "But on the other, you want to feel safe."

"I think I've forgotten what it feels like to feel safe," Lizzie said. "I just want to stay home with Flea."

"Because that's the *safe* thing to do," Flea said. "But it's not the *right* thing to do. Not for your future. You've got to let Dylan and Jake catch this person. And the best way to do that is to go about your business and not be stopped from living your life!"

"You are absolutely right, Flea," Holly

said. "I want my dear cousin safe, too, but you're right."

Lizzie sat up. "Great. First I have a madman after me and now I have to help catch him." She offered a weak smile. "I know you're right, Flea. But you're sure — about us going to the reunion without you?"

Flea nodded her head. "Absolutely. Besides, you know I hate parties. I'm way too shy."

"If we're going, we'd better start getting ready," Gayle said. "The reunion starts in forty-five minutes."

"I didn't bring anything fancy," Holly said. "I did bring a pantsuit I could wear."

"Let me guess," Lizzie said with a smile. "Beige?"

"Beige is classic," Holly said. "Goes with everything."

"Except for a good time," Lizzie responded with a laugh. "Beige and fun definitely don't mix."

Flea laughed. "She's got you there."

Gayle was still in Lizzie's closet. "Oh, Holly, I would love to see you in this — with your wonderful brown hair and blue eyes, a pale pink would be so dramatic on you, yet feminine — or . . . what about this!" She pulled a long, red silky dress from the closet. "Liz, what do you think?"

"That would look so great on you, Holly!" Lizzie said. "Try it on — pretty please?"

"It is pretty," Holly said, running a hand down the floaty material. It's so soft. And the color is beautiful."

Lizzie shooed Holly behind her old-fashioned dressing screen. "Chop-chop, Cousin. You've only got a half hour!"

Holly took off her dress slacks and blouse and slipped on the dress. It fit perfectly, skimming over her body. It felt like heaven against her skin.

"Does it fit?" Gayle called.

"Perfectly!" Holly said. "Lizzie, could I borrow a pair of shoes? I don't think my sensible beige, one-inch heels are going to cut it with this dress."

A pair of three-inch-high red sandals appeared in a hand behind the screen.

Holly laughed and slipped her feet into the shoes. Luckily, she and her cousin were the same size.

"Come on out," Flea said. "We want to see!"

Holly stepped out to a collective gasp.

"You look so beautiful!" Lizzie breathed. "Oh, Holly, you look like a princess!"

"You do," Gayle said. "Red is definitely your color."

"Just beautiful, Holly," Flea said, smiling

sweetly. "It's a really lovely dress. Not one of mine, but lovely nonetheless." She laughed. "All right, girls, you'd better all get ready or you'll be late."

In moments, Gayle and Lizzie removed their dress bags from Lizzie's closet and shimmied into their dresses.

Lizzie flopped down on her bed next to Flea. "I feel awful about this. Here I am, getting all gussied up for a party, and one of my best friends is holed up here, with a bandage on her head. I won't go."

"Lizzie Morrow," Flea scolded. "We've been through this. You're going and that's that. Besides, you look way too beautiful to stay home."

"You do, Lizzie," Holly seconded. Lizzie wore a long silky dress, royal blue, with a large royal blue flower on one strap.

"I can't get over how stunning you look, Holly," Lizzie said. "This dress says, 'Jake Boone, you will not be able to take your eyes off me!' "

"Lizzie!" Holly said, her cheeks flaming. "I do not want Jake Boone's eyes on me! Not that I think they're on me in the first place. In fact, quite the opposite."

"So you're not attracted to him," Lizzie stated. "Not at all."

"No," Holly said. "Not one bit."

156

"Liar," Lizzie singsonged. "I know you, Holly Morrow. And I know when you're very interested."

Holly hoped that didn't mean she was transparent. Could Jake tell she was attracted to him? He hadn't known when they were teenagers and neither had Lizzie, so clearly she wasn't that transparent.

"I saw the way you looked at him when he was here earlier this week questioning Flea," Lizzie said. "And I knew you were in love with him in high school."

She turned beet red. "I wasn't looking at him in any way," Holly lied.

Actually, she'd been unable to take her eyes off him. He looked so handsome, so . . . masculine. So . . .

She closed her eyes and pictured him, his face, his strong shoulders.

"Oh, yes, you were," Lizzie said with a smile. "And I know you loved him in high school. You didn't want to, because you wanted nothing to stop you from leaving Troutville. But you did love him. You think you could hide something like that from your cousin? I knew it, Hol."

"Me, too," Flea piped up from the bed. "And Gayle, too."

Holly bit her lip. "I —"

"We understood," Lizzie said. "You des-

157

perately wanted to leave Troutville. That was your dream. If you'd given in to your feelings for Jake, you might not have left."

"It was for the best that he heard what you said on prom night, Holly," Flea said. "Or he might have followed you wherever you were going, when it was his dream to stay in Troutville and prove everyone wrong about him."

"Followed me?" Holly asked. "Why would he have followed me?"

"Because he was in love with you," Flea said. "Madly."

"What?" Holly shouted. "Jake Boone was in love with me?"

Lizzie nodded. "Anyone could see it."

"Except me," Holly said quietly.

"Sometimes we see what we want to see," Flea said. "If you did acknowledge his feelings for you and yours for him, you would have ruined both of your dreams."

"But their real dream was to be together," Lizzie pointed out. "Wasn't it?"

"At the time, all I wanted was to leave," Holly said. "I'm ashamed of that now, but at eighteen, that was what was burning in my heart."

"Well, you're both adults now. And what happened was a long time ago," Lizzie pointed out.

158

"He hates me," Holly said. "He hated me on prom night and he hates me still."

"He doesn't hate you!" Lizzie said. "Right, Flea? You were there that night — was it hate you saw in his eyes? Or a broken heart?"

Holly glanced at Flea, who could be counted on to always tell the truth, even when it might hurt.

Flea said nothing for a few moments.

"Flea?" Holly asked.

"I don't know," Flea said. "He was very angry that night. But he was so young then."

Holly took a deep breath and glanced down at herself. "I think I'd better change. I'd be more comfortable in my pantsuit."

"You're wearing this dress whether you like it or not, Hol," Lizzie said. "If I have to take this fuchsia lipstick and draw on your pantsuit, I will."

"You would not," Holly said.

"Oh, but I would," Lizzie said with a devilish smile. "You'll forgive me eventually since it's a good cause — your love life." Lizzie waved the lipstick, then pointed it at Holly. "What's it going to be?"

Holly caved. "You win."

"I wish there was time for a pedicure for

you, Holly," Flea said. "Those shoes are screaming for a hot red pedicure."

Holly smiled. "Three-inch heels *and* a pedicure? One is enough for one night."

Miss Ellie would sure enjoy seeing Holly in shoes like this.

Would Jake? she wondered.

What am I thinking about? she scolded herself. *The man doesn't even want to work with me on the case; he's not the least bit interested in me as a woman. Perhaps he was, once, as Lizzie and Flea insist. But he isn't now. I can see it in the way he barely looks at me.*

She wondered why he didn't want to work with her, what his cryptic reason was. If not because of the past, then what?

You're now an amateur detective, she told herself. *And you have all of tonight to try to figure it out.*

If she didn't fall flat on her face in these skyscraper heels.

CHAPTER SEVEN

Jake surveyed the crowd in the ballroom of the Troutville Plaza Hotel. He'd spent the past few days researching his former classmates, especially those who still lived in Troutville. Of a class of two hundred nineteen students, seventy-six made their homes in Troutville.

He'd easily narrowed down the group of those who'd stayed in town to those who'd had anything to do with either Lizzie or Dylan. He focused on those who were romantically linked, romantically interested, or were known to dislike either Lizzie or Dylan. Eighteen former classmates (due to Dylan's popularity and Lizzie's undeserved reputation) came to light. Of those, five were attending the reunion.

Jake scanned his list. Prudence Dunhill. Arianna Miller. Corey Forge. Bobby Jones. Elissa Erikson.

Pru fell into the "disliked Lizzie" category. Arianna had dated Dylan during high school and still held a well-known torch for him. Corey Forge had dated Lizzie in high school as well and was devastated when she broke up with him, a fact Jake was privy to because he and Corey had both worked after school at Mott's Supermarket, and Corey talked nonstop about how Lizzie had done him wrong.

Jake smiled at the memory. Back then, he used to think, *Hey, at least you got to date the love of your teenage life.* Holly would come in to pick up groceries for her parents or for Lizzie's (Lizzie refused to enter Mott's because Corey would start serenading her with heartbreak songs at the top of his lungs), and Jake would act as nonchalant as he could. After all, Holly was his best friend, but inside he'd be shaking, his knees trembling, his senses on overdrive.

Corey Forge was now the chief mechanic at Troutville's best garage, and Jake had kept up a casual friendship with him. The man was always shaking his head about the many women he dated in his quest to find Ms. Right, how none measured up to the ideal he had in his head.

Lizzie?

Was Corey so enamored of Lizzie and so jealous of her engagement to Dylan that he'd gone over the edge?

Bobby Jones. Jake shook his head at the

thought of the lumbering, loud Up Hill boy. Bobby had been crazy about Arianna Miller. But Arianna only had eyes for Dylan. And more than once, Bobby had picked a fight with Dylan — and lost.

Bobby was a "real piece of work," as Jake's grandmother used to say. He was a boaster — and his boasting often included the girls with whom he'd been intimately involved. In high school, Bobby would keep a running list in a particular stall of the second-floor bathroom. Almost every day he'd add another conquest. Holly, Lizzie, and Gayle were always on his list. Sometimes Holly would appear twice in the same day — on a day when she wasn't even in school or a night when she'd been staying with her grandmother, who used to live three towns over. Every day Jake would cross out the names with black magic marker.

Once, for an entire school day, Bobby and his posse of idiots had taken turns waiting in the next stall to see who was x-ing out the list. The second the stall door opened and the hapless Jake came out to wash his hands, he was grabbed while the thug looked to see if the name added that morning was still there.

Jake was caught four times and punched

in the stomach four times. Twice, Bobby had jumped him after school and threatened to kill him if he ever "messed with my list of sluts" again. "Go ahead and kill me," Jake had yelled back, spitting blood from his injured mouth at Bobby's retreating back.

Jake had gone on x-ing out names and Bobby had gone on jumping him. Sometimes Bobby won the fight; sometimes Jake did. Once, in the middle of a fight in the grassy field behind the school, Bobby said, "I want you to know I respect what you're doing, but I still have to kick your ass." Jake had replied, "I want you to know I think you're the biggest loser there ever was." And so the fights continued.

The fights would have continued past high school had Jake not become a cop. Jake would walk past him in town, pat his holster, nod with a "Fine day, isn't it, Bob?" and keep going. Bobby never so much as littered in his presence. A typical bully, he quickly backed down in the face of real authority.

As for Troutville High suspect number five, Elissa Erikson was one of Arianna and Pru's friends. She was neither romantically linked to Dylan nor known for disliking anyone — she'd actually been known as the "nice" one, but she was a friend and potential ally of Arianna and Pru, here for the weekend, and therefore, worth watching.

The hotel ballroom began filling up with a chorus of, "It's so-and-so!" and "You look exactly the same!"

"Same old posing jerk," said a male voice.

Jake turned to find Corey Forge, in a suit jacket and jeans, rolling his eyes at Dylan, who had just walked in with Lizzie on his arm.

You could hear a pin drop.

Jake glanced around; all eyes were on the couple.

But Jake's eyes were on the woman who'd entered behind Lizzie and Dylan. A beautiful woman in a red dress, her shiny brown hair flowing to her shoulders.

Oh, Holly, he thought. *How is it possible that you still have this effect on me?*

"Now there's the original odd couple," Corey chortled, upping his chin at Dylan and Lizzie. "Those two? Please. Nothing in common. He's getting great sex, she's getting jewelry and fancy dinners. That's what it's all about."

"Sorry, Corey," Jake said, "but I think Dylan and Lizzie are the real deal."

He snorted. "I know the real deal — I've got it myself. I finally found myself the dream woman I've been looking for all my life." He waved over a redhead heading their way with two glasses of wine. "Gina, come meet an old buddy — Jake Boone. We used to work at Mott's together and . . ."

As Corey went on and on without a breath, his dream woman listening intently to every word, smiling and nodding, Jake looked around for Bobby and Erika.

"We're here, everyone! The party can begin! Whoo-hoo!"

Pru, Arianna and Erika had arrived. The three women elbowed their way onto the center of the dance floor and took over. There was a chorus of, "Omigod, it's Pru! It's Arianna. It's Erika! You look so beautiful. You haven't changed a bit!"

Pru and Arianna certainly hadn't. Pru grabbed Erika by the arm and pulled her over to whisper something in her ear. Erika grimaced and yanked away. Pru angrily pulled her over again, and Erika shoved her — right into the woman behind her.

Suddenly there was a fight breaking out.

Jake shook his head. Just figured. But before he could blink, the three women were hugging and laughing and dancing again.

"Good thing I wasn't on the dance floor

just then. I would have been history in these shoes."

Jake turned to find Holly checking out her high-heeled strappy sandals. God, even her feet were beautiful.

"You look very nice," he said in the understatement of the century. "I'm glad you came."

"Thank you," she said. "I suppose I'm supposed to say 'me, too' to being glad I came, but I'll have to reserve judgment on that."

"How does it feel to be here?" he asked.

"Odd. It's strange to see the same faces, well, ten years older, but to feel so removed from it all. Do you remember the holiday dance we all went to junior year?"

Jake would never forget it. He, Holly, Corey, Lizzie, Gayle and her date, and Felicia had all gone together in a group. That night had been over a decade ago, and he still remembered it so clearly. Remembered the white dress with the little pink roses that Holly had worn, the way her hair had smelled. And he remembered the name-calling and the fights, which had started moments after they'd walked in.

"Look, it's Lay Me Lizzie, Holly the Whore, the Fleabag, and Good Time Gayle!" Arianna had shouted. "Guys, start lining up!"

There had been laughter and a race as a bunch of boys ran to form a line. There were even mock fights about who was first in line.

"No, you drew the shortest straw so you get stuck with the Fleabag!" someone had called out.

"Hey, just stick a bag over her head — hell, her whole body except for the good parts — and she's like any other girl!" another boy yelled.

More laughter.

The four girls and their friends, stunned and frozen in place, stood in their unwanted spotlight like the clichéd deer in the headlights, until Felicia had run out. Lizzie had screamed, "I hate you all!" Gayle had yelled, "Go to hell!" at the boys forming their line.

And Jake had been powerless to do anything. So he did what he always did back then. He ran into the crowd of boys, fists swinging, joined by Corey and Gayle's date, a guy who'd joined the army and then moved away, and one or two other Down Hill boys. And as usual, they took a beating.

Dylan Dunhill had never been part of the jeering, leering, fighting crowd. He had been at the dance; Jake remembered noticing him dancing with Arianna, his girl-friend at the time, just before Lizzie and company had walked in. After Arianna's outburst, Dylan had whispered something in her ear and then left, and then the fight had started and Jake had lost track of Dylan.

He imagined Dylan berating Arianna for her cruelty and leaving in protest. That was the Dylan he knew now. Back then, though, he figured Dylan had told Arianna to meet him outside for a backseat ride.

That night had been one of the worst. It was the last time he and Holly had ever attended a Troutville High dance; it had taken a lot of convincing on his part to get her to go to the senior prom. And then she herself killed that night.

He looked at her now and didn't know how to process all that had happened. On one hand, the past was complicated, so complicated in how children and adolescents internalized the external when forming identity, and he wanted to wrap Holly in his arms and tell her they should forget it all and start over as adults. They were the best of friends once; they should be the best of lovers now.

But he himself had internalized too much.

Someone tapping a microphone shook Jake from the past. "Welcome to our reunion!" said Michael Donner, who had been class president. "It's so wonderful to see so many familiar faces . . ." As Michael went on, reading off a list of names of those attending, there were claps and snickers. At the mention that two of their class had recently gotten engaged, two of the least likely, Michael gleefully announced, the crowd buzzed with anticipation. Finally, he said, "Okay, folks, I won't keep you in suspense a moment longer. It's Dylan Dunhill, football star, prom king and most popular, and Lizzie Morrow!"

Dylan took that moment to dip Lizzie with a major kiss.

There were gasps and shrieks and "Oh, my Gods." But most people, Jake noted, couldn't care less. They went back to talking and eyeing name tags. Of course, there were a few who couldn't leave the topic alone.

"My brother, the philanthropist," he heard Pru Dunhill say with a snicker. "He feels bad for the underdog. Trust me, when he sees what a scheming opportunist Lizzie Morrow really is, he'll dump her. My brother won't marry that slut."

Gayle, who was standing right next to

Pru, gasped. Loud enough that Pru stopped talking and looked at her.

"Oops, did you hear that?" Pru asked, feigning concern before she giggled.

Holly glanced over at where Lizzie and Dylan were talking with a group of people. Jake could tell that Holly was relieved that Lizzie hadn't heard what Pru said.

"I think you need to get a life," Gayle responded. "Normally, I wouldn't waste my breath trading childish insults with you, but you really need to get a life."

Pru's expression darkened — for just a second — and then she laughed. "Pigs will fly before Good Time Gayle could possibly insult me."

Gayle shook her head. "You're sad. Sad and pathetic. And not worth my time or energy."

"Gayle, you're absolutely right," Holly said, stepping up beside her.

"Why don't I get both of you a glass of wine," Jake said to Gayle and Holly. He shot Pru a look and saw her stiffen; it was a tiny movement, that was how in control of herself Pru was. But he could see that Gayle had stung her. Pru wasn't used to being told off, and he knew she'd respond as though she hadn't even heard Gayle. But what Gayle said would bother her very much — more so because she'd said it in front of him. Tomorrow, if you asked Pru Dunhill if she and Gayle Green had exchanged words at the reunion, Pru could very well say no and believe it. She tended to do that — completely block out "unpleasantness," even when she started it. Jake had seen her do it once before, when a friend of hers had made a flip comment about her father's affairs. "My father never had an affair," Pru had said very seriously. The next day, when Jake had run into Pru in the coffee lounge and said that she shouldn't let gossip get to her, because it was just that, gossip, Pru said she had no idea what he was talking about.

There was a possibility that Pru Dunhill was behind the attacks on Lizzie and her friends. A possibility that she quite conveniently blocked out her behavior, too. Still, Jake didn't think so. Pru had always been a very straight shooter. She was a little crazy, but he wouldn't bet money that she was their girl.

A friend of Pru's pulled her away and onto the dance floor. A moment later, she was laughing and dancing as though nothing had happened.

"She's vile!" Gayle muttered. "Thanks for the wine, Jake. I could use a little before I go flirt my butt off with my handsome boss, who has just arrived. Whoohoo!"

Jake and Holly smiled after Gayle, who danced her way over to her boss.

"I admire Gayle and Lizzie so much for their ability to let things roll off their backs," Holly said, accepting a glass of white wine from Jake.

"It took me a long time to learn how to do that," Jake said. "I used to fly off the handle about everything. Take everything personally. I never realized that if I don't care about the person's opinion, it can't affect me."

It's why your opinion of me almost killed me, he wanted to add.

Jake Boone represents everything I'm running away from . . . leaving . . . everything I hate here. . . .

"I know what you mean," she said. "It's taken me a long time to get to that point in the first place. You know, I *almost* feel sorry for Pru. If she had an ounce of decency, I might feel sorry for her."

"Attention, everyone!" Arianna called out. "The Troutville Senior High reunion class poll sheets are now available on the alumni table."

Gayle hurried over. "Class poll?" she

said, raising an eyebrow. "Why do I doubt this was sanctioned by the reunion committee."

"Hey, I've got one that's not on here," bellowed a deep male voice. "Where's Most Likely To Buy Your Way Through Life? I vote for Dylan *Dunce*hill!"

There were gasps and murmurs from the crowd — and then a thud.

A red-faced Bobby Jones, waving a beer bottle in one hand and the class poll in the other, staggered a few feet, then tripped and fell over his own feet.

A crowd gathered around him. "I think he passed out!" a woman said.

Jake kneeled down beside Bobby and checked his pulse. The smell of liquor emanated from his pores. "He's out cold. How about some help getting him to a couch in the lobby?"

Three men came to Jake's aid; together they carried the very tall, very muscular man to a couch along the darkened hallway to the left, where Bobby could sleep in privacy until he either woke up or fell off.

"Now I really feel like I'm back in high school," Holly said. "All this stupid animosity!"

Jake nodded. "I know. It is stupid.

Carrying around grudges and old hurts doesn't do anyone any good."

Holly glanced up at him, her blue eyes serious. "We were all just kids. That's what's so hard to swallow now. Kids, innocent kids. Hurting each other. Them to us. Us to each other." She shook her head.

"Why don't we go breathe some fresh air," Jake suggested. Holly nodded and he led her outside, into the hotel's flower garden. "Seat?"

She sat on the white wooden bench and he sat next to her, aware of her nearness, the brush of her thigh, her shoulder against his own. For a moment, he was transported back to a time when he'd still had hope for them.

"What's Bobby's problem with Dylan?" Holly asked.

"Bobby had — still has, I guess — a huge crush on Arianna. And Arianna was only ever interested in Dylan. Once or twice she used Bobby to try to make Dylan jealous. Didn't work, of course. Only made Bobby jealous of Dylan."

She froze for a moment and clutched his arm. "Could Bobby be behind what's been going on? The notes, the stone?"

"Possible," Jake said, "but you'd think he'd be grateful to Lizzie for taking Dylan off the marriage market — leaving Arianna still available."

"Why, Jake Boone, I do declare I've been looking everywhere for you!"

Pru Dunhill.

"You found me," he said. "You remember Holly Morrow, of course."

"No, I don't believe I do," Pru responded, twisting on her high heels. She stood on his side of the bench, so close that he had to sit back in order to keep her breasts from brushing against him. "Dear," she said to Holly. "I'm sorry, but I seem to have forgotten your name already. I'm Pru *Dunhill*. Would you be a sweetie and get Jake and me two glasses of champagne? We have something to celebrate."

Holly's mouth dropped open. "I think you're confusing me with one of your servants."

Pru stared at her. She clearly hadn't expected Holly's retort. She recovered quickly, but Jake could see that being put in her place twice in the same hour had caught her off guard. Pru was used to being deferred to, used to intimidating everyone. Used to intimidating Holly and making her run away in tears.

Not anymore.

"Ooh, there's Laureen! I haven't seen

her in years. Jake, I'll catch up with you later. Save me a dance, darlin'."

And with that, she flitted away.

"She is unbelievable!" Holly said, shaking her head. She looked at him. "So are you and Pru —"

"Don't even suggest it," Jake interrupted.

She nodded. And, unless Jake was mistaken, he caught the hint of a smile.

"Hey, you two," Lizzie called, stepping out into the garden. "Take a look at this crap."

"Lizzie, I told you to throw that away," Dylan said, shaking his head. "It's just the usual bull. Liz, when you pay any attention to this nonsense, you give them what they want. This is our reunion and we're here to have a good time."

"You're right, honey," Lizzie said. She crumpled up the sheet of paper and tossed it in the wicker trash can next to the bench. "I knew there was a reason I was marrying you," she teased.

Dylan kissed her nose. "Hey, they're playing our song. Let's dance."

Lizzie smiled, winked at Holly, and Dylan twirled her all the way back inside the ballroom.

"They're so in love," Holly said.

"It's nice to see," Jake responded. "I was beginning to think the whole love thing was some kind of myth."

"You've never been in love?" Holly asked carefully.

He coughed, covering his surprise. "Once, actually."

"What happened," she asked.

"The usual," was all he would say. "We'd better get back inside, see whether Bobby is still out cold and what the witches trio is up to."

He felt her eyes on him, and he met her gaze and held it. And then a couple came out, laughing and pointing at the stars, and the moment was broken.

"Jake, wait a minute," Holly whispered, staring past him through the ornate cast-iron gate that led to a path to the woods. "Is that Pru?"

Jake squinted to see in the dim lighting. About three hundred feet away, partially blocked by a huge tree, stood a couple, a man and a woman, who appeared to be arguing, if their hand motions were any indication.

Ah, yes. There was the flash of blond hair as the woman dramatically shook her head, and an expanse of long, smooth, pale leg, the foot encased in a high-heeled sandal. It was Pru Dunhill.

But with whom was she arguing?

"Can you make out who she's with?" Holly asked.

Jake shook his head. The man wore what looked like a baseball cap; it was impossible to see the color or style of his hair, and Jake couldn't get a good eye on his face. He was tall, just over six feet, and powerfully built, but Jake couldn't determine his age.

"Let's move slowly, naturally, to the gate. Whatever you do, don't look in their direction. Let's just get closer for a better view or at least a different angle."

The strains of a Frank Sinatra song came softly through the open windows from the reunion room, and couples in the courtyard began dancing, dipping and twirling.

"Thanks to Frank, we've been given a perfect cover for moving over to the gate," Jake said, holding out his hand. "Shall we dance?"

Holly took his hand, and he slipped his other arm around her narrow waist. They stood close; he could breathe in her trademark perfume, the clean scent of her silky hair. Their mouths were inches away . . . so close. And yet so incredibly far. For a split second, he allowed himself to look at those lips, those luscious, berry-colored lips that he'd dreamed of for so many years —

"Oh, my God, Jake," Holly cried softly. "She just grabbed a stone from the ground!"

Jake danced Holly over to the gate. Pru did have a large stone in her hand. Good Lord, was she going to hit the guy, whoever he was, with the rock?

Pru threw the stone, hard, at a neighboring tree; a squirrel darted along a high branch and jumped to yet another tree.

The man was staring down at the ground, shaking his head. Pru seemed to be asking him for something that he didn't want to give.

What? And who was he?

Move over just a bit, he willed the man. *Shift over just a foot so that the leafy trees aren't blocking the moonlight!*

But the man stood still. He glanced up at the dark sky, at the ceiling of branches in the dense woods. And then he shook his head again and started walking away, deeper into the woods.

Pru ran after him, her hands gesturing wildly. But the man kept walking. Pru stood there, in her black dress, the warm summer wind blowing tendrils of long blond hair away from her face.

The man gone, Pru picked up another stone and threw it, then another.

Jake and Holly stared at each other, then back at Pru Dunhill.

"Perhaps she was showing him how hard she wants the stone next time — when it's Lizzie's turn to get hurt. Or mine," Holly said, her face pale. She closed her eyes and let out a deep breath.

"It doesn't look very good for her," Jake agreed, watching as Pru peered over toward the gate, then began walking very quickly toward the side of the hotel. He had a feeling Pru would reenter the hotel through the front door, then magically appear in the doorway to the courtyard as though she'd been in the reunion room the entire time.

Five minutes later, there she was, the loose tendrils of hair suddenly back in place, her red lipstick fresh and shiny. But as she fell in with a group of her girlfriends who were now shimmying to a Madonna song, one of the women, Laureen, pointed at Pru's high-heeled sandal and laughed.

For just a moment, the smile died from Pru's face as she scraped a leaf from her heel. And then it was business as usual. She danced and laughed and even accepted a pat on the rear end from a jerk in their class, as though she hadn't minutes ago been passionately arguing with a man in the woods.

Over what, Jake was determined to find out.

"Is she on your list of suspects now?" Holly asked, raising an eyebrow.

Jake looked at Holly and nodded. "It's more than suspicious that Pru is sneaking off into the woods during a crowded party when she's least likely to be missed, and arguing with a strange man."

"So you do agree it's likely that Pru hired him as her 'hit man,'" Holly said. "He's the one doing her dirty work."

"It's possible," Jake said.

"Fine," Holly said. "I'll take that. I assume she's high on your list of suspects now?"

He let out a deep breath and nodded.

Holly, Lizzie, and Flea were all so relieved that the rest of the evening had passed without incident that they all had hearty appetites the next morning. When Lizzie and Holly had arrived back at Lizzie's, Flea had been asleep on Lizzie's couch, the novel she'd been reading open on her chest. Holly and Lizzie had tried not to wake her as they shut off the television and the lights, but Flea was a light sleeper and was too anxious to hear about the reunion.

"You should have heard Gayle tell Pru Dunhill off!" Lizzie had said. "She was great!"

I just hope Pru doesn't try to retaliate, Holly had thought as she'd drifted off to sleep. If Pru *was* their suspect, who knew how she'd try to get Gayle back — or Holly.

Holly had spent the night tossing and turning, the possibilities of exactly what Pru Dunhill had been discussing with the man in the woods keeping her eyes wide open. Had she been plotting the next "accident"? Insisting the man get more violent? Such as taking a heavy stone and bashing one of them —

Flip. Flop. Flip. Flop. From her stomach to her back and back again, Holly had been unable to keep the terrible thoughts from her mind. She was scared. Very scared. And worried for her friends.

She debated telling Lizzie, Gayle and Flea about what she'd seen, but during a quick shower in the morning, she decided to hold off, as Jake suggested, until they had proof.

"It looks bad," Jake had said last night.

183

"But until we know for sure that Pru hired this man to hurt Lizzie and her bridal party, we're better off keeping what we saw — what we think we saw — to ourselves and working on finding out who that man is."

The shower helped clear her head, and Holly headed downstairs to work on her prize chocolate chip muffins. Baking always took Holly's mind off her problems. She would sift her flour and spoon in her sugar and start humming a song and suddenly a half hour would have gone by and the muffins would be in the oven before she even remembered she'd been troubled by something at the start.

An hour later, as Holly placed on the table her delicious homemade chocolate chip muffins, the three women all dug in.

"I'm so happy about last night that I'm off my diet — for the morning," Lizzie said, laughing.

"Yum!" Flea exclaimed, licking crumbs off her lips. "This is the best muffin I've ever had! Holly, I had no idea you could bake like this."

"Holly's a master baker," Lizzie said. "She has a side job and everything."

"Well, if anyone wants seconds, I made two tins," Holly said with a wink.

"You know," Flea said, sipping her orange juice, "I'm so glad to hear that nothing awful happened last night, but at the same time, it means Jake couldn't catch him or her red-handed. They're still out there."

"I know what you mean," Lizzie said. "I was half hoping someone would try to dunk me in the punch bowl just so Jake and Dylan could catch them and our lives could all go back to normal."

"Interesting that Bobby Jones was asleep most of the night and nothing bad happened to one of us," Holly said before biting into her muffin. According to Jake, Bobby had woken up early this morning on the hotel's couch, demanded another beer, and then been arrested on disorderly conduct.

Just when Holly thought it was one suspect — Pru — there was another just as likely.

Lizzie froze, muffin midway to her mouth. "Hol, you're absolutely right! I hadn't thought of that."

"And he does have a major ax to grind against Dylan . . ." Flea put in, "but not against Lizzie."

Lizzie sighed. "It's so stupid. Ugh — I'm glad the reunion is over. I'm not even sure

I'm glad I went. I mean, on one hand, I feel like we overcame something by going. But on the other hand, it felt like the same old thing. Like we were back in high school."

"Why?" Flea asked. "What happened? I thought *nothing* happened."

"Nothing except for the usual crap," Lizzie explained. "Name calling. Immature class polls."

"Class polls?" Flea repeated.

Lizzie shook her head. " 'Most Likely To Star In a Porn Video Despite Her Ugly Face and Bad Body — Lizzie Morrow.' 'Most Likely To End Up In the *Guinness Book of World Records* For Sex Partners — Holly Morrow.' That sort of thing."

Holly took a sip of her coffee. "Unbelievable. Do Pru and Arianna realize they're twenty-nine? That they're grownups?"

"I hate them!" Flea said through gritted teeth. "Sometimes I wish I could do something, anything, to get back at them!"

"Dylan made a really good point last night when he said that the best thing we could do is not pay any attention to their immaturity," Holly said. "And he's right. Getting upset is giving them what they want."

"Isn't Dylan just wonderful?" Lizzie said, her expression turning dreamy. "Do you know he came back over last night, after you guys fell asleep, just so we could sit on the front porch? Just talking, holding hands. Those are my favorite times with Dylan — when it's just me and him — no money, no fancy car or house or other people. Just us."

"I feel so bad that you all cut your night short for me," Flea said, arranging her black scarf around her neck, a telltale sign that she was uncomfortable. "You didn't have to do that."

"There's nothing we wouldn't do for you, Flea," Lizzie said with a smile. "There's nothing I wouldn't do for any of you."

Flea smiled. "I know you would, Lizzie. That's why I'm making you the dress from Bettina's. No — don't you dare say a word. I already ordered the material. It'll be here tomorrow."

Lizzie shot up and hugged Flea. "I love you so much! Do you think you'll feel up to coming to the engagement party?"

"I hope so, Lizzie," Flea said. "The doc said I should stay off my feet for two weeks, but let's see how I feel. I still feel pretty wobbly, but I've got six more days to rest up till the party."

Lizzie's face crumpled. "I can always postpone the party. How could I celebrate my engagement without one of my best friends?"

Flea smiled. "You'll postpone nothing. If I'm not up to going, I'll be there in spirit. You can bet I'll be dancing at your wedding, though."

"Felicia Harvey, dancing?" Lizzie said with a grin. "Now that I have to see!"

Flea laughed. "I'd better get going. Thanks for letting me rest up here last night. It was nice staying here instead of my room in the shop."

"Anytime, Flea," Lizzie said.

When Flea was gone, Lizzie cleared the breakfast dishes, and the cousins headed into the living room with their second cups of coffee.

"Sometimes I don't know if she's really okay about things or if she could use more support," Lizzie commented. "She's always so strong, but getting locked in her room, hit with that stone, missing the reunion and maybe even my party — and the dirty names . . . she deals with an awful lot."

"Flea's a strong woman," Holly said. "She's had to be. Like all of us. I'll spend some time with her today — make sure she's all right."

"Thanks," Lizzie said. "I'd better head to work. You'll come by for lunch?"

"I wouldn't miss your mom's mac and cheese for anything," Holly said.

A few minutes later, Lizzie had gone off to work, and Holly was alone. She headed upstairs to Lizzie's bedroom, planning on a long think-session. But the sight of the Troutville High yearbook on Lizzie's bed stopped her.

She lay down with the book and flipped through it. When she got to the pictures of her classmates, she turned directly to the B page.

Jake, unsmiling, his expression half serious, half pensive, as it often was, stared back at her. She traced his face with her finger. "I loved you, too," she whispered.

She carried the book to the window and nestled into the cushion on the seat Lizzie had built. She could hear a bird singing on the branch that scraped the window, and Holly parted the curtains.

And then she froze.

She shot up so fast she scared the bird and it flew away.

One story below, in the backyard, on the lawn, someone had used what looked like white spray paint to spell out: WHOREHOUSE.

189

★ ★ ★

In less than ten minutes of getting Holly's phone call from Morrow's Pub, Jake and Dylan had rushed over, where Holly, Lizzie, Gayle, Flea, and Lizzie's mom were sitting around a large table, their faces somber. The pub didn't open for business until noon, so they had the place to themselves.

"I feel terrible for calling you all out of work," Lizzie said. "But I want my fiancé and my mother and best friends to give me their honest opinions. Someone is out to get me. Out to hurt me, out to hurt my friends. I can't stand it any longer."

"Now, Lizzie —" Dylan began.

"No, Dylan," she interrupted. "They have won. I can't live like this. I won't live like this. And I won't subject my cousin — who left Troutville because of this very thing — to it. It's just not fair —" Even with security guards, this monster is managing to get to me, to get inside my backyard!"

Lizzie broke down into sobs and her mother flew to her side. "Lizzie, honey. It isn't fair. And someone is out to get you. But we are going to catch them. Do you hear me?"

"Lizzie, you can rest assured that I'm devoting all of my time to the case," Jake said. "I'm on this twenty-four/seven. And Mrs. Morrow is right — we will catch whoever is doing this. There just isn't a lot of evidence right now, but sooner or later they will make a mistake and the culprit is going to lead me right to him or her."

"So I'm supposed to have an engagement party and risk our lives?" Lizzie asked. "Dylan, how can I do that?"

"Jake, maybe she's right," Dylan said, running a hand through his hair. "Whoever's behind this crap is seriously unhinged. I don't want Lizzie hurt. And I don't want her friends hurt even more than they've already been."

"This is really between the two of you," Jake said. "It's your engagement party. And it's something you deserve to have and to celebrate with your friends and families. I wish I could guarantee security and safety, but I can't. On the other hand, there's no guarantee nothing will happen if you don't have the party."

Dylan and Jake sat back down. For a few moments, everyone ruminated on that.

"Holly, what do you think?" Lizzie asked.

All eyes swung to Holly. "I think the party should go on. Lizzie, it's not like you can just hide in your house all day, every day. You have to live your life. If you cancel the party, what's next? Canceling the wedding? You can't do that."

"I *won't* do that!" Lizzie insisted tearfully. "I want to have the engagement party. I want to plan the wedding of my dreams. I want everyone I love involved in the most important day of my life. But I also want everyone safe and sound!"

"Lizzie, there's no guarantee that canceling anything will stop this . . . psycho," Jake pointed out. "We don't know what we're dealing with here. Holly's right — you need to live your life, go on as planned."

"The party is on," Dylan said, rubbing Lizzie's shoulder. "We'll beef up security. Every guest must have ID and be checked against a master list at the front door, and all bags and purses will be checked. Maybe we'll set up a metal detector, too."

"That's a good start," Jake agreed. "I'll tell you what. Since it's my business to take care of these things, why don't all of you head back to work. I'll arrange the security detail."

Holly opened her mouth to speak, but then thought better of it. The despicable greeting in the backyard had scared her senseless. It wasn't only the ugly message;

192

it was the invasion. Of privacy. Of space. Of everything.

It was almost as though Holly could feel the person's breath on the back of her neck, warning her that he or she was close by, just waiting for the right opportunity to do away with Lizzie and her friends.

She shivered and felt Jake's eyes on her.

Once she could have run straight into his arms for warmth, for safety, for comfort. And now those arms were a man's arms, muscular, strong.

God, how she wanted to run into those arms, even if it was for just a few minutes.

CHAPTER EIGHT

The Dunhill Mansion ballroom could comfortably hold two hundred guests. Currently, it held two. Yet Jake had never felt more claustrophobic.

Victoria Dunhill, wearing an ornate, sequined peach gown, walked up and down the length of the ballroom, conducting her inspection as she always did thirty minutes before each Dunhill party. Jake walked beside her, scanning the guest list her personal assistant provided for him. He recognized most of the names. He wondered if one of them was Pru's mystery man from the reunion.

"How is Lizzie's little friend — the one who got hurt?" Victoria said. "I don't believe I know her name."

"Felicia Harvey. She's one of Lizzie's *closest* friends. She's a member of the *bridal party*."

Mrs. Dunhill fluttered her eyelashes. "Oh, Jacob, please. You can't expect me to recollect all of Lizbeth's friends. I know she is the little one with the —" She paused dramatically. "We don't need to mention her other more *permanent* injuries, do we? She's reminded of her scars from that fire her own father set every time she looks in the mirror, poor dear."

Mrs. Dunhill was insufferable. Plain and simple. If Jake hadn't become such close friends with her son, he would have cut ties with Victoria years ago.

"Mrs. Dunhill, it was town gossips who accused Felicia's father of setting the fire. And he was completely cleared of having anything to do with it."

"Are we still talking about that unpleasantness?" Mrs. Dunhill said, waving her arm in the air. She clapped her hands twice, and a maid came running. "There's a crease in this curtain," she snapped to the young woman.

The maid nodded, pulled a walkie-talkie from her apron pocket, and ordered a porter to bring a stepladder and a portable steamer at once.

Jake rolled his eyes. How Dylan ended up so down-to-earth was beyond him.

But Jake had more pressing concerns — such as Felicia's name appearing on the guest list when she had called to say she would not be attending, after all. How accurate — or inaccurate — was the list?

"Speaking of unpleasantness," Mrs. Dunhill said, "I'm surprised Lizbeth and Dylan didn't cancel tonight's party given what happened to Lizbeth's little friend a couple of weeks go. But what really shocked me — shocked quite a few people — was their callousness at attending their high school reunion last weekend while Lizbeth's dear friend lay with a grave injury. That doesn't sound like friendship to me."

"She prefers to be called *Lizzie*," Jake said for the hundredth time in the past week. "And Lizzie didn't want to go to the reunion, but Felicia insisted she'd feel worse if her friends canceled their plans because of her."

Mrs. Dunhill could not have looked more bored. Perhaps what he would say next would interest her.

"Besides, there was a very good chance that whoever's behind these 'incidents' would be at the reunion," Jake said.

Mrs. Dunhill perked up. "And was he?"

"He?" Jake asked.

"Or she," Mrs. Dunhill amended.

"I never discuss my cases," Jake said. "You know that."

"Yes, I do," she said flatly.

"And as far as tonight is concerned," Jake continued, "Lizzie and Dylan aren't going to let some jerk stop them from celebrating how much they love each other."

Mrs. Dunhill raised an eyebrow. *"Love?"* She leaned close to Jake. "Come now, Jacob. You can speak straight to me. You mean *lust*."

"No, I mean love," he corrected. "You haven't spent a lot of time with Lizzie or with Dylan and Lizzie as a couple. You'll see — as time goes by — how much they love each other."

"Jacob, my dear boy," Mrs. Dunhill said, her eagle-eyed gaze inspecting every curtain, every square of wood on the floor. *"Love* is what I felt for my husband. From the first moment I saw him and until the day he died six years ago. Twenty-nine years of marriage. *That* is love."

No, that *is your story and you're sticking to it,* Jake thought as Mrs. Dunhill, apparently satisfied with the rest of the ballroom, snapped at her butler, who stood awaiting her every request. The man hurried to the bar, returned with a scotch on the rocks, and resumed his post.

"Yes, Jacob, love is much more than sex," she added as she sat in one of the high-backed chairs lining the walls. She sighed and stared upward at the ornate ceiling, a huge crystal chandelier its magnificent centerpiece, and seemed lost in thought.

Dylan Dunhill II had been cheating on Victoria from the moment they met, through their courtship and their marriage. He'd been cheating on his wife when he died of a massive heart attack, a high-priced prostitute on top of him.

Jake had been the police officer who'd responded to the call at the Troutville Plaza Hotel. The prostitute, scared out of her mind, had phoned the front desk for an ambulance, then ran out the front door, never to be seen again, according to the night manager. Jake had gone to Dunhill Mansion and was ushered into the library, where he met Victoria Dunhill for the first time. Upon hearing the news, the details of which he relayed as sensitively as he could, she blanched for just a moment, then recovered instantly. She led Jake into her private office, snapped for her scotch on the rocks, sat very straight in her desk chair, and spoke with absolutely no emotion in her voice.

"With Dylan's heart condition and previous heart attack, I have no doubt that his heart simply gave out, especially under such . . . activity," she'd said. "So I'm under no delusion that the autopsy report will reveal this . . . call girl had anything to do with his death. Dylan . . . enjoyed young women and he always survived his dalliances."

"We'll have the report in a few hours —" Jake began.

"The cardiothoracic unit at Troutville General is in the Dylan Dunhill II wing, did you know that?"

Jake shook his head. "I didn't know that."

"Young man," she said, reaching into her desk drawer and removing what looked like a checkbook. "It's very important to me that one particular detail of my husband's death not be reported to the media — or to anyone. I'll pay you — what? Ten thousand good enough to keep that mouth of yours shut about the woman Dylan was with at the time of his death? I don't need to have this conversation with the managers at the Troutville Plaza Hotel. We've had an . . . understanding for years."

Jake's stomach turned. "Mrs. Dunhill, I am very sorry for your loss. I've never been married, but I did lose my mother to a heart attack, and I understand the pain and grief firsthand."

She lifted her chin for a moment, regarding him out of the corner of her eye.

He cleared his throat. "I will require the autopsy report before I file my own report, and if the autopsy indicates that no foul play was involved, you can be assured that I won't breathe a word of the circumstances to the press or to anyone. I don't require payment for being a decent human being."

She'd looked at him very closely, suspicion narrowing her blue eyes. "How can I be assured of your discretion if I don't have a canceled check to hold over your job?"

"You'll just have to accept my word," Jake had said. "It's the only guarantee you need."

"What's your name?" she asked. "Your family name."

"Boone."

"Boone," she repeated flatly. "I'm not familiar with the Boones of Troutville."

Boones of Troutville. Jake almost laughed at how absurd it sounded. Though his family had been in Troutville for three generations, his father and grandfather in the police department.

"I wouldn't think you would be," he said. "I'm from Down Hill."

"That, I guessed," she responded. "You're a cop. It's a noble job, but a blue-collar one."

Jake hadn't bothered wasting his breath or an ounce of his time or energy enlightening Mrs. Dunhill on societal perceptions of the police.

"I have your word about my husband's death?" she repeated.

"You do."

She looked him directly in the eye. "My son won't find out about this?"

"I doubt I'll ever have occasion to speak to your son, Mrs. Dunhill," Jake said, his gaze lifting to the many framed photographs of a boy and a girl in various ages and stages lining the credenza behind her desk. "But in the event that I do, you can trust that I will not tell him. Your husband died of a heart attack in the Troutville Plaza Hotel. End of story."

She nodded and returned the checkbook to her drawer. "My husband checked into the five-star hotel rather than drive the ten minutes home since it was so late and he didn't want to wake me," she said. "My Dylan was such a thoughtful man."

She seemed to be internalizing the story, committing it to memory *as* a memory as she made it up.

"He died all alone, poor man," she continued. "Such a tragedy. Clutching a photo of me that he always carried in his wallet."

"Again, Mrs. Dunhill," he said. "I'm very sorry for your loss." He wanted nothing more than to get away from her, get away from this cold, heartless mansion.

A few hours later, the autopsy had revealed that Dylan Dunhill II died of a heart attack due to a heart condition.

And as Jake had sat at his desk at the precinct, he could see Victoria Dunhill smiling. Had her husband been murdered by the call girl, Jake was ninety-nine percent sure Mrs. Dunhill would have it obliterated from all records — and her memory.

Exactly one week later, the matriarch phoned and asked that he pay her a visit at her home. She thanked him for his discretion and said he had earned her trust, something no one except her son had ever managed. For that, she was indebted to him, and should he need anything, he was only to call. During that visit, Dylan Dunhill III, who Jake knew of from high school, had been conducting a tutoring session in the house library with a teenager he was working with at the Boys' Center, and Jake had been truly surprised. He'd never talked to Dylan Dunhill in all the years they'd gone to the same school, and here he was, tutoring a Down Hill teenager in fractions, using basketball as a guide. The teenager was getting it and seemed to be enjoying the lesson.

Dylan had invited him to the center to volunteer, and that was that. The two had become friends. Dylan, Jake was surprised to discover, didn't discern between Up Hill and Down Hill. He wasn't a snob. In fact, he was one of the kindest people Jake had ever met. And with Victoria constantly inviting Jake to family functions as a "wonderful officer of the law, representing the best of Troutville's public service citizens," Jake and Dylan had run into each other often and discovered they had a lot in common — the law, for one.

"I know what you did for my mother," Dylan had said one afternoon on their way to the center's basketball courts.

"I don't know what you're talking about," Jake said.

"For my twenty-first birthday, my father brought me to Chez Jacqueline's, a very high-priced brothel in a nearby town," Dylan said. "He said I was officially a man now, since I had just inherited a sick sum of family money, so it was time I joined him in the Dunhill male tradition of enjoying all Chez Jacqueline's had to offer. I was outraged, of course, and told him I preferred to sleep with women I loved. Sleep with the *woman* I loved, not that I loved anyone or had slept with very many women then. He said he didn't know where I got my ethics from, since I certainly didn't get them from him or my mother."

"Jesus!" Jake said.

"Don't be so shocked," Dylan responded. "I never was. And I don't judge them. They can live the way they want, I'll live the way I want."

Jake nodded. He had no idea what to say. His own parents' marriage was wonderful. In their mid-sixties now, they loved each other and had retired to a lively apartment complex in Florida.

"My father told me he'd been three-timing my mother from the moment they met," Dylan continued, shooting for the basket — and missing. "He'd fallen for her at first sight at a cocktail party — her and two other women. So he circled the room, pretending he had to mingle, and romanced them all. He married my mother because of pressure from his own parents — she had the best pedigree — and he continued to see the others and hundreds more during their marriage."

"*Hundreds?*" Jake repeated.

Dylan nodded and shot for the basket.

"Does your sister know any of this?" Jake asked. He wondered if it contributed to Pru's prickliness, the bitter part of her personality.

Dylan shook his head. "My mother likes to pretend that they had the perfect marriage. She's worked very hard to make sure Pru and I believe that. I know better because my father told me himself, but it's not the kind of thing he'd tell Pru. She was daddy's little girl."

The sounds of laughter and glasses clinking shook Jake from his reverie.

"Jake, dear, you were a million miles away," Victoria Dunhill scolded. "Did you even notice my first guests arrive? Have you met the delightful Chipwells?"

He hadn't, but the delightful Mrs. Chipwell, who'd made it clear she couldn't believe Dylan had passed up her beautiful daughter in favor of "that . . . that Down Hill girl," was on his list of suspects.

Jake stood, shook the couple's hands, and engaged the delightful Mrs. Chipwell in a subtle investigative conversation.

"This limo could almost make me forget

my troubles," Lizzie said, crossing and un-crossing her legs in the luxurious limou-sine that Dylan had insisted on renting to transport Lizzie, Gayle and Holly to the party. Her smile faded. "Almost. I wish Flea were here."

"I stopped by her shop before I headed to your place, Lizzie," Gayle said, tossing her heavy red hair behind her shoulder. "She's still wincing a little from the pain. And yet there she was, cutting and pat-terning your dress, working with those tiny scissors, straining her eyes."

"I spent some time with her yesterday," Holly said. "She said that working on the dress will make her feel like she's at the party."

"What would I do without Flea?" Lizzie said, tearing up and glancing out the window. "What would I do without any of you?"

"Hey, come on now," Gayle said, patting Lizzie's knee. "Don't forget that gorgeous, kind fiancé of yours!"

Lizzie let out a deep breath. "Gayle, I'm so sorry about what happened at your workplace. I don't know if it was the person who's after me going after my friends or if it was Pru or what, but I'm so sorry."

Gayle smiled weakly. "Don't you worry, Lizzie. My boss was never going to go for me anyway, whether or not he thinks I'm some good-time girl. Besides, it's nothing he didn't hear every day in the halls in high school."

A few days ago, Gayle's boss had received a typed letter from an anonymous source in Troutville, insisting that she be fired, that Good Time Gayle had no business being the receptionist at such a professional establishment as his law office. The letter went on to say that Gayle partied every night of the week till all hours, drinking and carrying on with who knew who, and who knew what confidential secrets she was spilling? Her boss would be well advised, the letter continued, to fire her.

Gayle's boss hadn't fired her, but he had, with some embarrassment, shown her the letter so that she'd be aware, given what was going on with Lizzie.

Gayle's beautiful green eyes teared up. "Sticks and stones, right?"

"It was Pru!" Flea said through clenched teeth. "For telling her off at the reunion. Probably why she waited a week — so you wouldn't necessarily connect it to that."

"I'm sure you're right," Gayle said. "But

it's not like I can confront her without proof."

"If it was her, Gayle," Lizzie said, squeezing Gayle's hand, "I'm just sorry you'll have to see her tonight. Feel free to ignore her. I don't want you thinking you need to be polite just because of me. She's certainly not polite to me and I'm marrying into her family."

"Are you okay, honey?" Holly asked Lizzie. "Remember, tonight is about you and Dylan celebrating how you feel. It's not about the psycho. It's not about Pru. It's not about anything but you and Dylan."

Lizzie nodded and offered a smile, but as the limo turned onto Dunhill Place, she bit her lip and then burst into tears. "I'm a nervous wreck," Lizzie said, dabbing at her eyes with a tissue. "I'm trying to put on a good front, but I'm scared to death. For myself, for you two, and Flea, for Dylan. And then there's Mrs. Dunhill. Pru is nothing compared to her."

Holly held Lizzie's hand for support. "Honey, I thought you said Dylan's mother was being civil."

"Meaning she's not insulting me to my face," Lizzie explained, her face crumpling.

"She'll come around," Gayle put in.

"Trust me, after tonight, when they see firsthand how in love you and Dylan are, his mom will welcome you into the family."

"I hope so," Lizzie said, brightening just a little. She glanced out the window. "Especially because we're here."

The three women stared out the window at the stately white mansion up a manicured slope of lawn. Holly had been here once before. Not inside, though. When she was eleven, her aunt Flora, who worked in the house as a maid, had forgotten her brown-bag lunch on the counter at home, and Holly had been sent with it on her bicycle. When she'd arrived, she was careful to leave the bike in the street so that its handlebars or wheels wouldn't touch the lovely grass, and she'd started up the walkway to the majestic front door, wondering where the special entrance was that her aunt had told her about. Once at the front door, she'd peered around the side of the house for the workers' entrance, but saw only a garden and rosebushes. And so, brown bag in hand, she tiptoed to knock the heavy brass knocker. The housekeeper, her aunt's boss, had answered the door, and had smiled at Holly and taken the bag, but Pru Dunhill, who Holly had never seen before (she attended a special boarding school then) had been coming down the stairs.

"Is this a beggar girl?" Pru had asked the housekeeper. "Why is she dressed that way?"

As the housekeeper explained that Holly was the maid Flora's little niece, come to bring her forgotten lunch, Holly glanced down at herself and saw for the first time the difference between the way she was dressed and how Pru was dressed. She had never noticed such a thing before. Pru, in a pristine white dress, her hair held back with a pink headband, looked like a princess. And Holly, in her cousin Lizzie's hand-me-downs (Lizzie was so much taller than Holly that she outgrew her clothes faster than Holly) felt shabby, despite how clean and well mended her shirt and pants were. She didn't "look" like Pru did, with her shining blond hair and polished Mary Janes.

"Well, if she's related to a maid, she can't use the front door," Pru said matter-of-factly. "She has to use the servants' entrance."

The housekeeper had reddened, smiled at Holly and shooed her away, and the heavy door closed in her face. That had been Holly's first experience with Pru Dunhill, with Dunhill Mansion. With feeling "less than." Here she was, twenty-eight years old, a self-assured teacher with her own home, and yet being in Troutville, being in front of this house again, was able to call up that old feeling so vividly. Now, she would be walking through the front door, a guest at a family party. It didn't seem like a victory, though. In fact, she was feeling a little sick. She'd like to slap Pru Dunhill and wasn't sure if she could stop herself if Pru provoked her.

Watch it, Holly, she cautioned herself. These people were going to be Lizzie's in-laws, and for her, she would respond to the Dunhills as though they were any family she was meeting for the first time.

"Ready?" Lizzie asked as the driver came around to open the door for them.

As we'll ever be, Holly thought, exiting the limo.

"How do I look?" Lizzie asked as they headed up the walkway. "Is my hair too wild?"

Holly looked Lizzie up and down in an exaggerated way. "From toe to head, my dear cousin, you look absolutely beautiful. And your hair is amazing."

"You look incredible, Lizzie," Gayle said. "Even Mrs. Dunhill won't have a thing to say about the 'appropriateness' of your dress." She giggled. "You look — almost —

like a Dunhill's wife!"

Holly and Lizzie laughed. "Well, except for the cleavage," Lizzie said, shimmying her shoulders. "And the bright color. And the flowery print." She laughed. "This is the most conservative dress I own!"

"I know this one isn't," Holly said, glancing down at herself, at the pretty black dress with its flouncy hem Flea had insisted on giving her yesterday. She felt so light, so feminine — and so not herself again. She loved the dress, loved the shoes Lizzie had loaned her, but she'd love it a lot more on someone else. She hated calling attention to herself, to her body. To anything that might make people notice her. In high school, she'd worn big dark shirts and corduroys to hide her body, to help her fade into the hallways. But the comments had kept on, regardless.

The heavy door was opened by a butler. "Your name," he said to Holly.

"Holly Morrow."

"You may enter," the butler said.

Oh, may I, thought Holly.

Gayle went through the same process.

"And you are?" he said to Lizzie.

Lizzie smiled. "Hello, Walker. It's me, Lizzie Morrow. We met once —"

The butler scanned the list. "I'm sorry,

but you are not on the guest list." He turned to Holly and Gayle. "If you two are coming in, please do so now."

The three women stared at the butler. "She's the bride-to-be!" Holly said incredulously.

"Half of the guest of honor!" Gayle said.

The butler's expression didn't change. "I'm sorry, but her name is not on the list. I'm under strict orders not to allow any person in whose name is not on the list."

"Oh, brother," Lizzie said. "Talk about humiliating. I can't even get into my own engagement party!"

Gayle handed Lizzie her cell phone. "Here, Liz, use my phone to call Dylan."

Lizzie punched in the numbers. "Hi, sweetie," she said into the phone. "I can't get into my own party! I'm not on the list!" She listened for a few moments. "Okay. We'll be here." She clicked off and let out a deep breath. "He says of course I'm not on the list — I'm not a guest!"

Holly supposed she could understand the mix-up. *Supposed* she could.

In a moment, Dylan appeared behind the butler. "Walker, don't you remember my fiancée, Lizzie? Of course she's not on the list. The party is *for* her — for us."

The butler paled. "Oh. I'm terribly sorry,

213

sir. Sorry, ma'am. I'm under strict orders not to let anyone in who isn't on the guest list."

Lizzie smiled. "Believe me, I of all people understand the need for tight security. And I appreciate it, too."

Holly wasn't sure if the butler deserved Lizzie's generosity, but she admired her cousin's ability to turn the other cheek.

Dylan enfolded Lizzie in a hug. "You look smashing, sweetheart. You're going to knock them all dead."

"I wouldn't use that word if I were you," Gayle joked.

Dylan smiled. "Come on in. Just about everyone's here. I can't wait for them all to meet my Lizzie." He kissed her hand.

Dylan led them inside a packed ballroom. There were at least a hundred people in the elegant room, but the first person Holly saw was Jake. He was in his beautiful dark suit, and his dark hair shone under the lights of a chandelier. He was so handsome, so intensely handsome, that she had trouble looking away.

He caught her staring. He upped his champagne glass at her and moments later, he was at her side with a glass for her.

"Thank you," she said, taking it from him. She was glad to have something to do with her hands.

"You look beautiful," he whispered. "I hope you don't mind my saying that."

She felt herself blush. *Just say thank you,* she ordered herself. But her mouth felt as though it were stuffed with cotton. She smiled shyly instead, and he smiled back.

"Can you bring me up to date on where you are suspect-wise?" Holly asked, mostly to have something to say. He hadn't made a point of talking to her when he'd come by Lizzie's to discuss the case. He seemed to be trying to avoid her.

Holly cleared her throat. "If you don't mind, I'd like to know who your top suspect is, so that I can pay close attention to him or her tonight. Or perhaps we could begin with the top two — we could each take one — surreptitiously follow them around, listen to their conversations."

"I thought we'd begin with a glass of champagne," Jake said, clinking his glass with hers.

Holly felt her cheeks pinken. She was so aware of him standing next to her, his masculinity. She could smell just a hint of his soap, a hint of his aftershave.

He was in love with you in high school . . .

Was it true? Had this gorgeous man really loved her?

"You promised me my first dance, Jake

215

Boone," came a seductive, feminine voice.

Holly and Jake turned to find Pru Dunhill in a skintight, low-cut, short black dress. Somehow, she managed to look elegantly sexy, instead of inappropriate. With her long blond hair and blue eyes, Pru's angelic beauty was offset by the severity of the black, and she made a dazzling picture.

Pru took Jake's hand and put it to her waist. "Lead me around the floor," she purred.

"Sorry, Pru, but I'm in the middle of something," Jake said.

Pru stared at Holly with one of her famous dirty looks. "I'm sure your friend here — what was your name, dear? I believe we met at the reunion, but I'm at a loss . . ."

Holly stared at her, stunned at how outwardly obnoxious she was. Perhaps Jake was right about Pru; she was so forthright, it seemed uncharacteristic of her to skulk around, leaving notes and scratching cars and hiding behind Bettina's Bridal to hurl a stone. Holly could imagine Pru Dunhill standing right in front of someone with a stone in her hand. She could also imagine her sending an obnoxious letter to Gayle's boss.

"Her name is Holly Morrow," Jake said.

She caught the impatience in his voice, that old disdain for Pru. *Or was it impatience at being with me, disdain for me, when perhaps there was something going on between him and Pru, as unbelievable as that was. Perhaps he didn't like her, but she was stunning and she sure did come on to him in a very strong sexual way. Maybe . . .*

Holly well recalled seeing the two of them together on the train platform. Granted, Pru had been all over Jake, not the other way around. But still, maybe they slept together, casually.

Jake Boone doesn't do anything casually, said a voice from somewhere inside her. *He's not sleeping with Pru Dunhill.*

Pru shot Holly a cold smile. "Ah, that's right. *Holly Morrow.* It's a shame for you that cousins aren't considered 'family' by marriage. Lizzie will be a Dunhill, of course, by name and marriage, if not pedigree. But you won't be. It doesn't work that way. Sorry, hon."

If Holly hadn't been exposed to Pru Dunhill from the age of eleven, she would not believe what had just come out of her venomous mouth. The woman was despicable, there was no other way around it.

"Pru, what makes you think Holly is the least bit interested in whether or not she is or isn't a part of the Dunhill family?"

"*Isn't*," Pru assured them. "And please, who wouldn't want to be a part of the Dunhill empire?"

Holly stifled a laugh. Surprised that she could laugh at Pru, Holly realized that the woman had lost the power to hurt her, to have an impact on her self-esteem or worth as a person. Pru never had, not really, but she had managed to hurt Holly, more at the injustice at being treated badly than at anything Pru actually said. Holly had always been proud of her name and she always would be.

"Come, Jake," Pru said, trailing a finger up his chest to his lips. "Come dance with me."

"Pru, I'm talking to Holly," he said, stepping back from her.

"Holly must be used to waiting around," Pru said. "Of course she doesn't mind if I steal you for one little dance."

"Actually, I do mind," Holly said, surprising herself again. She blushed and glanced down. She wasn't quite sure how that had come across. She felt Jake's eyes on her.

"Why, Holly, I didn't know you cared," he said somewhat teasingly.

But there was the edge of something

218

dark in his voice. A hint of sarcasm.

"As a matter of fact, Pru," Jake said, "I'm surprised you're interested in dancing with anyone other than your new boy-friend."

Yes! Holly thought, impressed by Jake's good use of the opportunity to slyly confront Pru.

The blood drained from Pru's face and she took a small step back. "What are you talking about? I don't have a boyfriend. I'm not even dating anyone right now."

"Oh?" Jake said innocently. "I thought I saw you having something of a lover's spat."

"I have no idea what you're talking about," Pru said. "You must have me mistaken with someone else."

"You're difficult to mistake, Pru," Jake said.

Pru glanced at Jake, yet not angrily, Holly noticed. Instead, Pru seemed . . . nervous. Very nervous.

"Well, either you need to get those gorgeous eyes of yours checked, Jake Boone, or you're not as good a private investigator as you think."

"So you weren't having an argument with a man during the reunion?" Jake asked.

The color returned to Pru's cheeks. Hot red spots. "I most certainly was not. In fact, I had the time of my life at the reunion."

"Well, that's interesting," Jake said. "Because I'd bet my life it was you I saw."

Holly held her breath. Had Jake baited her to the point that she'd crack?

"Now, now, Jakie," Pru said, reaching two slender hands toward his neck. She tugged on his tie. "I —"

"Pru! There you are!" Arianna said, grabbing Pru's hand. "I've been looking all over for you. Wait till you see what Clarissa Leedwill is wearing! You can see her thong underwear through her gown!"

Whatever Pru had been about to say about Jake and his life had been forgotten. But Holly would bet her life that Pru had been about to retort with a thinly veiled warning.

"So sorry to interrupt your little reunion," Pru said to Jake. "Come find me when you're through rehashing old boring times," she added with a press against him, before flitting away.

Holly rolled her eyes. "Not too subtle, is she?"

"She's the opposite of subtle," Jake said, leading Holly to an empty space by a wall. "Which is why, despite what we saw, my gut says she's not our gal. I'm not saying she's not high on the list — she is — but my gut says she's not the one."

"Then why was she arguing with a strange man in the woods during the reunion?" Holly asked.

"Maybe it really was a lover's spat," Jake said. "I hadn't considered that, actually."

Holly shook her head. "But she said she wasn't even dating anyone."

Jake let out a deep breath. "I'm more confused about Pru than I was five minutes ago. I expected her to say, 'You caught me, Jake Boone. My new man and I sneaked off into the woods for a private moment, but then we got into a little lover's quarrel. Everything's peachy now, of course.' But she didn't say that. In fact, she denied she was dating anyone. Denied having a fight with anyone the night of the reunion. Why?"

"Why, is right," Holly said. "She could have covered her butt, pretended that the man she hired to hurt Lizzie and her bridal party is no one other than her new boyfriend."

"I'll need to trail her," Jake said. "It's the only way I'll find out who the man is. And when I find out who he is, I can pressure him into revealing something."

Holly nodded. "I'll keep an eye on her tonight."

"Holly —" Jake began.

"Just an eye," Holly said. "I'm not talking about becoming an amateur sleuth. Who knows — perhaps our mystery man will show up here tonight."

Jake nodded. "Another thing I don't understand is her motive. If she is our gal, why? She doesn't have a super strong motive. She might not want Lizzie as a sister-in-law, but it wouldn't personally affect her."

"But it would personally affect Victoria Dunhill," Holly pointed out. "Lizzie marrying into the family, her only son —"

The sound of a bell ringing interrupted Holly. She craned her neck around a group of people in front of her and Jake. Victoria Dunhill stood in the center of the room, bell in hand.

"Attention, please," Mrs. Dunhill called, her peach sequins glittering in the dim light. "Thank you all so much for coming to celebrate the engagement of my son Dylan to the woman of his choice" — she emphasized *choice* — "Miss Lizbeth Morrow." She gestured at the couple, who stood arm in arm nearby, to join her.

Dylan took Lizzie's hand, brought it to

his lips, kissed it, and then gallantly led her to his mother. *To the wolves,* Holly couldn't help but think.

After a round of applause, Dylan held up a hand. "Thank you all so much for helping us celebrate our incredible happiness," he said. "For the first time in my life, I am absolutely madly and truly in love, and I'm honored that the woman of my dreams, my beautiful, sweet Lizzie, has consented to marry me."

There were some ahs and cheers and claps, and also stony faces and silences. Holly tried to pay attention to who was stony, but there were too many and too many Holly didn't recognize. She glanced around for Pru and found the woman standing in a far corner with Arianna, whispering and laughing and pointing. Suddenly, Pru joined her family in the center. She whispered something in Lizzie's ear, and Lizzie turned bright red, her eyes full of panic.

Oh, no. What did Pru say to Lizzie? Should I go see what's wrong? Holly wondered.

Before Holly could move, Lizzie began backing her way through the crowd, against the wall, heading for the exit. Everyone was staring at her.

"Lizzie?" Dylan said. "What's wrong?"

Beet red, Lizzie continued backing out of the room. "I'll be right back, sweetie."

Dylan signaled the band to continue playing, and once music filled the room, everyone went back to talking, drinking, and dancing.

Holly glanced at Pru, who was smiling. Arianna slithered next to Pru, and they high-fived each other.

Oh, God. What had Pru said to Lizzie?

Holly rushed after Lizzie and found her standing against a wall in the foyer outside the ballroom, asking a maid where the powder room was.

"Lizzie!" Holly called, hurrying to her. "What's wrong?"

"I need to get to the bathroom right away!" Lizzie said, tears in her eyes. "Pru said my dress split up the back and that you could see my thong!"

Holly stood behind Lizzie as the maid directed them to the powder room. She locked the door, then checked Lizzie's dress. "Lizzie, there is nothing wrong with your dress. It's not split. It's not even torn. It's absolutely fine."

"What?" Lizzie said, trying to get a good glimpse of her back in the mirror. "Are you sure?"

"It's in as perfect condition as it was

when you left your house," Holly assured her.

"Then why would Pru —" Lizzie stopped and closed her eyes. "Oh, that's right. She was just having a little fun by ruining my engagement party for me, right in the middle of my future mother-in-law's toast to me and Dylan." She burst into tears, then wiped them away angrily.

"You know what, Liz? You're not going to let that immature, spiteful *person* ruin anything for you. You're going to go back in there, tell Mrs. Dunhill exactly what happened and that Pru was *mistaken* about your dress, and that she should feel free to continue on with her toast."

Lizzie took a deep breath, collected herself, and nodded. "You're right, Holly. I'm not going to let Pru's immaturity ruin my night. My money's on her for our culprit," Lizzie added. "She's the only person close to the family who hasn't asked how Flea's doing."

"That's because she doesn't care about anyone but herself," Holly said. "But Jake doesn't think Pru is the one, and I'm beginning to think he's right. Pru is so outward in her animosity. She doesn't strike me as someone who'd sneak around to get her way."

"I guess that makes sense," Lizzie said. "Oh, I just hope nothing goes wrong tonight. I don't even kid myself anymore about being welcomed into the family — I just want the night to pass in a civilized way."

It was a shame that that was the best Lizzie could ask for herself. But given what Holly had seen of the family so far, her cousin was being realistic.

Holly stood behind Lizzie and smiled at her reflection. "Let's go back out there and show these people who owns this town!"

"Yeah!" Lizzie exclaimed, smiling. "Oh, Hol, I don't know what I'd do without you."

"You'll never have to find out," Holly said. "C'mon. That handsome fiancé of yours is probably going crazy wondering what was wrong."

Indeed, Dylan was pacing in front of the bathroom, and he was all over Lizzie the moment she exited. She assured him she was all right, that she thought her dress had split open, and had been mortified until she checked it out.

"Is that what Pru whispered to you?" Dylan asked.

"Forget it, Dylan," Lizzie said, kissing him on the cheek. "It's no big deal. Maybe she thought it had split for some reason. The lighting . . ."

Dylan shook his head. "I'll never understand my sister." He slung an arm around Lizzie. "Don't worry about Pru. She'll come around. When she gets to know you, Lizzie, she'll love you like I do. And if she doesn't get to know you, well, then it's her loss."

Holly had to admit she liked Dylan. The more she got to know him, the more she liked him.

"I've been on the lookout for your mom, Lizzie, but I haven't seen her," Dylan said. "She is coming, isn't she?"

"Your mother personally invited Mom by telephone," Lizzie said. "So she knows where and when. I'm also surprised she's not here yet." She glanced at her watch. "She's an hour late. I hope everything's all —"

"Lizzie, I'm sure your mom's fine," Dylan said. "She's probably just delayed at the bar or in deciding what to wear."

Aunt Louise had two good dresses — one slightly fancier than the other, and Holly knew her aunt would choose the fancier one, a lovely royal blue that accentuated her bright blue eyes. She wasn't delayed in getting dressed. Which meant . . .

Oh, God. Why hadn't they insisted

Holly's mother come with them in the limo? Mrs. Morrow had determined to drive herself — she was nervous about meeting the Dunhills as her in-laws-to-be, and she wanted to get ready at her own pace and drive herself the five minutes Up Hill to the mansion. Maybe something had happened. Maybe the culprit had gotten to Aunt Louise!

"I'm sure she's fine," Dylan said, but Holly caught the worry in his tone. So did Lizzie. Dylan handed her his cell phone. "Call her."

Lizzie punched in the numbers. "Mom? Is everything all right?" She listened and relief came over her features and shoulders. "We were so worried! We expected you an hour ago." She listened again. "No, the party's not starting at nine o'clock — it's *ending* at nine. The party started at *seven!*"

A two-hour discrepancy? Had Mrs. Dunhill told Lizzie's mother the party was starting at nine o'clock?

"Mom, you must have misunderstood Mrs. Dunhill. Why would she tell you nine o'clock when she herself was the one who decided the party would start at seven?"

Holly let out a harsh breath. She could answer that question.

"I'm sure Mrs. Dunhill meant seven, too, Mom," Lizzie was saying, but the truth of what had happened was in the tears she was trying to blink back. "Well, it's only a two-hour party, and if you're just getting ready now, you'll get here when it's ending."

"We'll extend the party, Lizzie," Dylan said.

Lizzie shook her head, her eyes glistening with tears. "Mom, why don't we set up a lunch, you and me and Dylan and his mother. Yes, for next week. I know, I'm sorry, too. No, no, Mom, it's okay."

Holly watched Lizzie try to hold on to her composure as she and her mother talked a bit more and then hung up. "Lizzie? I'm sure it was a misunderstanding. Let's all go back in and enjoy ourselves."

"Enjoy myself?" Lizzie repeated. "My sister-in-law-to-be hates my guts, and my mother-in-law-to-be personally invited my mother to show up when her daughter's engagement party was *ending*. I don't think I can enjoy myself."

"I can't believe this," Dylan growled. "What the hell is wrong with my family!"

"You're marrying *me*," Lizzie said. "That's what's wrong with them."

"Let's go back in there and talk to my mother right now," Dylan said. "A little two on one. We'll see how she likes being taken away from the party she's throwing."

"Actually, she already left," said Jake.

Holly, Dylan and Lizzie turned around to find Jake, the faint remnants of a pink kiss on his cheek. *Gee, I wonder whose lips left that,* Holly thought sarcastically.

"I've been unable to find Mrs. Dunhill for the past fifteen minutes," Jake said. "And no one has seen her."

"Great, she couldn't stand being at our engagement party," Lizzie said.

"Lizzie!"

Lizzie whirled around at her mother's voice. "Mom! You got here so fast!"

"I wouldn't miss my baby's engagement party for the world," Mrs. Morrow said. She looked lovely in her blue dress. "Oh, how beautiful you and Holly look. Where's Gayle? Flirting with a handsome man, I assume."

Lizzie wrapped her mother into a hug. She was clearly so overjoyed that her mother had come, Pru Dunhill's antics and Mrs. Dunhill's whereabouts were forgotten. Lizzie and Dylan offered Mrs. Morrow an arm each, and they led her into the ballroom.

"Shall we?" Jake asked Holly, offering her his own arm.

Holly took a deep breath and slid her hand through his arm.

CHAPTER NINE

They're playing our song, Jake thought as he led Holly back into the ballroom. "Unchained Melody." Their first — and only — slow dance at the Troutville Senior Prom was to that song. He wondered if she even remembered.

He glanced at her, and she met his gaze.

"They played this at our prom," she said softly.

So she did remember.

She stood very still, seeming lost in thought, and it was all Jake could do not to pull her into his arms and dance her away, far, far away, away from the threats and fear and danger, where they could be alone. It amazed him how his tender feelings for her had come rushing back despite what had happened between them. He should hate her. But he didn't. Couldn't.

She was so beautiful in her black dress, her shiny brown hair in a low knot at the nape of her neck. He could smell a delicate perfume, not the one she used to wear.

God, how he wanted her. He'd been unable to take his eyes off her all night.

Keep your distance, man, he cautioned himself. *Keep your distance.*

As Lizzie and Dylan began a dance in the center of the floor and all the couples joined in, Jake placed his hand at Holly's waist and led her onto the dance floor.

So much for listening to myself, he chided himself. *I'll really be able to keep my distance when I'm an inch away from her.*

She glanced up at him, and he could see the famous two spots of pink on her cheeks. He smiled to himself.

The moment her soft hand touched his, he was undone. He held her so close he could smell her soap, her shampoo. He breathed deeply and closed his eyes, remembering back ten years ago, when he was an eighteen-year-old boy at his prom with the date of his dreams. Then, they'd danced to a few songs, and every time a slow tune started, they stood back awkwardly and mumbled something about punch. Until the next to last song, when a beautiful slow melody began and Jake gathered his courage to hold Holly against him. He remembered how she accepted his hand as he led her onto the dance floor, and how she looked into his eyes before laying her cheek against his shoulder.

They'd had only that one slow dance, yet it had given Jake the courage to confess his feelings. Thank God he hadn't told her how he felt.

Now, they danced silently, as they did that night so long ago, and for a moment, Holly was once again his closest friend, the girl he'd loved.

"This is like old times," Holly said softly, as though she'd read his mind.

In a way it was, much more so than it had been at the reunion. Tonight was about love and celebrating love. The reunion was more about pride and defense. Despite the threat in the air, there was spirit and warmth and love. That was owed to Dylan and Lizzie's love, he was sure.

And my feelings for Holly . . . whatever they are.

He said nothing in return.

"All right," she said. "We'll stick to business."

"Probably best," he said flatly.

She glanced up at him, with those dark blue eyes that had always mesmerized him.

"I'm glad Lizzie's mom was able to come, after all," she said finally. "Lizzie would have been devastated if her mom had missed the party — especially given the reason. Do you think Mrs. Dunhill purposely gave Lizzie's mom the wrong time?"

He shrugged. "I wouldn't put it past her."

"Where is she, anyway?" Holly asked. "Why would she leave her own son's engagement party?"

Yes, Victoria, where are you? Jake wondered. The woman had been complaining about the engagement from the moment Dylan and Lizzie had sat her down with the big news. *"Engaged? The two of you? Why, that's simply preposterous! You have nothing in common. Lust, my dear children, should not be confused with love."* Dylan had a lot of patience, especially where his mother was concerned, but he drew the line when his feelings — or Lizzie — weren't respected. Dylan had gotten up, escorted Lizzie out of the room, and refused to talk to his mother until she apologized for her lack of respect for his feelings and Lizzie. Mrs. Dunhill, who couldn't bear the silent treatment from her son, acquiesced in three hours.

Would she risk the silent treatment for the rest of her life to stop the marriage? Jake wondered. He shook his head. He didn't think so. Mrs. Dunhill had motive, but Dylan simply knew her too well.

If not Victoria Dunhill or her daughter Pru, then who? Who wanted to break up Dylan and Lizzie and for what gain? Arianna Miller was the likeliest choice, but given that everyone in town knew how Arianna felt about Dylan, she would be the first choice on anyone's list. Which tended to make Jake think she wasn't the one, either.

"Her Jaguar is gone, which means she did leave the mansion and drove herself," Jake said. "But, that doesn't make her guilty, Holly. Everyone knows she's none too pleased about the engagement. She might have left because she was unhappy — not because she's plotting some terrible crime against Lizzie."

Holly glanced at him. "You care about Mrs. Dunhill, don't you." It was a statement, not a question, and there was a mild accusation in it.

"Care isn't quite the right word," Jake said. "*Understand* her is more like it."

She was quiet for a few moments. "I still think it's suspicious that she left."

"And not," Jake said. "I'm sure a few people noticed her absence. Let's say you and Lizzie head home to find another terrible note. Mrs. Dunhill would be immediately suspected. She's not stupid."

"Then where did she go?" Holly asked. "You said her car was gone."

"That, I don't know," Jake said. "But I will find out."

"How?" Holly asked.

"By asking her directly."

"I suppose you could just ask her, since you're so close," Holly said.

"Close isn't quite the right word, either," Jake said. "But I am considered a confidant, part of the family. I'm so much a part of the Dunhills' lives that it seems strange to think I once wasn't."

"You were, in fact, the opposite of a 'part of their lives,' " Holly pointed out. "What was it that brought you together in the first place, if you don't mind my asking?"

"The fact that I keep my word," he answered.

"Your word?" she prompted.

"I was privy to something personal," Jake explained, "and I assured her I would keep her confidence. She's treated me like family ever since."

"Must have been some confidence," Holly commented. She was quiet for a few moments. "What did you think of Mrs. Dunhill when you first met her?"

"What I always thought," he said, "rich,

condescending, bigoted, and rude. And then I got to know her a little, and though I was still astonished at her way of thinking, I began to accept her for who she was."

"But how can you accept a vicious person?" she asked. "Isn't that who she was and is?"

"Mrs. Dunhill has her good traits," Jake responded.

"I find that hard to believe," Holly retorted. "Granted, I don't know her well."

"That's right, you don't," he said quickly. "You don't know any of them."

"I know Pru," she said. "I know it was Pru who made my life and Lizzie's and Gayle's and Flea's a living hell in high school. I know it was Mrs. Dunhill who fired my Aunt Flora and accused her of stealing for no good reason. And I know it was Dylan's group of friends who told everyone they'd slept with me and Lizzie every night behind the Tastee-Freez. Didn't the reunion remind you of that?"

"The reunion was about a few select people ruining it for everyone else," Jake said. "A few very immature people. I'm not going to let them prevent me from enjoying my life, Holly."

"Is that what I'm doing?"

"I think you give them too much power," he said. "Are you dirt?" he asked.

She stared at him.

"Are you?" he repeated. "If you're not and you know you're not, there's no good reason for the immature idiot spouting it or the comments themselves to get under your skin. I'm saying that's what I've learned."

She was quiet. He could tell she was ruminating. "I am surprised by Dylan."

"How so?"

"I've gotten to know him a little," she said. "Through Lizzie more than one-on-one with Dylan. He does seem to love her very much."

"He does," Jake confirmed.

"It has made me think," she said, "about judging him to be as awful a person as his sister or some of their friends are. I just assumed he was like them, one of them, and he's not at all."

"It would be like someone making an assumption about me because Dylan is my closest friend, or because I'm close with Victoria Dunhill."

She nodded. "I guess I've been something of a snob in reverse."

"You've been through some tough stuff, Holly," he said. "The important thing is to always remember that *you* hold the power."

"But now someone else is holding the power," Holly said. "Whoever's trying to destroy Lizzie and Dylan."

"No," Jake said. "It's not power they have. It's anonymity. And when we take that away, he or she or they will have nothing but a jail cell to look forward to."

She said nothing for a moment. Then she took a deep breath, and he could see how upset she was, how worried. Holly had enough on her plate without him telling her how to *feel*.

"Let's just stick to business," Jake said. "I'm sorry I let the conversation veer off track into something personal."

"I'm not," she whispered.

He closed his eyes for a moment, then opened them slowly and glanced away from her, from *them,* to regain his composure.

And found Pru Dunhill and Arianna Miller staring at Holly with hatred in their eyes.

"The witches don't look happy," Jake whispered.

Holly glanced over and Jake saw — felt — her startle. He was standing so close to Holly that he could feel her heartbeat quicken.

"Looks can't hurt me," she said. "Not

239

dirty looks from those two, anyway. I don't know who's number one on your suspect list, but number one on mine is shared by those two."

"Arianna has the strongest motive," Jake said. "She's in love with Dylan and always has been. She always expected that Dylan would come back to her, that he'd have his dalliances but that he would come back to her when it was time to settle down."

"Did he ever go back to her," Holly asked, "since high school?"

"A few times," Jake said. "They'd get back together because Arianna would talk a lot of sweet junk about becoming a nicer person and volunteering at the Girls' Club or at the hospital, and three weeks later, she'd be as selfish as always, spending her days getting manicures."

"I just realized something," Holly said. "I'm surprised she's even here. I mean, would Dylan have invited her? I know Lizzie didn't."

"Pru did," Jake explained. "And I'm sure Mrs. Dunhill was more than okay with having Arianna on the guest list."

"Surprised again," Holly said. "If Arianna's in love with Dylan, why would she want to attend his engagement party? Why would Pru invite her to something that would hurt her?"

Jake raised an eyebrow. "Do you really need to ask that question? Pru isn't exactly going to win friend of the year."

Holly nodded and glanced over at Arianna. She and Pru were now whispering. Discussing how to next hurt Lizzie?

"I wouldn't be surprised if Pru and Arianna are trying a last-ditch attempt to make Lizzie look bad while showing off Arianna's assets," Jake said. "Let's keep close tabs on them tonight. With Lizzie here and Dylan watching out for her very closely, I'm comfortable that she and you and Gayle are safe."

"What about Flea?" Holly asked. "Oh, God, maybe one of us should have stayed with her or —"

"I have a guard watching her home and shop," Jake said. "He's posted in a dark car a block down so as not to attract attention, but he's got a clear view."

Holly relaxed. "Thanks, Jake."

Their eyes met and held for just a moment. Again Jake was mesmerized by how beautiful she was.

"Hey, Jake," came a teenaged male voice. "I made it."

Jimmy. Surprised the teenager had taken him up on his invitation, Jake wasn't surprised to find the boy in jeans.

"Didn't I tell you the party was formal?" Jake asked. "Jeans aren't formal."

"Didn't you also tell me that clothes don't make the man?" Jimmy retorted. "That it shouldn't matter what you wear, just what you are inside?"

"He's got you there," Holly said, winking at Jimmy.

Jimmy beamed at Holly.

"Hey, just because you made the lady smile doesn't mean you're off the hook, kid," Jake said. "When you're invited to a formal party, you need to dress appropriately."

"Even if I had worn that monkey suit in my closet, I'd still feel way out of place here," the teenager said. "I'm outta here."

"Jimmy," Jake said. "Stay the three seconds long enough for me to introduce you to Holly Morrow."

The boy glanced up at Holly. "Hi," he said.

"It's nice to meet you, Jimmy," Holly said.

"So can I go now?" Jimmy said to Jake. "When you told me to come, you said I could leave if I wasn't having fun and I'm not."

"Why do I doubt you've given the party

a chance," Jake said, ruffling Jimmy's sandy-blond hair. "How long have you been here?"

"Five, six minutes," Jimmy responded. "The bartenders won't let me drink any of the good stuff, all the girls are older than me, and Dylan's too busy with his girlfriend to have time for me — as usual."

"Lizzie is his fiancée," Jake corrected. "Not his girlfriend. And this is their engagement party. Lovey-dovey comes with the territory."

"Well, it makes me sick," Jimmy said. "I'm outta here." He stepped away, then turned back. "It was nice to meet you, too," he said to Holly, then stalked off.

"Well, well," Jake said. "That last bit of politeness threw me. Just when I think I have the kid pegged, he does something surprising."

"He doesn't seem too happy with Dylan," Holly said. "What's their relationship? And how do you know Jimmy?"

Jake explained how he came to meet Jimmy and how his attitude had changed lately. "It kills me to have him on my list of suspects, but the way he's reacted to Dylan's engagement . . ."

"Sounds like he's hurting pretty bad," Holly said. "My heart goes out to him.

And to you, too — it's clear you care a lot about him."

"I do," Jake said. "And so does Dylan. Most of me thinks he's incapable of some of what's been happening, but a part of me has to be realistic about how angry he is, how rejected and abandoned he feels."

Holly squeezed Jake's hand and he squeezed back, then dropped her hand. "I have that sensation again, that someone's staring," she said.

Jake glanced around, sure it was Pru Dunhill who was staring. But Pru wasn't even looking in his direction. Instead, she was heading out the door with Arianna.

"Jake, Arianna and Pru are leaving," Holly whispered. "Should we trail them?"

He glanced at his watch. "It's a little past nine. The party's ending. I want to be the last to leave so that I can monitor who leaves when. If you don't mind sticking around, I'll see you and Gayle home."

"I don't mind," Holly said.

Neither did he.

The band suddenly stopped playing and a bell tinkled over and over until there was silence. "Thank you all so much for coming," boomed the voice of Victoria Dunhill, her silver bell in hand.

She stood in the center of the ballroom,

on a little box. Her butler stood next to her, his hand on her elbow.

Mrs. Dunhill, I'm sorry, but you are not the queen of England.

"In celebration of this occasion, the bride-to-be has chosen an adorable party favor," said Mrs. Dunhill. As you leave, you'll find the favors in lovely lavender gossamer sacks on the marble table in the foyer. Please help yourself to one, and again, thank —"

A piercing shriek from just outside the ballroom interrupted her.

Jake grabbed Holly's hand and rushed into the foyer. Mrs. Chipwell, one of Mrs. Dunhill's close friends, was sitting on a chair by the front door, fanning herself with the invitation to the party as she caught her breath. A small group of people gathered around her.

"Look at this!" Mrs. Chipwell shrieked. "I took one of the party favors — and this was what was inside the little bag!"

She held up a bride and groom cake topper. It was wood and painted, Lizzie's and Dylan's names inscribed across the bottom.

And a little noose around both of their necks with a note:

You'll be dead before you're wed!

245

CHAPTER TEN

Holly felt Lizzie sway beside her, then wobble, and just as Lizzie's legs gave out, Dylan caught her.

He lay her down on the red velvet chaise in the foyer, brushing back her hair. "Lizzie, sweetheart. Lizzie?"

Holly kneeled down next to Dylan and held Lizzie's hand. "Lizzie, if you can hear me, everything's all right. Everything's going to be all right."

Lizzie's eyes fluttered open. She looked at Holly, at Dylan, and then at the many eyes peering down at her, and she began to cry. "That's it," she said. "We have to call off the wedding. I can't take another minute of this."

"Lizzie," Dylan said. "Just rest." He brushed her hair back from her face and caressed her temples. "Just catch your breath and relax."

Lizzie slowly sat up. "Who would do this?" Lizzie cried. "Who *is* doing this? *We* brought those favors over straight from my *house*. So either someone broke in and ran-

sacked through them, or the culprit was —
is — here tonight!"

"Don't you worry, Lizzie," Jake said.
"We're going to find out. You can count on
that."

"I still think we should cancel the wedding, Dylan," Lizzie said, tears pooling in
her eyes. "Mrs. Chipwell's heart could
have given out!"

"Dear girl, I am not frail!" Mrs.
Chipwell scolded.

"Lizzie, remember what we talked
about," Dylan said, taking both her hands
and bringing them to his lips. "We're not
going to let some psycho ruin our plans.
We love each other and we're getting married and that's all that matters."

"But, Dylan —" Lizzie began.

Dylan shot up. "Do you hear that,
Psycho?" he shouted, glancing wildly at the
guests who crowded into the foyer. "If
you're here, if you're one of us, one of our
friends, your evil isn't working. And trust
me, when I find out who you are, watch
out!"

Mrs. Dunhill, who'd been standing quietly by the entrance to the ballroom,
pushed through the crowd and stood in
front of her son. "Dylan Dunhill!" she
said, her usually calm voice raised. "Are

you insinuating that one of my dear friends is the person behind the unfortunate incidents troubling Lizbeth and her friends?"

"It's *Lizzie*, Mother," Dylan said. "And no, I'm not *insinuating*. I'm flat out saying that it's entirely possible — probable — that our culprit is in this room."

As the guests gasped and murmured and muttered and began looking around, looking for the guilty party, Holly squeezed Lizzie's hand.

"The party is over, everyone," Dylan announced, his expression grim.

"Dylan, how dare you be so rude!" his mother scolded. "I am hosting this party."

"Mother, I do believe you made the same announcement fifteen minutes ago," Dylan said through gritted teeth. He kneeled beside Lizzie. "Honey, do you think you can stand? I want to get you out of here."

"I think so," she said, sitting up.

Jake leaned over to Dylan and whispered something in his ear. Dylan nodded and helped Lizzie to her feet.

"Holly," Jake said, "Dylan's going to take Lizzie home and stay with her until I bring you back to her house. I'd like us to do a little work here first."

Holly nodded. She gently put an arm

around Lizzie's shoulder. "I'll be back soon, Lizzie. Jake and I are going to find out who's behind all this. I promise you that."

Lizzie offered a tearful nod, and Dylan escorted her out.

Henrietta Dunhill, the elderly aunt of Victoria Dunhill, reached for one of the favors as she was slowly making her way out with the help of her cane.

"No, no, Mrs. Dunhill," Jake said gently. "These favors have been tampered with."

"What's that you say?" Henrietta asked. "Lovely favors. Since the place has cleared out, I'll take two," she added with a wink. She grabbed the favors and opened one. "Just adorable."

The bride and groom topper she held had no noose, no note. Jake glanced at Holly and they lunged for the marble table, opening the little lavender sacks as quickly as possible. Only two others contained nooses and notes.

"And only three of the guests are members of the bridal party," Holly said slowly. "Lizzie, Gayle and me."

"Well, whoever altered the favors clearly wasn't concerned with who actually ended up with those three favors. Mrs. Chipwell isn't a member of the bridal party."

"Maybe he or she figured whoever got the tampered-with favors would scream bloody murder about it."

"Meaning it wouldn't matter if one of us got them, since the message would make its way to us," Holly said.

Jake nodded. "And it did."

Yes, it did, Holly thought, a weariness settling over her.

"All this unpleasantness has made me very tired," Victoria Dunhill said, reaching for the banister of the stairs. "Walker," she droned to her butler. "See me up the stairs, will you. And fetch Louis to accompany us."

"Before you go, Mrs. Dunhill," Jake said, "I'd like to ask you a few questions."

She offered him a smile. "Jacob, dear, it's late. I'm tired. And under a great deal of stress. Why don't you come see me in the morning."

"I will," he said. "You don't mind if I have a look around, do you, Mrs. Dunhill?"

She stopped on the stairwell, then turned just a bit so that she was facing nothing in particular. "Of course, dear. Go right ahead."

Jake waited until she had ascended the stairs, then turned to Holly. "A guest at this party tampered with those favors. And we're going to find out who if we have to spend the night here."

Holly glanced up at him. Spending the night with Jake Boone didn't sound so bad.

As an antique grandfather clock ticked-tocked on the wall across from where he sat, Jake breathed very slowly, very calmly — which was difficult as Holly was leaning against him, her head on his shoulder.

She was fast asleep.

God, she felt good.

He didn't dare move a muscle, lest she awaken and startle to find herself in such an intimate position.

Intimate. It was funny to think of it that way. A decade ago, Holly had often fallen asleep sitting next to him, resting her head on his shoulder. They'd be on one of their living room sofas watching a video, or down by the lake, tossing pebbles into the water, and Holly would fall asleep. Back then, she'd awaken as comfortably as she'd fallen asleep, her head on Jake Boone's shoulder as familiar and normal as talking to him.

Only he'd be stock-still, listening to her breathe, watching her chest rise and fall with each breath, smelling her shampoo, watching every slight and tiny movement, her lips, a hand, a tiny coo.

And he'd want to stay like that forever. Then, in those moments, she was his.

Now didn't feel so different. She lived far away from him. They weren't even friends. But she was Holly Morrow, and she was sleeping against him.

He very gently caressed her hand, then stared at the brass hands of the clock.

It was midnight, three hours since the party ended. Three hours since they'd combed through the Dunhill mansion and the grounds, looking for something, anything to shed light on who had brought the nooses for the party favors. A crumpled receipt thrown away foolishly in a trash can. A wrapper or a bag from the store where the items had come from. Something dropped or missed. Or something right out in the open.

People were careless when they committed crimes. Nerves got the best of them, and they slipped up, made mistakes.

But Jake and Holly had found nothing.

After two hours, they'd gone to Jake's office to talk over the case, where things stood, what they did know, what seemed to be, what could be. The best they could come up with was that their culprit was very careful and right under their noses.

"There's Pru and Arianna, individually or together. There's young Jimmy. There's Bobby Jones. There's Victoria Dunhill. They all have motives."

"And unfortunately, just about anyone who's seen an old movie had access to Lizzie's home," Jake pointed out, "thanks to the keys she left under the doormat, under a flowerpot, above the doorjamb. Perhaps our psycho let him or herself in, saw the party favors and tampered with a few."

"And a lot of people in town have their own key to her house — her mother, her friends, her handyman, Dylan. Lizzie's unusually trusting with everyone."

"Even I have a key," Jake conceded. He shook his head. "Before I became a cop, I thought that only happened in the movies. I had no idea people left keys right in front of their doors for anyone to use. It's practically a cliché to hide a key under the mat, or above the door or under a plant."

Holly nodded. "Like I said, Lizzie's unusually trusting. She's never had much reason to trust people, given how she's been treated since puberty, but she always has trusted." She glanced down at her feet. "It's one of the biggest differences between us."

"Do you want to be more trusting?" Jake asked.

She shrugged. "I honestly don't know. Part of me thinks it's safer not to trust, safer to keep your guard up — as long as you're open, I guess. And the other part thinks that as long as your guard is up, you can't really be open."

"I suppose there's a middle ground," Jake said. "Reasonably cautious."

"I guess that could describe me," she said. "Do you think I'm —" She stopped and pulled her shawl more tightly around her shoulders. She didn't finish her question.

I wouldn't know, Jake finished silently for her. *I used to know if reasonably cautious fit you, but I don't know the woman you've become.*

She took a deep breath and stared up at the ceiling for a moment. "Jake, after the mound of dirt was left on her bed, she got rid of the keys around the property and had the locks changed. The only people who have new keys are Dylan, me, you, and her mother. So if Dylan has a key, it's possible that Pru could have gotten her hands on it and made a copy."

"It's possible," Jake said.

The words *anything's possible* seemed to hang in the air between them, even though neither spoke them aloud.

It was interesting — back then, when they were as close as two people could be, it wasn't possible for them to become a couple. Now, when they barely knew each other, it was very possible.

Perhaps that was how it worked. Couples hooked up all the time because of that very fact.

Now who's cynical, he thought.

Holly stirred, jolting him out of his reverie. He watched her slowly open her eyes and glance around, then she bolted upright when she realized there was a body next to her. "Did I fall asleep?" she asked, suppressing a yawn.

"You took a twenty-minute catnap."

"Was I leaning against you the whole time?" she asked nervously. "I'm sorry about that."

"It was fine," he said. "I'm used to it."

"Putting women to sleep?" she asked with a smile. And then she laughed, and he laughed, too. Her humor was unexpected.

And it broke the ice.

"I can make that joke only because I know how untrue it is," she said. "Boring is not an adjective that describes you, Jake Boone."

"Glad to hear that," he said and laughed again.

She smiled and the warmth in the room held and spun around them. "It's nice to be with you again, Jake," she said, looking at him shyly for a moment, then looking away. "You don't realize how much you miss something . . ." She shook her head. "I won't even bother with that because it's not true. I missed you fiercely right away."

"I missed you, too," he said quietly, so quietly he wondered if he thought it or said it aloud.

Tears came to her eyes, and he knew he'd said it aloud.

He stared down at the hardwood floor. "Perhaps if we'd been this direct with each other, our friendship wouldn't have ended."

Why had that come out of his mouth? He wasn't supposed to say that. Now *he'd* brought up their past.

"Meaning?" she asked.

"Meaning I didn't know what low regard you held me in."

She gasped. "Low regard? Jake, are you kidding? I thought you walked on the moon!"

"I'm the last man on earth you'd marry, Holly. I heard you say it yourself."

Her face crumpled. She stared at the ground, then slowly back up at him. "Jake,

I've regretted saying that from the moment it left my lips."

"But you said it. And you said it because you meant it."

She buried her face in her hands for a moment. "At the time, to be with you would have meant staying in Troutville. That was your dream. Mine was to leave. Back then, it was so black and white. Stay or go."

He raised an eyebrow. "You marry a person because you're in love, because you belong together. I'm not so sure it matters where you are."

"It is if your spirit dies in that place," she whispered.

He looked at her.

"The divorce rate is awfully high, Jake. Marriage starts out about love. And then life intrudes on that private happiness. Troutville would have intruded on us. Of that, I have no doubt."

He closed his eyes for a moment, not sure how he felt about what she was saying. Much of what she said was realistic.

"Let's say I asked you to leave Troutville and follow me where I was going," Holly said. "Would you have?"

Would I have left Troutville if you asked? I

257

would have bought a bus ticket to anywhere to be with you. It didn't matter to him that she wouldn't have stayed in Troutville for him. He knew how much she hated the place. He never would have asked such a thing of her. But he'd never gotten the chance to ask to come with her. And just when he'd worked up the courage to do just that, he'd discovered her real feelings for him.

She hadn't said: *Troutville is the last place I'd spend my life.* She'd said: *Jake is the last man I'd ever marry.*

The whole thing was complicated. Jake's dream had been to stay in Troutville, join the police force the way his father and grandfather had. Overcome the obstacles. Live where he wanted to live, which was right here in Troutville, despite how the Up Hillers treated him. He'd had big ideas to build up Down Hill, contribute to making the area a nicer place to live, safer for children and the elderly. And he'd done so.

But Holly hated Troutville. He never would have asked her to stay.

He shook his head. What was the difference?

She glanced into his eyes. His expression was unreadable. "I . . . I felt terrible about what happened . . . how things ended."

She looked down at her feet. "Oh, Jake, I don't know what to say. There's so much I want to tell —"

His cell phone interrupted her. He pulled it out of his pocket with a mouthed *excuse me,* then glanced at the incoming telephone number.

Dylan.

"Dylan? What's up?"

"Jake, Lizzie and I just got to her house — we took a long, soothing drive and then walked the Troutville Bridge, her favorite spot — and we found another note in her house. This time written on Lizzie's bedroom wall, over her bed. Part of it is in Magic Marker, and part is in what looks like blood."

"Blood?" he repeated.

Holly whirled around. "What's happened?" she asked, her voice panicked. "Did something happen to Lizzie?"

"Another note," he whispered. "Dylan," he said into the phone, "we'll be right there. Hang on, okay?"

"Lizzie locked herself in the bathroom and won't come out," Dylan said. "She's crying, terrified — I can't get her to open the door or calm down. Oh, God, Jake, I'm really worried. I've been able to calm her down before, but now I can't."

"What did the note say?" Jake asked.

"You'll see," Dylan said. "I'd rather not even repeat it."

During the four-minute drive to Lizzie's house, Holly was barely able to think. *Please let Lizzie be all right,* she prayed. *She's been through enough!*

Before Jake had fully parked in Lizzie's driveway, Holly was out of the car, racing up to the porch to ring the bell.

"Thank God you're here," Dylan said, gesturing for Holly and Jake to come in. "Holly, you're probably the only person who can help calm her down."

"Is she upstairs in her room?" Holly asked.

"In the master bathroom," Dylan said. "She locked the door."

Holly ran for the stairs, but Dylan gently took her arm.

"Wait, Holly," Dylan said. "I think Jake should go with you."

She looked at Dylan, then at Jake, and then she nodded, understanding setting in. The note had to be that bad.

Slowly, Holly pushed open Lizzie's bedroom door. The bed faced the door, so the large Magic-Markered letters could be seen from the doorway.

Lay Me Lizzie Is Pregnant!

It was underlined in blood.

Holly felt her knees wobble. She grabbed onto the doorway for support.

"I've got you," she heard Jake say from behind her, and she could vaguely feel his arm around her shoulder.

"Lizzie, honey?" Dylan was saying. "Holly's here, sweetie."

Lizzie's name shot a jolt of adrenaline through Holly's entire being. "Lizzie!" She ran to the bathroom door. Dylan was leaning against it, a hand flat on the door, as if he could communicate his feelings through the door.

He loves her, she thought with absolute conviction.

"Should I try?" Holly asked.

He nodded, tears in his eyes. She watched him walk over to her bed and sit down, his elbows on his knees, his hands covering his face. He was crying.

Jake sat down next to him and slung an arm on his back. Dylan raised his head and took a deep breath, wiping at his eyes.

"Lizzie, honey, it's Holly. Will you open up and let me in?"

No answer.

"Lizzie, I just want to hold you. We don't have to talk. I just want to hold you

261

and tell you everything's going to be okay."

She heard a sniffle. And then a few movements. And then the door lock sliding.

"It's open," Lizzie said softly.

Holly turned to offer a reassuring glance to Dylan, then slowly opened the door and slipped inside. She shut it behind her. Lizzie, who was sitting on the floor, jumped up and fell into Holly's arms. They slid down against the wall until they were half sitting, half lying down.

Lizzie's sobs shook her entire body. Holly held her against her, stroking her hair, whispering, "Let it out. It's all right. Just let it out. Everything's going to be all right."

In a few minutes, Lizzie was quiet. They continued to sit that way for another five minutes.

"It's true," Lizzie whispered. "I am pregnant."

Holly lifted Lizzie's face with both her palms. "Congratulations, Lizzie." She smiled gently. "Congratulations, mom-to-be."

Lizzie offered a weak smile. "I'm going to be a mom, Holly. Just like I always dreamed."

"And you're going to be a great mother,"

Holly said. This little one is sure lucky to get you," she added, very gently touching Lizzie's tummy.

Lizzie smiled and touched her stomach. "I'm sorry I didn't tell you. "I wanted to, but —"

"It's okay, Lizzie. I'm just so happy for you. Getting married, having a baby. All your dreams are coming true. This psycho" — she gestured toward the door — "isn't going to get his, her, whoever's, hands on your dreams. Do you hear me?"

Lizzie bit her lip and nodded. She took a few deep breaths. "Oh, Holly, I feel so much better. Someone is out to get me, big-time, and it's so damn scary not knowing who it is." She froze. "Oh, my God."

"What is it?" Holly asked.

"I haven't told anyone I'm pregnant, except for Dylan, of course. No one else knows. Not my mother, not you, not Dylan's family. No one. But clearly someone *does* know."

"Is it possible you were overheard talking about it with Dylan?" Holly asked. "Or maybe someone saw you at your doctor's office? Where were you when you told him?"

Lizzie thought for a moment. "I went to

surprise him at the Boys' Center. That's where he happened to be when I found out. He has an office there, and that's where I told him. There were some boys walking in the halls, one was dribbling a basketball, one was listening to a portable CD player. But there were no adults around. And I didn't recognize anyone there."

"So you and Dylan were alone in his office when you told him?" Holly asked.

"Yes. And we were very careful to talk about the baby only when we were absolutely sure we were alone. I know how gossipy this town is, and we don't need to add any fuel to the fire about why we're getting married so quickly."

Holly let out a deep breath. "Could the culprit be guessing?"

"Maybe," Lizzie said. "But it's a pretty good guess."

"The 'Lay Me' part could be a good clue," Holly said. "That's from high school. So that can hopefully narrow things down."

"I've heard the 'Lay Me Lizzie' crap around town for the past ten years, Hol. It didn't stop with graduation. And I heard it from a few people who didn't go to our high school. I guess it's just catchy."

Holly shook her head with disgust. "Well I've got an assignment for you for tonight. You're to do nothing but think happy thoughts about the baby and your wedding. Okay? Leave the junk to Jake and me."

"You two are spending a lot of time together," Lizzie commented, the twinkle coming back in her eyes.

"It's nice," Holly whispered.

Lizzie squeezed her hand. "Shall we go let the boys know everything's all right in here?"

Holly nodded. "Dylan's a wreck out there. He was crying, Liz."

She gnawed her lower lip. "You know, all this crap has been directed at me, so I've been getting all the comforting. I've forgotten how this affects him. How much comforting he could use. I'm the woman he's going to marry and the mother of his child, and I'm being threatened."

"All right, then," Holly said. "You two go comfort each other, and Jake and I will do some investigating. We'll get them, Lizzie."

She nodded, then wrapped Holly into a hug, and opened the door. Then she flew into her fiancé's arms, and Dylan led Lizzie out of the bedroom and down the stairs. Jake and Holly followed behind.

"I'm going to take Lizzie to my house for the night," Dylan said. "We'll call you both in the morning. Thanks for coming over."

"You bet," Jake said. "Lizzie, you take care. I'll call the police and make sure they conduct a thorough investigation."

Lizzie offered a weak smile over her shoulder, and then they were gone.

Jake and Holly stood on the porch and watched as Dylan's car turned onto the main road. "I think we should start fresh in the morning," Jake said. "It's late, and we're both so exhausted, there's no way we can do any good investigative work under these conditions. Let's let the police do their job first."

Holly nodded. "I can't stay here. I can go to Flea's or Gayle's —"

"You'll stay with me," he said.

He neither asked nor did she answer.

It was simply understood that she would.

CHAPTER ELEVEN

Two hours later, Jake put cookies and two mugs of steaming tea on a tray and headed back into the living room of his apartment. Holly was standing by the wall of windows, looking out onto Troutville.

"You can see so much from up here," she said, her arms crossed over her chest. "Even this late, between the stars, moonlight and street lamps, I can see the high school, the lake, the skating rink. The town center. Even the dividing line between Up Hill and Down Hill."

"One of the reasons I love this view," Jake said, setting down the tray on the coffee table, "is that from up here on the sixth floor, the line doesn't look like much of anything. Just a sloping hill, quite pretty and green. It helped me with perspective, that it's really just a hill, with no meaning."

She glanced at him. "I wouldn't say 'no meaning.' "

"People gave it meaning," Jake amended. "Nature made it just a beautiful slope."

Holly turned from the window. "I sure

could use a cup of hot tea."

"Come sit down, then," he said. He patted the sofa, then sat on one end so she'd feel comfortable on the other. "I'm sorry I don't have much in the way of a late night snack to offer you."

Holly smiled. "Your mom must go nuts when she comes to visit. I remember how she loved to cook. I'd never seen a pantry and refrigerator stocked like your mom's."

Jake smiled back at her. "She still sends me care packages — all sorts of healthy stuff. When she comes to visit, she doesn't even bother opening the refrigerator or cabinets. She stops at the supermarket before she comes and practically buys the place out."

"It was your mom who taught me how to bake," Holly said thoughtfully.

Jake could see Holly, at nine, ten, every age up to eighteen, sitting on a stool in his family's kitchen, her nose and apron dusted with flour and stained with icing. She loved helping his mom bake. And Jake loved gobbling down at least two huge portions of whatever delicious treat they whipped up, from cupcakes to lavish layer cakes. He'd stuff himself silly, then zigzag around exaggeratedly, patting his stomach, and fall on the floor. Holly would crack up, and no matter how bad his stomach ached from eating too much, he'd feel great.

"I was surprised you didn't become a pastry chef," Jake said. "I know you were set on a super steady career, but somehow I always thought you'd chuck 'steady' and chase your passion."

She glanced at him, clearly surprised. "I wouldn't think you'd take me for a 'chase your passion' kind of person."

"You're forgetting how well I know you," he said.

She looked at him, but said nothing. Then she reached for a cookie.

"You're either uncomfortable or you *are* trusting," Jake said, smiling.

"A little of both, I guess," she said. She took a nibble. "The cookies are just fine." She glanced around. He'd had it right with *uncomfortable*.

"So you didn't become a pastry chef," Jake said. "You became a teacher instead. I can see that, too. I'll bet anything you're a wonderful teacher."

"I do love teaching," Holly said. "I love my kids, love seeing eyes light up with learning. But I think I became a teacher to try to inspire those kids who seemed a little less motivated for whatever reason — kids who were picked on, or who seemed to have problems at home. Kids who are having a tough time."

"Like we had," Jake said.

She nodded. "One of our English teachers was so wonderful," Holly said. "Do you remember Mrs. Vogel, junior year?"

Jake nodded. "I sure do. She managed to get me interested in reading Shakespeare."

"Exactly. Because she cared about us as individuals, not just a lump of eleventh graders. She tried to find in each of us the spark that would relate to the text we were studying. That's what I try to do with my kids. And it really works. It helps them see in sixteenth-century plays or nineteeth-century novels what's relevant to their own lives right here in the twenty-first century. And suddenly, they want to read. They want to think. They want to write their papers. Not all of them, of course. I don't mean to say I'm Miss Perfect Teacher, but every little bit helps."

"Your students are lucky to have you," Jake said. "And Hoboken — you like it there?"

Holly nodded. "It's a great place to live. So close to New York City, just across the river. And there's so much to do right in town. It's a really bustling place. And then there's Miss Ellie and Herbert."

"Miss Ellie and Herbert?" Jake asked.

"They're the most romantic couple I've ever met. Miss Ellie is in her seventies and Herbert is in his eighties, and they fell madly in love at the senior center where Herbert lived and Miss Ellie was volunteering. They married right before I left for Troutville."

"Newlyweds, at their age!" Jake said, smiling. "That is romantic."

Holly nodded and grinned at the thought of the special couple. "I lived next door to Miss Ellie for years, and then Herbert moved in with her after their wedding. Miss Ellie made me feel like I had family right next door. I don't know that I would love living there quite so much if she weren't my neighbor."

"She sounds like a very special person," Jake said. "I'm glad she found herself a groom."

Holly smiled at the memory of Herbert and Miss Ellie kissing on the platform as they waited for the train to take her away to Troutville. And then the thought of Troutville turned her mind back to Lizzie.

"I hope Lizzie's all right," Holly said, her brows furrowing. "I'm so worried about her."

"She's in good hands with Dylan," Jake

said. "You did such a great job of calming her down."

"It was heartbreaking to see Dylan cry," Holly said. "Ten years ago, I wouldn't have thought he had tear ducts."

"Not every rich Up Hiller is a bad person, Holly."

"Dylan does seem true-blue," Holly said. "He seems to really love Lizzie."

Jake nodded. "He does. And he told me while you were with Lizzie before that she's pregnant. He's going to be a great father. I have no doubt about that. He cares so much about the kids we mentor." He smiled. "And you're going to have a baby cousin." He raised his mug of tea to her. "Congratulations."

"I'm so happy for Lizzie," she said. "She's always wanted to be a mother. And she'll be great at it."

"Do you?" he asked.

"What?"

"Want to be a mother," Jake said.

She stiffened. "Sure."

"And?"

"And what?" she asked. "I'm not even dating any —"

"Why?"

"Is this twenty questions?" she asked, annoyed.

"Yes," he responded with a smile.

She wrapped her hands around the mug. "I just haven't met the right man. It's that simple."

"I was in love with you in high school, Holly," Jake said quietly. So quietly he wasn't sure he'd said it aloud.

She blushed. "I didn't know."

"I took great pains to hide it," he said.

"Why? Why didn't you tell me how you felt?"

"Because I knew I wasn't what you wanted," he said. "You wanted out. I was Troutville. I wasn't the great beyond, I wasn't something new, I wasn't possibilities. I was just plain old Jake Boone you grew up with, as Down Hill as you could get, and you wanted to escape that."

"I loved you, too," she said softly. She glanced up at him shyly, then put down her mug. "I did, Jake. I loved you very much."

He didn't want to talk. He didn't want to continue the conversation. He didn't want to ask why he was the "last man on earth she'd marry" if she loved him so much.

He just wanted to believe it, to soak it in.

He stood and moved down the couch, then sat down next to her. He took her hand and brought it to his lips. He cupped her chin in his palm and tilted her beautiful face to his and kissed her.

Warm. Sweet. Stirring.

He deepened the kiss and she stiffened at first, then he felt her relax and go limp against him. One kiss. That was all it took. Ten years, he'd waited for that kiss, this moment. He scooped her into his arms and carried her to his bedroom, laying her down on the soft blanket covering the bed.

He lay down beside her and kissed her again, passionately. He knew she could feel his response to her. He pressed against her, then rolled on top of her and lifted up on his arms to look down at her. "I've wanted you for so long, Holly."

"Make love to me, Jake," she whispered.

Her soft moan was all he needed. He undid the zipper of her dress and slipped the sides apart, exposing an expanse of skin and her lacy white bra. He made quick work of removing the bra, then ran his hand over her breasts, so full and beautiful and pink tipped. She moaned again, arching her back, and he took her nipple in his mouth and teased it, suckled until she was arching her entire body against his. He pressed against her, and she slid a hand between them to reach his zipper. In moments, his pants were off, joined by his shirt and her dress.

She now wore only white cotton panties, and the sight of them drove him wild in his desire for her. He slid them off, down her long, slender, silky legs, and then caressed every inch of her, from her feet to her knees to her velvety thighs, until he found the center of her womanhood.

"Now," she breathed in his ear.

He entered her, slowly, looking into her eyes. And as he fought for control, she shuddered and moaned, and it was all he could do to keep from exploding. He made love to her, hard, then slow, then fast, then hard, until she screamed his name and he could hold on no more.

He lay against her, listening to her heart beat, listening to her catch her breath. He grasped her hand and she tightened her fingers around his, and then he closed his eyes.

He was sleeping.

Holly stole a glance at Jake, his bare chest rising and falling with each breath. God, he looked beautiful. The early morning sunlight played on his silky brown hair, and she wanted to run her fingers through the strands, but she feared waking him. For a few moments, she wanted to study him, commit every inch of him to memory.

I loved you in high school . . .

She knew he didn't love her now. Couldn't and wouldn't. But last night, for a little while anyway, he had.

Thoroughly. Completely. And very well.

Holly stretched luxuriously. She wasn't a virgin, but she had never experienced anything like last night. She had been in a few relationships, nothing long-term, and she'd tried to fall in love, willed herself to fall in love with the perfectly fine men she'd met or been set up with. And though she enjoyed male companionship and dating and sex, she never felt her heart move. Not the way it had in high school for Jake Boone.

Last night, her heart had stirred.

And now he had stirred. He stretched beside her, the blanket lowering to reveal six-pack abs. His eyes opened slowly, and then he quickly glanced at her, as though suddenly remembering she was there.

He said nothing.

She said nothing.

Awkward silence.

"Um, did you sleep well?" she asked, feeling stupid. She had no idea what to say, what she was supposed to say.

"Just fine. You?"

"Just fine," she echoed.

"Great. Uh, why don't I go order in

some breakfast from Doreen's Diner, and we'll go over the case."

He reached for his pants and slipped them on, then hopped off the bed, throwing his shirt on over his shoulders as he left the bedroom.

Talk about uncomfortable.

Holly felt tears prick the backs of her eyes.

Her cheeks burning, she reached for her clothes and quickly dressed, then headed into the bathroom to wash her face and brush her teeth with her finger and some toothpaste. The moment she turned on the faucet, her own waterworks began. Gripping the sink for support, she cried into the water. Finally, she smushed her face into a towel and calmed herself down.

At the bedroom door, she hesitated, feeling like a nervous thirteen-year-old about to enter the school dance. One deep breath later, and she pulled open the door and affected what she hoped was a nonchalant expression as she stepped into the living room.

Jake was at the front door, paying a delivery boy. He placed two white bags on the dining room table. "Omelets and coffee okay? I remember you loved omelets."

He could bring up the past, yet he

couldn't face what they did last night? Holly wondered what he was thinking. She wanted to just ask, be as blunt as he had last night, but she saw he needed space and she wanted to give it to him, no matter how much it hurt.

"Sounds great," she said. "I'm starving. And I could use an entire pot of coffee."

"Good thing I ordered three cups each," he said with a smile.

They sat, they ate, they drank. In silence.

"I'm dying to call Lizzie," Holly said. "But it's so early. I think I should wait till at least nine."

Jake nodded. "I'll call Dylan in an hour and he'll put Lizzie on the phone for you."

"Thanks."

He looked nervous. Uncomfortable. Unsure. "So, I think I'll hop in the shower. The newspaper's on the coffee table."

She nodded. They looked at each other for a moment, each waiting for the other to say something, perhaps. Neither did.

How could you be so intimate, as physically intimate as two people could get, and be so emotionally distant the next morning? she wondered. She wanted to know what he was thinking. How he felt about what happened between them last night. But instead of asking, instead of being as direct as she should be, she sat back, unable to say anything.

"Um, so just make yourself comfortable," he said and then disappeared into the bathroom.

Holly sighed and stared at the ceiling.

No, don't think, she told herself. *Don't think. Concentrate on something.*

She drummed her fingers against her thigh, stared at the ceiling, sipped her coffee.

Part of her wanted to rush into the bathroom and join him in the shower, to show him how she felt.

How do *you feel?* she asked herself.

I don't know. I only know I feel like I belong. When I'm with Jake, when I'm with Lizzie, I feel like I belong. Like I'm home.

But how was it possible to feel that way here in Troutville, a town she hated perhaps even more than when she left a decade ago?

Because no matter where you are, when you're with Jake, when you're with Lizzie, when you're with Aunt Louise or Gayle or Flea, you're home.

Home is where they are, where the people you love are.

Tears came to her eyes and she blinked them back. She didn't want Jake to come out of the shower and find her crying on his couch. These feelings were all so new that she wasn't ready to share them.

Especially with Jake, who clearly wanted to forget last night had happened.

I loved you in high school . . .

Perhaps last night had been about unfinished business for him. Perhaps he wanted to take what he wanted for the boy he once had been.

Again she stared up at the ceiling, confused.

Stop thinking, Holly. Read the newspaper instead.

She picked up the *Troutville Gazette*, a paper she used to despise, and leaned back against the couch. The *Gazette* was a local paper, pretty small-time, but had a certain cachet in town and was read religiously by almost everyone. Holly had avoided it because of the coverage of Bride Under Peril. According to Jake, the two reporters covering the "incidents" were more interested in the whodunit aspect than in reporting the facts. Jake had hoped the reporters might help shed light on the case, but instead there was a tabloid quality to the coverage.

Her heart beating a mile a minute, she looked for coverage of last night's "incident," and was relieved to see there was none. It must have occurred too late for the paper's deadline. Besides, they hadn't reported it to the police, and she and Jake had combed the house and the grounds for clues and had found nothing.

Nothing. Always nothing. How could the culprit be so careful?

Holly was about to toss the paper to the coffee table when the Town Tattler column caught her eye. The Town Tattler was just a gossip column written by a wealthy sixty-year-old woman whose husband had once owned the paper, but it was read and discussed gleefully in town. The headline read: "So That's Why He's Marrying Her."

Holly sucked in her breath and prayed what she was about to read had nothing to do with Lizzie. But there, in the first line, was her name. Her heart sank and she crumpled up the page and threw it. Then she imagined Lizzie hearing about it if not reading it herself, and she ran over to pick up the page so that she'd know how to counterattack.

Bile rising in her throat, she sat back down on the couch, smoothed the page and read:

Word has it that Dylan Dunhill III and Lizzie Morrow are marrying because Lizzie is pregnant with his child and forcing him into the union. What she has over his head is anyone's guess. Or perhaps Dylan, the most eligible bachelor in the county, is a stand-up guy.

How do we know Miss Morrow is with child? Hmmm . . . It's been reported from three Troutville locales that she has been requesting decaffeinated coffee and cappuccinos, when the woman's coffee consumption — the real stuff — is well known. And, according to sources who attended the lavish engagement party hosted by her future mother-in-law, Victoria Dunhill, Lizzie didn't have a single glass of wine or champagne. Plus, she clearly has cravings — or perhaps she's always been a very good eater. Sources say she consumed an entire platter of fries and two hot dogs with the works at a recent charity baseball game for The Troutville Boys' Center for which her handsome fiancé kindly volunteers time out of his busy schedule.

It's a good thing Lizzie is a strong and sturdy Down Hill girl, because the terrible events plaguing her and her friends must be causing her a great deal of stress, and we know that stress is not good for a baby.

Holly heard the shower stop running. "Jake!" Holly called. "I have to go see Lizzie right away!"

282

Jake rushed out of the bathroom, a green towel wrapped around his hips. Water dripped down his chest. She thrust the page at him, and he read it, his expression similar to Holly's own.

"What garbage!" he muttered. "Complete garbage. How dare she write this trash!"

"I can only hope Lizzie dismisses it as the usual mean-spirited nonsense," Holly said. "But I'm afraid this might be the last straw. I don't know how much more she can take."

"Give me two seconds to throw on a shirt and jeans and we're out of here," Jake said.

Moments later, they were at Dylan's house, located just a quarter mile away. But Dylan and Lizzie weren't there.

And the *Troutville Gazette* was torn in half and lying in the garbage can awaiting pickup.

Both Lizzie and Dylan were unreachable by cell phone, and Holly and Jake had no idea where they'd gone. They sat in Jake's idle car in the parking lot of the Cooper County Park, Lizzie's favorite. They'd hoped to find Lizzie and Dylan walking along Lizzie's favorite trail by the dog runs or by the lake, tossing bread to the ducks, but the couple was nowhere to be found.

Jake glanced at Holly. She looked so worried that it was all he could do not to turn to her and take her into his arms.

But why? Why was he acting this way?

He'd woken up early, overwhelmed to see her in his bed. He'd lain there for a while, unable to think, or to process his feelings. He'd been so overwhelmed that he'd closed up and acted like a jerk.

"I don't know where else to try looking for them," Holly said, breaking into his thoughts. "We've tried everywhere I can think of."

He hoped he wasn't adding to Holly's worries. She had enough to think about with her cousin without having to try to figure out what was going through his mind.

But what was he supposed to say? he wondered. That last night meant more to him than he could ever express, so he was closing up and acting like it never happened?

"Can you think of somewhere Dylan would go to get away? A favorite place he likes to go to think things through?"

"He often shoots hoops when he has to think," Jake said. "At the Boys' Center. But

I'm not convinced he and Lizzie would be playing basketball right now."

"Perhaps they're walking the grounds? The surrounding woods?"

"It's worth a try."

Ten minutes later, they arrived at the Boys' Center. Dylan's car wasn't in the lot. But Jake found it parked in a deserted stretch by the woods.

"Oh, thank God," Holly said. She turned to him. "Is it possible they want to be alone? I mean, us included? Maybe they'd rather not have us barge in? I didn't even think of that until just now."

"Well, they did turn off their cell phones," Jake said. "Since you can see who's calling, it might mean that they want to be alone, just the two of them. Our hearts were in the right place by trying to find them, but perhaps we should give them a little space."

"Maybe I should head back to Lizzie's and just be there," Holly said. "So when she comes home, she can talk to me about it if she wants."

"Good idea," he said.

He felt her stiffen for a moment. *Because you can't wait to get rid of me?* she was no doubt wondering.

Hardly, he told her silently.

Jake turned the car around and headed toward Lizzie's. They drove in silence.

Four hours and much pacing later, Holly heard the front door open and slam shut. A moment later she heard a crash — the sound of breaking glass.

"Lizzie?" Holly called, hurrying down the stairs. She peered into the living room. It was empty. "Lizzie, are you okay?" she called out.

No response.

Holly headed into the kitchen. Lizzie was kneeling in front of a broken mug, a broom and dustpan in her hands. But she was just staring at the red pieces of ceramic. "Lizzie?"

No response. And then tears.

"Lizzie, honey?"

"Did you read the *Troutville Gazette* today?" she asked. "I'm canceling my subscription, that's for sure," she added before bursting into tears.

"Oh, Lizzie," Holly said, pulling her cousin into her arms. Lizzie sobbed against her.

"I'm trying to be strong about this," Lizzie said. "Dylan said it's my — our — best defense. But it's so hard. It was just so mean. And so personal. Because of the baby, I guess. This innocent, sweet baby shouldn't have to be the center of this disgusting animosity. I won't stand for it." Her anger chased away her tears. "Oh, Holly, you had the right idea by leaving this town!"

"You have every right to live in this town in peace," Holly said. "Troutville is your home."

"But I'm completely helpless against these horrible attacks — if it's not the culprit, it's a gossip rag or Pru Dunhill attacking me."

"So let's fight back."

Lizzie turned to her. "How?"

"Write an editorial," Holly suggested. "At least you'll be able to say what you want, get your side told. If no one chooses to believe you, that's their problem. But you might feel better."

Lizzie liked the idea. She jumped up and grabbed a pad of paper and a pencil and sat down at the kitchen table. "What should I say?"

Holly smiled and sat down beside her. "Tell this town who you are and how you feel. That's it."

"I'm going to do just that," she said, heading to the refrigerator. She pulled out a jar of pickles and a bottle of ketchup. She sliced two pickles, arranged them on a plate, and then squirted ketchup all over them. She popped one in her mouth, then added more ketchup to the pickles on the plate.

"You're pregnant, all right," Holly said, winking at Lizzie.

Lizzie laughed. "For the past few weeks, I've been doing my best to ignore my strange cravings," Lizzie said. "Just in case anyone was paying too close attention — which they were! If I'd known I'd be outed in that gossip rag anyway, I would have been eating my ketchup-pickle slices and cheddar cheese cubes all over town." She popped a couple of gooey pickle slices in her mouth. Then she shoved the plate away and burst into tears.

"If you'd found out by reading the column . . . I would have been devastated. I'm so glad I got to tell you first — well, sort of, anyway. At least I told my mom before she heard about it in town. I had to call her at the crack of dawn. Oh, God, Holly, everything is so crazy." She placed her hand on top of Holly's. "Oh, hell. I'm doing it again. I'm pregnant, Holly-Molly! That's what's important. I'm so happy. And Dylan, he's beside himself with joy. We're going to have a baby!"

"I'm so happy for you, Lizzie."

"And this means a little first cousin once removed for you," Lizzie said. "Or is that second cousin?"

Holly laughed. "I have no idea!"

"If it's a girl, Dylan wants to name her Lizzie, after me. Isn't that sweet?"

Holly nodded, her heart too full to speak. "And if it's a boy?"

"Dylan Dunhill IV," Lizzie said.

"I'm so happy for you, Lizzie," Holly said, squeezing her cousin into another hug.

"I know you are, Hol," Lizzie said. "I'm sorry for not telling you sooner than I did. There's so much I haven't told you, so much I've been keeping to myself."

"You can tell me, anything, Lizzie. And I promise I'll never judge you again."

And she wouldn't.

"I wonder what Dylan's mother is thinking right now," Lizzie said.

"She's going to be a grandmother," Holly said. "I'm sure she's thrilled."

"Well, my mother was thrilled, that's for sure. But my mom loves me. Dylan's mother doesn't even like me," she added with a frown. "And she might not be too thrilled about my being pregnant before the wedding."

"I have a feeling she'll be so happy about her little grandchild-to-be that she'll forget about the timing," Holly said.

Lizzie didn't look convinced.

CHAPTER TWELVE

"I wouldn't be surprised if the value of our companies' stocks plummeted," Mrs. Dunhill muttered, slamming the *Troutville Gazette*, open to the Town Tattler, on her desk. "This is an absolute disgrace!"

Jake and Dylan sat across from Mrs. Dunhill. Jake glanced at his friend; the guy looked like he was about to explode.

"Mother," Dylan said between gritted teeth. "It's not a disgrace. It's a *blessing.* And it's too bad you can't see that. That's what's a disgrace."

"Dylan Dunhill the Third," Mrs. Dunhill said, "If your father heard the way you just spoke to me he would turn over in his grave."

Exasperated, Dylan shook his head. "Jake, talk some sense into my mother, will you?"

"Jake isn't running around fathering babies out of wedlock," Mrs. Dunhill snapped. "Or being forced into marriage because of it."

Dylan started to rise, no doubt to walk out on his mother. Jake put a calming hand on his shoulder. "Mrs. Dunhill, with all due respect, I'm with Dylan on this. You're having a grandchild. That's something to celebrate."

"I'm not about to arrange a parade for news of an illegitimate child," Mrs. Dunhill said.

"Well, Mother, I guess Lizzie and I will just celebrate on our own," Dylan said. "In fact, I'll be leaving now to do just that."

"This isn't about my being old-fashioned," Mrs. Dunhill said. "It's about morality. Propriety. Social standing. People in town look up to us."

As Dylan and Jake stared at her with incredulity on their faces, Mrs. Dunhill picked up the receiver of her antique telephone and dialed. "Pru, dear, it's Mother. I'd like to see you in my office, please. Yes, dear, it's important. I said *now*, Pru. Not in five minutes."

A few moments later, Pru Dunhill, looking as though she just walked out of a beauty salon, popped her head in. At the sight of Jake, she went into power flirtation mode, thrusting out her chest and twirling the ends of her hair. "Why, Jake Boone, what have you possibly said to upset my mother so?"

Oh, brother.

"Pru, come in, please," Mrs. Dunhill said. "Have a seat." She gestured to the chair next to Dylan. "Have you read the *Gazette* today?"

"I assume you're referring to the news about Lizzie's pregnancy," Pru said, examining her nails. "I didn't read the column myself. Arianna read most of it to me over the phone. I was too bored to listen to the whole thing."

"Bored?" Mrs. Dunhill said. "You find it boring that you're going to be the aunt of a bastard child?"

"Well, if it's a bastard, I'm not the aunt, am I?" Pru said.

"She's got you there, Mother," Dylan said, shooting his sister a look. "So you have nothing to worry about. The baby won't be your grandchild if you consider him or her illegitimate."

Mrs. Dunhill seemed to take this in. "Are you threatening me?"

"Threatening you?" Dylan asked. He looked to Jake and threw up his hands. "What the hell is she talking about?"

"Don't you dare use that language in this house!" Mrs. Dunhill yelled.

"Oh, but bastard child is all right?" Dylan said.

"Can I go now?" Pru said. "I have an appointment for a pedicure. This color looks simply awful with this dress, don't you think, Jakie?" She lifted her knee so and rested her foot on the edge of her chair. Her white, flowered underwear was visible. She spread her knees ever so slightly.

"Pru, I can see your underwear," Dylan said. "A little decorum from the daughter of the Ettiquete Queen, please."

"Pru Dunhill!" Mrs. Dunhill snapped, reaching over the desk to slap down Pru's knee.

"Mother, I'm late," Pru said, getting up. "It's not like news about the pregnancy is any worse than news about the marriage, so why get all upset?"

Dylan stared at the ceiling and began counting to twenty. Again Jake put a calming hand on his shoulder.

"Jake, let's go," Dylan said and stood.

"I'm not finished," Mrs. Dunhill responded.

"I am," Dylan retorted.

The moment they were outside the front door, Dylan kicked the brick wall so hard that he winced.

"Dylan, let out your aggression at the hoops, not here," Jake cautioned. "The last thing you want is a broken foot."

"You're right," Dylan said, jogging down

the steps to his car. "Let's get the hell out of here."

Once in Dylan's car and on the road, Dylan calmed down. "I think Lizzie's cousin had the right idea by leaving Troutville. I can't even stand my own family anymore. And I'm beginning to hate this small-minded, gossipy, crappy town. I've been thinking a lot lately of leaving. Lizzie wants to stay, but I think we'd be happier somewhere else. Somewhere new. Where we can start a new life together without all these ridiculous prejudices and feuds."

"Well, if you two do move, move to a bordering town," Jake said, tossing his friend a smile. "The Boys' Center needs you."

"I know," Dylan said. "I'd never leave the center, although there are needy kids everywhere."

"Speaking of the center," Jake said, "according to Lizzie, she told you about the pregnancy at the center. She said there were several boys around. Do you recall if any of the boys could have overheard you? Or were any of them waiting outside the door as you and Lizzie were leaving?"

"I'm trying to remember," Dylan said, turning onto Troutville Plaza. "I was so

stunned by the news that just about everything went out of my head. Oh, wait — I
do remember seeing Billy Mayville and
Logan Jefferson before Lizzie came in.
They wanted help with their three-point
shots. And Jimmy Morgan was waiting for
me as Lizzie and I were leaving, but I was
so rocked by the news of the pregnancy
that I barely acknowledged him."

Jake's heart sank. "Have you seen him
since?"

Dylan shook his head. "I didn't even remember him until right now. I owe him an
apology. Until a couple of weeks ago, I
spent a lot of time with him. And now, it's
dwindled down to nothing."

As Dylan pulled his car into a parking
space near their offices, Jake could barely
breathe.

Please don't let Jimmy Morgan be our guy,
he thought.

"Holly, right?"

Holly turned around to find Jimmy
Morgan, the teenager she'd met at the engagement party, sitting on a bench,
throwing pebbles at a stray cat who was
trying to eat from a can of tuna that
someone had left for it. Every time the cat
neared the can, Jimmy tossed a pebble.

Not hard enough to harm the cat, Holly noticed, but enough to frustrate the poor animal.

Lizzie's mom had come over with hugs and congratulations about the pregnancy, and Holly had slipped out for some fresh air. She needed to think about this morning with Jake — and last night.

"That's right. Holly Morrow. And you're Jimmy."

"Surprise, surprise," he said, jamming his hands into his pocket. "Usually I'm beneath noticing."

"Of course I remember you," she said. "You're Jake's friend."

"I used to be," he responded, throwing another pebble at the cat.

"Used to be?" Holly repeated. "Stop bothering that poor animal."

"Forget it," he said. "Just like Jake's forgotten me."

"Jimmy —"

The boy jumped up. "Whatever. First Lizzie and now you. Before you came to town, Jake had time for me. And he was all I had left since Dylan went into la la land with his marriage plans."

"Dylan and Jake both care very much about you," Holly said, knowing she needed to be very careful with what she said. The boy looked as though he might explode at any moment.

"Funny way they have of showing it," he muttered. "And now that Dylan and Lizzie are gonna have a kid, I can really forget about him helping me with my game or working with me on my algebra."

You know about the baby? she thought. She doubted Jimmy read the gossip pages. Then she remembered Lizzie's words: *There were some boys in the hall at the center when I told Dylan I was pregnant . . .*

Oh, no, Holly thought. For everyone's sake, please don't let Jimmy be the one.

With a shrug of resignation, Jimmy ambled off.

Slowly, Holly neared the cat. When the cute stray was convinced she wasn't going to throw a rock, it rubbed against her jeaned leg. She scratched behind its ears. "You eat up your lunch, little guy," Holly said, stroking the cat's silky fur. For a stray, the cat was clearly well tended to. "Someone will take you home, I'm sure," she said.

Jimmy clearly felt like a stray, she thought. But enough to take his anger and resentment out by hurting the person Dylan loved?

Holly gave the cat a final pat on the head

and headed through the park, her mind heavy with questions to which she had no answers. A group of boys were playing basketball, some children were horsing around in the playground, but Holly barely heard the cacophony of sounds. She began jogging toward the pay phone by the public restrooms. Great — it was unoccupied. In an age when just about everyone had a cell phone except for her, pay phones usually were free.

Unfortunately, the pay phone ate her quarter and was out of service. There was another pay phone, if it was still there, by the tennis courts about a quarter of a mile away. Holly turned and started to head in that direction when she was suddenly grabbed from behind.

"Hey!" she screamed.

But something was placed over her head, something scratchy and heavy, like burlap. She resisted and kicked wildly, but whoever had her had too strong a grip on her.

Panicked, Holly tried to scream, but the burlap was tight against her mouth. She could barely breathe. She felt something going around and around her neck.

No! she screamed silently, flailing wildly to get free.

Suddenly she was shoved hard, and she

fell against the ground. She heard footsteps.

"Help me!" she tried to scream against the burlap. "Help!"

She realized she was free. No one was restraining her. She pulled wildly at what felt like a rope around her neck. Finally, it loosened and she pulled it away, then ripped off the burlap sack.

She breathed deeply until she had enough air in her lungs again. And then she opened her eyes and looked all around her. There was no one. She'd been pushed behind the restrooms; behind her was a bank of trees. If her attacker had wanted to kill her, she most likely would be dead right now.

Catching her breath, Holly angrily tossed the burlap away from her.

And that's when she noticed the note taped to the front of it.

On an ordinary piece of lined paper was typed: *Go back home, Holly the Whore. Or next time, I will kill you.*

Will had been underlined twice with red marker.

Panic rose again and gripped her. Her legs too shaky to support her, Holly fought for control. *Just get up and get the hell out of here,* she ordered herself. *Get up!*

Finally, she found the strength to stand. And then she ran.

"Jake, Miss Morrow is here to see you. She says it's an emergency."

Jake hurried to the door to his office and threw it open. Holly stood, pale and trembling, by his secretary's desk. Her arms were wrapped around herself. She looked scared to death.

"Holly?" he said, rushing over to her. With his arm firmly around her, he led her into his office. Once the door was closed, she collapsed against him. "Holly, what happened?" She shook her head, but couldn't seem to speak. He held her, stroking her hair. "Let it out, Holly. It's okay. You're okay now. You're safe."

She began to calm down. She straightened up and he led her to the sofa by the window. "I —" She stopped. "I was attacked." She reached into her tote bag and pulled out a burlap sack, some heavy string, and a white piece of paper.

Jake took it all and read the note. "Oh, God. Tell me what happened, Holly."

She took a deep breath and relayed the terrible story, starting with running into Jimmy Morgan and ending with being shoved against the ground.

"I didn't want to think it was Jimmy," she said. "But the timing, Jake. It looks very bad for him. He was so angry. And the way he was throwing the pebbles at that poor, hungry cat."

"It doesn't look good at all," he said. "But if Jimmy is the culprit, he's not just some lonely teenager mad at the world. He's a deeply disturbed teenager who is going to face some very serious consequences for his actions."

"I can still feel the rope against my neck," she said, rubbing at her tender skin.

He could see angry red marks on her creamy neck. Fury rose in him and he tried to push it away. Holly needed his support right now. *One thing at a time,* he told himself. *Help Holly right now. Then find the creep who did this to her.*

"Let me take you to Lizzie's," Jake said. "You need rest and some tea. I'll report what happened to the police and have an officer come by to take your statement."

"No, I don't want to go to Lizzie's," she said quickly. "After everything that's happened, I'm afraid this might be too much for her. That kind of stress isn't good for the baby."

"I understand what you're saying, but we will have to tell her at some point. It's not safe for her not to know exactly what she's dealing with. What we're all dealing with. Our psycho seems to be on an accelerated schedule — he or she isn't happy the wedding wasn't called off after last night's party and wall decoration and now this. We're going to step up security, that's for sure."

She nodded. "I just need some time to regroup myself before I face Lizzie," Holly said. "I don't want her to see me scared out of my mind."

"I understand," Jake said. "Why don't we head over to my place. You can rest in peace there."

The sudden vision of Holly in his bed came out of nowhere. No, not nowhere. The image had been there ever since he had woken to find her sleeping tangled in his white sheets. He'd tried in vain not to remember, but the picture was still there. Probably always would be.

"I'm not so sure I want to go to your apartment, either," Holly said. "There are some unresolved issues for me there."

"Then perhaps we need to resolve them," Jake said, surprising himself. Did he really want to talk about how he felt? When he didn't know how he felt?

You know how you feel, he chided himself. *You just don't want to acknowledge it.*

★ ★ ★

The moment Jake opened the door to his apartment, the memories assailed Holly. His kiss. His touch.

His lovemaking.

Fool making, was more like it, she told herself. *Don't confuse what happened last night with love. It was a night of false intimacy, that's all. Of passion. Of lust. Nothing more.*

Yet the moment he stepped away from her and headed to a closet in the hallway, she felt bereft.

She wanted him to carry her over to the sofa and hold her, just hold her.

Fool! she chided herself. *You can't seek comfort from Jake Boone.*

He was as distant as he was that morning when he'd left her in bed and gone about his day as though they hadn't made love.

He must feel uncomfortable about her being here, she thought. Or perhaps he was simply dreading the conversation.

She wasn't so sure she wanted to have it herself. Honesty was good, and all that. But sometimes ignorance was a sort of bliss. When she didn't know for sure how he felt, she could still dream that there was some kind of hope for them.

Hope. She wanted to have hope. For

303

Lizzie. For herself. But things were so damned frightening in their lives right then, so out of control, that she was beginning to lose hope.

How were they supposed to fight against something hidden?

By seeking it out, Holly answered for herself. If something is threatening you, and you can't run, you have to stay and fight.

So stay and fight for Jake, she told herself. *Don't be afraid of what you don't know for sure. Find out.*

Jake returned with a pillow and a throw blanket. "Come sit," he said. He fluffed the pillow. "Lie down."

Her heart heavy, she did as she was told. She sank against the soft cushions and instantly felt better. Yes, she needed to lie down. Needed to close her eyes. Needed to think. She needed to think about what happened at the park. Clues. Smells. Noises. There had to be something to give away her attacker. Something.

Yes, Holly. Think of that and put all thoughts of Jake Boone and his nearness out of your mind.

He sat down on the easy chair adjacent to the sofa. "Holly, why don't you try to sleep. We can talk about what happened when you wake up."

"What happened in the park or what happened here last night?" she blurted out.

Idiot! she chastised herself.

"Well, I guess I was talking about what happened at the park," he said. "But I do want to talk about what happened here. About why I . . ." He faltered. "Why I acted the way I did."

"Do you even know why?" she asked.

He shook his head. "No." He shook his head again. "Actually, that's not true. I do know why."

She took a deep breath. "Because you regret it."

He didn't contradict her. He didn't say anything for a few moments.

Tears stung the backs of her eyes.

"I don't regret it, Holly. How could you think that?"

Relief shot through her. And suddenly, she felt so tired she could barely keep her eyes open. "I need to . . ."

Before she could even finish the sentence, her eyes closed and she felt the pull of sleep.

She thought she felt a hand gently caress her cheek before a blanket was settled over her, but she wasn't sure if she was dreaming or not.

CHAPTER THIRTEEN

When Holly had woken after a couple of hours of much needed rest, she'd immediately begun talking about the attack and anything she could remember, which wasn't much. She hadn't heard her attacker sneak up on her. She hadn't smelled women's perfume or men's cologne. The attacker hadn't spoken. There'd been nothing to indicate whether the attacker had been a man or a woman.

Once the police had left, Jake and Holly had gone to Lizzie's together to tell her and Dylan what had transpired in the park. And then with Holly and Lizzie safe under Dylan's watch and a security guard parked outside Lizzie's home, Jake had gone to see Jimmy Morgan. He'd gone to his house Down Hill, hoping to catch Jimmy at home, but neither the boy nor his mother was there. He then tried the center, and found Jimmy tossing pebbles at the chain-link fence a few feet away.

"What is this, some kind of interrogation?" the boy muttered.

"Jimmy, all I asked you is where you went after you saw Holly at the park earlier today."

"And all I asked you was whether this is some kind of interrogation."

"Jimmy, Holly was attacked in the park."

The boy's eyes grew wide. "She was?"

"Yes, she was."

"Was she hurt bad?" he asked.

"No, but she was shaken up," he said.

Jake waited, his breath held, for Jimmy to ask the wrong question or give a piece of information that only the attacker would know.

But Jimmy gave nothing away. He seemed truly surprised by the news of Holly's ordeal, but as well as Jake thought he knew the boy, he couldn't allow his feelings for Jimmy to color the investigation.

"Jimmy, I want you to know something," Jake said. "You're not losing Dylan and you're not losing me. Right now, Dylan has a lot going on with planning his wedding and planning for the baby, and I've got a lot going on with the case of who is trying to destroy their happiness. But all this doesn't mean that Dylan and I don't love you, man. Do you understand that?"

The teenager jumped up angrily. "Yeah, you love me like an older brother. Please.

307

If you or Dylan cared about me, you'd show up when you're supposed to instead of missing stuff the way my father did. First he started showing up late and then he just didn't show up at all."

"Jimmy —"

"Forget it," the boy yelled. "I don't care anymore! I don't need either of you!" Tears streamed down the boy's face. Jake tried to pull him into a hug, but Jimmy, strong and muscular, fought him. "You're nothing but a fake! Acting all nice now when you think I'm the one who hurt your precious girlfriend! You're nothing but a fake and I hate you!"

Jimmy tore away so fast and was over the chain-link fence before Jake could even think about chasing after him.

The boy was angry as hell, that was for sure.

And it sure was looking bad for Jimmy Morgan. Very bad.

"See, now that we're not leaving the house, everything is fine," Lizzie said, trying very hard to be cheerful. She placed her mug of coffee on the kitchen table and peered out the curtains on the back door. "I'm never going outside again."

"You guys have been cooped up in here

for two days," Gayle said. She bit into one of the chocolate chip muffins she'd brought over. "You're going to need some fresh air soon. And Lizzie, you're going to run out of chocolate soon. You know you can't go a day without chocolate."

"I'd rather stay alive than breathe fresh air," Lizzie said. "Or eat chocolate."

"Lizzie, don't say that," Flea said, tears coming to her eyes. "I'm scared. Really scared. Security or not. I'm so afraid for all of us."

Holly placed her hand over Flea's. "We all just need to be strong. We have to remember that we're going to beat this creep at his or her game."

Gayle nodded. "And maybe Psycho is done. It's been two days since —" She glanced at Holly. "I didn't mean to bring it up."

"It's okay, Gayle," Holly said. "There's no use pretending it didn't happen, and not talking about things only gives them more power."

Lizzie sat back down at the table. "I wish I could be strong like you three. I wish I had an ounce of your self-possession."

"Lizzie, honey, you're stronger than you know."

"A strong waterworks, maybe," Lizzie

said, her eyes shimmering with unshed tears.

Holly smiled and playfully tugged one of Lizzie's springy long curls.

"In a way," Lizzie reflected, "the fact that nothing has happened for two days is creepy in itself. It's like the calm before the storm."

"Don't be negative," Flea said. "I believe in answered prayers."

"I hear you," Gayle said, nodding gravely. "I've been praying like mad."

"I don't mean to discount your faith," Lizzie said, wrapping her hands around her coffee mug, "but I can't rely on prayer. Something awful is going to happen. I've been having nightmares, and I keep seeing Flea hurt on the floor and Holly —" Tears filled her eyes. "Here I go again," she said. "I'm sorry, guys. I'm trying to be strong, but . . ."

Lizzie had been devastated by news of the attack. She'd blamed herself and locked herself in the bathroom again. It had taken an hour for Holly to calm her down. And then Lizzie had gotten the idea in her head that Gayle was next.

"Oh, my God," she'd screamed, then slapped a hand over her mouth. "Does this mean that something is going to happen to

Gayle? First Flea was locked in her back room and then hit by the stone, then Holly was attacked in the park. Is Gayle next?" She'd been shaking and crying, and Dylan had held her close and tried to assure her that security had been beefed up, but nothing would calm Lizzie down.

Thank goodness for Gayle, strong, solid Gayle. She'd flexed her muscles at Lizzie and made her feel them, and even Lizzie had been impressed enough to stop crying and concede that Gayle was very strong and could probably handle herself against any opponent.

"I've been taking self-defense at the community college since that nasty letter was sent to my boss," Gayle said, demonstrating some of her moves. "Hey, Dylan, c'mere. I'll use you as an example."

"You're not going to hurt him, are you?" Lizzie asked.

"Ah, see," Gayle said. "You do have faith in my ability!"

Lizzie's eyes widened and she smiled. "I guess I do."

"Gayle's going to be fine because she's going to have security watching her at all times," Dylan said. "Lizzie, sweetie, we've got the best bodyguards in the county shadowing all of us."

Lizzie headed to the window and peeked through a space in the curtain. "In that black car?"

"Yup," Dylan said. "Right out there in the open."

"That does make me feel better," she said. "And there's someone watching Gayle's and Flea's houses too?"

Dylan nodded. "And my apartment and my mother's house."

But your mother managed to slip out the night of the engagement party, Holly wanted to say. *Security isn't guaranteed. Security hasn't stopped a single thing from happening.*

She hadn't wanted to bring that up; questioning the effectiveness of security with a roomful of frightened people wouldn't have done any good. Holly had simply cautioned everyone to be careful *despite* the security, not to feel safe just because they were being guarded.

"So how does the dress look?" Gayle asked out of the blue, muffin in hand.

All eyes swung to her. "What dress?" Holly asked.

"Lizzie's wedding gown," Gayle explained.

Last night, Flea had brought over the wedding gown that she had made for Lizzie. When Flea had unzipped the dress bag and taken out the dress, Lizzie and

Holly had gasped. The gown was an exact copy of the one Lizzie had fallen in love with at Bettina's Bridal. But Lizzie hadn't been in the spirit to try it on last night.

"You still haven't tried it on?" Gayle asked. "Lizzie — the wedding is in less than one week. What if it needs alterations?"

"I'm just not feeling very brideish," Lizzie said. "I want to put the gown on and feel happy. But I'm afraid I'll look at myself in the mirror and cry."

"Oh, Lizzie," Holly said. "You're getting married. To the man of your dreams. Go ahead and try on your dress. You deserve to be happy. Remember that. This psycho isn't allowed to take anything away from you."

"Holly's right, Liz," Flea said. "It's a joyous occasion to try on your gown. I'm dying to see what it looks like on you."

"Flea! I've been so incredibly self-absorbed. Did I even thank you for the gown?"

"Of course, you did," Flea said. "Profusely. And making it was my pleasure. I wish I could have made the bridesmaids gowns, too, but with all the orders I have, there was just no way."

"I like what we came up with for the

bridesmaids dresses," Lizzie said. "I like the idea of all of you wearing a dress of your choice of the same color even if it is from your closets. It's more special that way."

"Well, at least it adds the 'something old,'" Gayle kidded.

"Go ahead, Lizzie," Holly said. "Run upstairs and try on that beautiful gown!"

Lizzie smiled. "All right." She got up, and hurried out of the kitchen.

"I can't wait to see how it looks on her," Holly said. "Flea, you're amazing. I wish I had your kind of talent."

"It's more just practice," Flea responded modestly, picking at her muffin. "Since I was a teenager I've spent most nights sewing. One of the plusses of not having dates."

Holly glanced at Flea. Flea very rarely spoke of her love life — or lack thereof. She was quite lovely, if you really took the time to look, which most people didn't. Flea walked with her head down, and she dressed in black baggy clothes, a black scarf always tied around her neck, and not necessarily in a fashionable way. The way she wrapped it around her neck almost seemed to accentuate it. All the black, though, did highlight her beautiful skin, pale, Snow-White skin, and the fine bones of her face. She had pretty blue eyes and shoulder length brown hair that she teased out at the ends, most likely, the friends had once decided, to cover her neck even though a scarf always did the job. During all of her teenage years, she'd never had a boyfriend, and from what Holly had heard from Lizzie over the last ten years, she never dated.

Once, in high school, Flea had been invited to a dance. He'd asked her in the school cafeteria, in the lunch line, Lizzie, Gayle and Holly right there to witness it. Flea had stuttered a yes to the boy, an Up Hiller, and then had practically fainted when the boy smiled and headed away.

"Did I fantasize that?" Flea had asked. "Or did that cute guy just ask me to the junior semiformal?"

The friends had assured Flea that he had indeed asked. For the first time, Flea was going to a dance with a date, as were all her friends. Holly and Jake were going as friends, Lizzie was going with a boy who worked after school as a dishwasher at Morrow's, and Gayle was going with a boy she'd started dating a few weeks before. Flea had spent a week making the dress of her dreams. For once, it wouldn't be black.

It would be pale yellow, her favorite color. It would be feminine and floaty. She'd sewed and sewed and when it was done, Lizzie, Gayle and Holly's jaws had dropped to the ground at her talent. The dress was exquisite. And Flea, a matching pale yellow scarf tied playfully around her neck, looked absolutely beautiful in it. Lizzie had insisted on making up Flea's face — just a little mascara and lip gloss, and when her date came to pick her up, even his jaw had dropped to the floor.

"Wow," he said, staring at her. "Wow."

She'd blushed and smiled up at him.

"Look, why don't we just go have some dinner in town," he said. "My uncle owns a fancy restaurant. Let's go there instead."

"But this is my first dance," Flea managed to say. "I really want to go. Maybe we could go to the restaurant after."

The boy bit his lip and seemed to be ruminating about something. "All right," he said.

And off they went.

But when they arrived at the dance, the boy was patted on the back. Handed ten-dollar bills.

And Flea had discovered that he'd been dared to invite her and bring her as his date.

He'd made over two hundred dollars that night.

He'd tried, very hard, actually, to tell Flea that he felt terrible about the whole thing; he'd even flung the money up in the air and insisted that he didn't want it. He'd said over and over that he was sorry, that if he could take it all back and ask her again, for real, he would.

But the damage had been done. The boy had tried to apologize again the next day, but Flea wouldn't come to the door.

On her way to visit Flea the day after the party, Holly had seen the beautiful yellow dress and scarf in the trash bin in front of Flea's house. She'd wanted to take the dress out and clean it and save it, but she'd left it there. Lizzie and Gayle had come over, too, and Flea had cried for hours. Then that Monday, at school, she'd said she was over it, that she wasn't going to think about it anymore, and she'd never brought it up again. She'd also never gone to another dance again. A few times before, she'd gone solo when at least one of her friends was solo, too.

A scream shook Holly from her memories.

"Lizzie!" Gayle shouted.

The three friends jumped up and raced

up the stairs into Lizzie's bedroom.

Lizzie was on her knees, holding her wedding gown.

What was left of it.

The beautiful dress was slashed. And across the bodice, in Magic Marker, was written: *Whores don't wear white.*

"Whoever slashed the dress came into the Lizzie's house last night or early this morning," Holly told Jake as she paced back and forth in his office. "How is the psycho getting past the security guards? I don't understand this!"

"Holly, sit down," Jake said. "You've got to calm down. I understand why you're so upset and rightly so, but I need you calm."

She took a deep breath and sat down. "I just don't get it. Who is behind this? And why can't we find them? Why aren't there any clues? Why?"

"Because it's an inside job," he said without thinking.

Her eyes opened wide. "Inside job? Meaning Pru?"

"Meaning any one with easy access to Lizzie. Anyone who's able to slip in undetected."

"But how is anyone able to slip in undetected?" Holly asked. "The security guards have completely failed us. Whoever it is is slipping right past everyone!"

Including me, he thought, frustrated. This case wasn't making any sense.

He'd painstakingly conducted handwriting analyses of the major suspects — no matches. He'd even analyzed Lizzie's friends' handwriting, Dylan's, his own, to check if the psycho was clever enough to frame someone in Lizzie's circle.

No matches.

Damn.

He was ninety-nine percent sure they could cross off Arianna Miller and Jimmy Morgan unless they had accomplices. He'd tailed them both for the last two nights, and neither had gone near Lizzie's home. Last night, when Lizzie's dress must have been slashed, Jimmy was at the arcade at the pizza parlor, and Arianna had been making out with two different men at a party to which Jake had also been invited; he'd gone because he knew Arianna would be there and he wanted to watch her every move. During the hours that someone could have sneaked into Lizzie's house and slashed the dress, Arianna was straddling a wealthy businessman in the front seat of his Mercedes on Lover's Lane. It was past midnight when Jake saw her removing her shirt and bra and then bouncing up and down with a smile, her hands in the man's hair. *Hey, at least she's not holding her breath for me,* he'd thought. He'd tailed the car until Arianna was safely back at her apartment. He watched the man and Arianna embrace as they said their good-byes. Jake had had the feeling that this was a relationship and not a one-night stand or just a pickup. But the guy was probably married — otherwise why would he sneak around and do it in the car?

He shared all this with Holly. "But if it's not Arianna and Jimmy, and it's not Bobby, and it's not Mrs. Dunhill, then who?" she asked.

"Well, unless it's you, Gayle or Felicia," Jake said, "I'm afraid to say I don't have any idea. I've been stumped by cases before, but this is one of the toughest."

Holly sat back and seemed to be taking it all in. "Jake, what do you think of the fact that Dylan and his groomsmen haven't been threatened or attacked? Only Lizzie and her bridal party are being hurt."

"I've thought about that," Jake said. "But that brings us back to Jimmy Morgan and Pru and Arianna. Jimmy wants Dylan and me to have time for him again, so he figures by scaring Lizzie and you out of town, he gets us back. He doesn't get what he wants by hurting Dylan or me."

"Do you think it's Jimmy?" Holly asked.

"He has a motive," Jake said. "And he was there in the park with you fifteen minutes before you were attacked. Trying to hurt a stray cat doesn't bode well for him, either. But I saw him at the pizza parlor during the time that Lizzie's dress was shredded. As for our other suspects," Jake said, "Arianna, Mrs. Dunhill, and Bobby Jones all have alibis for at least three of the incidents."

"And Pru?"

"She's been tougher to trail," Jake said. "In the past three days, I lost sight of her twice. I was tailing her, and it's like she disappeared."

"Disappeared?"

"I can't make sense of what happened," Jake said. "I followed her as she walked along Troutville Plaza. She went into a store and then never came out."

"I don't understand."

"I don't, either," Jake said. "The store was crowded, and maybe I missed her leaving, but I don't think so. That happened twice. Right before you came, I saw her just sitting down to lunch in the Troutville Café. I'd like to tail her when she leaves."

"Can I help?" Holly asked.

Jake nodded. "I'll need an extra set of eyes for Pru."

She offered a grim smile. "Jake, I'm just going to throw this out there. It doesn't mean anything, okay? I'm just thinking out loud."

"What?" he asked. "Go ahead."

She hesitated, then said, "Is there any chance, any at all, that Dylan Dunhill could possibly be behind all this?"

Jake let out a deep breath. "As much as it's pained me, I have considered him. He's like a brother to me, Holly, but I've run him through the mind mill of suspects. He's had alibis for several incidents. I really don't think it's him. In fact, I know so. He loves Lizzie like mad."

She nodded. "I think so, too." Tears came to her eyes, and they slid down her cheeks.

"Holly?" he asked gently, coming around his desk. He knelt beside her. "Are you all right?"

"Jake, I'm so scared," she said. "For Lizzie, for everyone."

Me, too, he thought. He took her hand and held it and they stayed that way for longer than either intended.

CHAPTER FOURTEEN

Pru Dunhill looked left, then right, seemed satisfied that no one was paying her any attention, and then walked into Wanda's Wig Salon.

Jake and Holly, sitting low in Jake's parked car across the street, stared at each other. Holly's mouth dropped open.

"Why would a woman with gorgeous, long, thick blond hair need a wig?" Holly asked, narrowing her eyes. "Unless she wanted to be in disguise."

"Let's just keep our eyes peeled on that store," Jake said. "Don't take your eyes off the door. That's how I lost her the last two times."

No one entered or left for over ten minutes. Finally, a woman came out. She had long, curly brown hair and black sunglasses.

"Jake," Holly said, sitting up, "That's Pru! I recognize her shoes. She went in wearing knee-high black boots with laces up the back, and that woman is wearing those boots."

"You're right," Jake said. "The hair and outfit are totally different, though."

Pru had gone in looking the way she always did, in a very expensive designer outfit. Now, she had wild hair — the brown wig — and she wore a tight red shirt and a denim miniskirt. There was even a tattoo on her thigh, just above her knee.

"Does Pru Dunhill have a tattoo?" Holly asked, incredulous.

"Not that I know of," Jake said.

"Well, she's going through an awful lot to alter her appearance," Holly said. "And my guess is that's because she's about to do something awful to Lizzie or one of us and doesn't want to be caught!"

"It is suspicious," Jake agreed. "I have a feeling she's going to meet her mystery man. Let's follow her."

Jake and Holly got out of the car and trailed Pru down Troutville Plaza from across the wide boulevard. They watched Pru stop dead in her tracks and suddenly turn to face a store window. She was staring at a display of drugstore items on sale.

"What the —" Holly began. "Why is Pru so interested in dishwashing liquid all of a sudden?"

"Look who's coming up the street," Jake said, gesturing.

Mrs. Dunhill, walking Louis, her butler a few paces behind, was headed right for Pru. Pru seemed to be holding her breath. Mrs. Dunhill passed right by her own daughter.

Pru turned around as her mother passed by and let out a deep breath. Then she continued walking, picking up her pace.

"Jake, she's headed Down Hill!"

"She seems to be," Jake said, frowning. "Holly," he added. "I think you should head to Lizzie's and let me handle this."

"No," she said. "We're in this together."

"Holly, I have no idea what we're walking into."

"That's why I'm not letting you walk into it alone," she said.

"You were always very stubborn," he tossed back.

"Takes one to know one," she retorted.

"Okay, now I know we're back in high school."

"Is she going into the auto body shop?" Holly asked. "She's heading straight for it."

"Without a car," Jake said. "Interesting."

"What the heck is going on?" Holly asked, doubting that Pru Dunhill would enter an auto body shop even if she were driving a car in need of work.

"Let's go in," Jake said.

Troutville's Auto Body Shop was a large operation. Jake held open the door for Holly, and they waited in front of the reception desk for the woman sitting there to finish her telephone conversation.

"Could you hold on, hon," she said into the phone, then placed it against her chest. "Yeah?" she asked.

"Did you see a brown-haired woman come in just a minute ago?"

"A brunette?" the receptionist asked. "There's a brown-haired guy who works here."

"No," Holly said, "A brown-haired woman. Long, curly brown hair, wearing a skirt and high heeled, knee-high boots. You couldn't possibly have missed her."

The young woman wrinkled her face at Holly. "Well I must be blind, then, because I didn't see her. No brown-haired woman came in here."

"But we just saw her walk right through that very door," Jake said, pointing at the glass doorway.

"Look, I gotta finish this call," the woman said. "If you need a car fixed, let me know. Otherwise, I can't help ya." With that, the young woman went back to her call.

And Jake and Holly went back to scratching their heads.

How could Pru Dunhill, in a getup like that, not be noticed? And more, how had she managed to vanish into thin air?

After a half hour of hanging around outside the auto body shop, waiting for the woman formerly known as Pru to make an appearance, Jake leaned against a tree and let out a long breath.

"I know that Pru is a smart cookie," he said, "but when she begins to outsmart me — or you, actually, one of the smartest people at Troutville High — something is seriously wrong."

Holly smiled. "Don't worry, Jake. It's not that Pru's smart; it's that she's shrewd. There's a difference."

"Maybe so, but her shrewdness has us loitering in front of an auto body shop."

Holly glanced at her watch. "Let's go get something to eat and talk this out. Between the two of us, we'll figure out what game Pru is playing. And we'll beat her at it."

Jake's stomach rumbled at the mere mention of food. "No wonder I can't figure out how the most visible woman in Troutville disappeared into thin air. I'm starving."

Holly laughed. "C'mon. Let's go have burgers at the best burger joint in Troutville."

Jake grinned and led the way across the street to Morrow's Pub, where in addition to two frosty sodas, the most delicious hamburgers in Troutville and a basket of golden onion rings, they received hugs from Holly's Aunt Louise.

"Aunt Louise," Holly said, "have you noticed a flashy young woman with long, curly brown hair around here lately? Perhaps with a tall, muscular guy wearing a cap?"

Louise refilled their mugs from a pitcher of soda. "Funny you ask. A couple of weeks ago I did see a flashy gal with long *blond* hair with a guy wearing a cap. And then just a few days ago, I saw a brunette with the same guy."

Jake and Holly exchanged glances. "You saw the same guy with a blonde? Are you sure?" Jake asked.

"Very sure," Louise said. "I was about to walk inside the pub when I noticed a young couple walking down to the railroad tracks. A woman with beautiful, long blond hair, white-blond, like Pru Dunhill's."

Holly almost gasped. "Pru Dunhill? Was it her?"

"I don't know," Louise said. "The couple wasn't facing me. But I don't think it was Pru. I mean, why in the world would Pru Dunhill be walking along the railroad tracks Down Hill with a mechanic from the auto body shop next door?"

Jake and Holly looked at each other. "How do you know it was a mechanic? Jake asked, sitting on the edge of his seat. "And which one was it?"

Louise shook her head. "Can't tell you which guy it was — as I said, the blonde and the guy were facing away from me, but I know it was a mechanic because I recognized the dark blue jumpsuit and the cap."

The cap! Jake thought. Pru's mystery man at the reunion had been wearing a cap.

"Tall guy?" Holly asked, clearly thinking the same thing. "Muscular?"

Louise nodded.

"Were they arguing?" Jake asked. "Could you tell anything from their body language?"

"If they were arguing," Louise said, "I didn't hear. They were too far away, almost by the tracks when I spotted them. From their body language, I wouldn't say they seemed friendly. Well, maybe the blonde. She touched his arm a couple of times, and he sort of pulled away. I don't know —

maybe they were arguing."

"And then you saw the same guy a few days ago with a brunette?" Holly asked.

"Yes, and it was strange because I saw them in almost exactly the same place, down by the tracks, almost hidden from view. I saw them for only a moment, though, before they disappeared around the bend." Louise smiled. "Hey! Is this official private investigator business?"

"Just might be," Jake said.

Two businessmen entered the pub, and Louise excused herself to lead them to a table.

Jake leaned back in his chair. "Well, at least we now know we're not crazy — we did see Pru walk into the auto body shop. And now we know why — her mystery man works there."

"Okay, so we're not crazy, but I, for one, am more confused than ever!" Holly said. "We saw Pru as Pru, not in disguise, at the reunion with the mechanic — at least, we're pretty sure it was him, from Aunt Louise's description of him. They were arguing. Then, Aunt Louise saw them a few weeks ago, and this time, Pru was trying to get friendly and the mechanic wasn't buying. Then Louise sees Pru in disguise as the brunette with the mechanic just a few days ago, but she couldn't tell if they were arguing or not." Holly let out a breath. "What the heck is going on? Who is this mechanic? And how do he and Pru know each other?"

Jake polished off the rest of his burger. "And how do he and the brunette know each other? Does the mechanic know it's Pru in disguise?"

Holly shrugged. "Okay, let's try some possibilities. Let's say that Pru wanted to hurt Lizzie and her friends and needed a hired thug. I could see her going to a Down Hill guy and offering a potload of money to do her dirty work."

"But would a Down Hill guy hurt Lizzie Morrow? Lizzie's loved Down Hill. She works in Morrow's, where everyone knows her. It doesn't add up."

"Especially a mechanic who works at the shop across the street from Morrow's," Holly added.

Jake took a sip of soda. "And, where does the disguise fit in? Why is Pru meeting the mechanic as herself and in disguise, as well?"

Holly shrugged. "I don't get it."

"Okay," Jake said. "Let's say that Pru isn't our culprit. Let's say she didn't hire this mechanic to scare Lizzie out of marrying Dylan. What reason would she have for arguing with him? What could their relationship be?"

"Well, we can discount romance," Holly said.

"Although, our lady did protest a bit too much," Jake reminded her. "Remember how vehemently she denied that she was dating anyone?"

"That's true," Holly said. "But you don't really believe Pru Dunhill would be dating a mechanic, let alone one from Down Hill!"

"The odds are a million to one," Jake agreed. "And, anyway, when we saw them at the reunion, they were anything but lovey-dovey. And when your aunt saw them, same thing."

"So what is their relationship?" Holly asked. "No matter how I try to figure it out, I come up with nothing."

"Me, too," Jake said. "Think your Aunt Louise would mind getting involved in some official private investigator business?" Jake asked.

"I'm sure she'd be thrilled," Holly replied. "What are you thinking?"

"Louise could go over, tell that prize of a receptionist that she'd like one of the mechanics to have a look at her car, that it's making a funny sound. And that one of the guys did some work on her car last year and he was so good she'd love to have him work on her car again, but she forgot his name, could she take a peek at the mechanics; she'd know him right away."

"Good idea," Holly said. "We'd get an ID and his name."

Jake nodded. "Mystery man no more. And perhaps I'll do a little undercover interviewing of our guy and see what I can get out of him. Something along the lines of, 'You lucky devil, I've seen you around town with not one, but *two* Troutville lovelies.' "

"Pru as herself. Pru in disguise. Same guy." Holly shook her head. "Arg! What is her game?"

"We'll find out, Hol," Jake assured her, pulling some bills from his wallet. "I promise you that." Without thinking, he laid his hand atop hers, startled for a moment by how soft hers was.

"Jake Boone, you'd better not be thinking of paying for that lunch," Louise gently scolded. "You know your money is no good in here." Louise's gaze stopped on their hands, and Jake could tell she tried to hide her smile.

Holly slipped her hand away, but not before she acknowledged how very good it felt to have his warm, strong hand on hers.

Later that night, as Jake and Holly were parked outside the Dunhill Mansion in a rented car, hoping, praying, waiting for Pru to make an appearance so that they could trail her again, Holly found herself staring at Jake's hand, resting on the wheel. The same hand that had rested on her own just hours earlier.

Suddenly, the thought of that hand on her face, on her neck, around her waist, touching her, came to her unbidden. She willed herself to think of anything but, yet instead of thinking about Jake's touch, she started feeling his touch. Well, *imagining* feeling his touch.

She sighed.

"Thinking about the case?" Jake asked, glancing over at her.

Her cheeks pinkened. *If only you knew,* she thought. "Um, yes," she said. "I hope Pru makes an appearance soon."

Lie. Total lie. Holly could sit in Jake's car forever. For most of the time they'd been waiting outside the mansion, they'd sat in companionable silence. She was so aware of him sitting so close to her. So aware of his muscular legs. Those hands.

Those shoulders, so close to her own. The clean, soapy, warm, male scent of him.

Get a grip, Holly, she scolded herself.

At that moment, the front door of the mansion opened, and Pru Dunhill came out.

"There she is!" Holly said, nudging Jake in the ribs.

"Thanks for making it easier, Pru," Jake said. "She's dressed as herself tonight."

"Perhaps her disguise is in her overnight bag," Holly noted, eyeing the small black duffel bag Pru had slung over her shoulder.

They watched her walk down the path and head toward the Volvo instead of the Jaguar she preferred to drive.

"Off we go," Jake said, trailing Pru's car down the street at a safe distance.

"She's headed to Down Hill," Holly said. "Back to the auto body shop?"

"We shall see," Jake said.

She didn't head to the auto body shop. She drove to the parking lot at the Down Hill square, turned off her car's lights and ignition, and then tucked her hair up inside a hat and slipped on the sunglasses. She got out of her car, slinging the duffel bag over her shoulder, and ran into the public restroom near the playground.

"Why do I doubt she suddenly has to use the facilities?" Jake said.

"Yup, I have a feeling our brown- or red-haired rock-and-roller is going to emerge."

Ten minutes later, she did. As Pru Dunhill came out of the women's restroom, Holly's mouth dropped open. The brown wig was teased a bit wilder, the makeup a little heavier, the skirt a little shorter. Pru looked like a Down Hill babe on her way to a hot party.

Pru threw the duffel bag into the trunk and grabbed a small purse, then she crossed the parking lot and headed for the auto body shop. There was a skip in her step.

Or so it seemed, Holly thought Pru was going toward the shop, but it wasn't the shop she was headed for.

"Oh, God, Jake," Holly said, panic rising. "She's headed into Morrow's Pub! For someone about to do some dirty business, Pru sure seems cheerful. Is she going after Lizzie's mother?"

"Let's go in," Jake said.

They got out of their car and raced to Morrow's. "Wait, Jake," Holly said. "Maybe we should spy through the window first, find out what she's up to."

"We don't have to be careful," Jake said.

"She has no idea that we're on to her. Just be mindful of not staring at her or acting any differently. You're just Holly Morrow, stopping into your aunt's pub for some dinner."

He was right. Okay, Holly-girl. Deep breath and head on in. Act naturally.

"Just remember that, in disguise, she has no reason to get nervous about us being in there," Jake whispered to Holly. "And it's perfectly natural for us to be here. Nothing will happen to your aunt while we're there, Holly. I promise you that."

Holly took a deep breath. "Okay, Jake. Let's go."

The moment they walked in, they were greeted at the door by Lizzie's mom and given the best seat in the house, near the window overlooking the back garden. Pru was sitting alone at a table for two, facing toward the wall. She'd exchanged the sunglasses for regular glasses, leopard-print red frames. Holly had never known Pru Dunhill to wear glasses.

"She seems to be really studying the menu," Holly noted.

"Or pretending to," Jake commented. "If she noticed us come in, she's giving nothing away."

Pru ordered a pitcher of beer, a platter of

buffalo wings and an order of nachos. Nothing that the elite Miss Dunhill would ever consume normally.

"What is going on?" Holly whispered. "I assume she's meeting the mystery man, but it's looking more like a date."

Jake shrugged. "Things are getting weirder by the minute."

The door opened and an attractive man, early thirties, Holly figured, wearing a mechanic's jumpsuit with the name tag Dan on the chest pocket, glanced around, smiled at the sight of Pru's back, and then sat down at her table.

The mystery man!

"Jake," Holly whispered, "that has to be our guy! He's the same height, same build. Put a baseball cap on him, and he's our guy!"

"Perhaps," Jake said, confusion on his handsome face. "But he's also a *good* guy."

"You know him?" Holly asked? "Who is he?"

"Dan Martin," Jake whispered, leaning close. "He was a couple of years ahead of us in school. He's definitely one of the mechanics at the auto body shop. He handles imported cars, the fancy ones, like our gal there drives. I've played poker with him a few times. He *is* a good guy. If he's involved in hurting Lizzie and her bridal party, I'd be absolutely shocked."

Holly seemed to absorb all that. "I wish we could hear their conversation."

"I think we should go say hi to my old buddy," Jake said. "I want to see who he introduces us to. And how she reacts."

Holly smiled. "Good idea."

They acted as though they were heading to the jukebox. "Dan Martin?" Jake asked. "Is that the best poker player in town sitting right here?"

"One and the same," Dan said, smiling.

Holly quickly glanced at Pru and smiled. Pru was looking up at Holly and Jake with a pleasant expression on her face and as though she'd never seen them before in her life.

Pru Dunhill was one heck of an actress.

"It's been a long time," Jake said to Dan.

"Yeah, because you're driving American and are a terrible poker player."

Jake laughed. "Dan, this is Holly Morrow. Her aunt Louise owns the place." He looked at Pru, waiting for an introduction.

"Well, Jake, meet Suzy, love of my life," Dan said, taking Pru's hand. "We met just a week ago and can't get enough of each other. Suzy, this is Jake Boone. He's a private investigator."

Suzy? Holly thought. *What is Pru up to?*

Pru smiled at Jake and Holly. "Nice to meet you," she said in a high-pitched voice.

If Holly wasn't one hundred percent sure this woman was Pru Dunhill, she wouldn't have recognized her. Aside from the wild wig, tinted eyeglasses, and rock-concert-esque outfit, she wore glittery eyeshadow and lots of pinky-red lipstick.

"And this is Holly Morrow," Jake said. "Nice to meet you, too, Suzy."

Pru offered a small smile. "You, too," she said in a voice that wasn't her own. Had Pru been taking how-to-disguise-your-voice lessons?

What the heck was going on?

"Well, good seeing you, Dan. Nice to meet you, Suzy," Jake said, and then, smiles and pleasantries over, they headed back to their own table.

"They're holding hands, smooching over the table," Holly said, incredulous. "I don't get it. Blond Pru and Dan argue and fight, yet redheaded Pru and Dan are in love?"

"Let's just chow down on some wings and listen in and hope she gives something away," Jake said.

Two baskets of wings later, Holly's stomach so full she couldn't even take another sip of her soda, Pru Dunhill had given nothing away. For an hour, Pru in disguise had had the time of her life, talking, kissing, even dancing to a couple of songs on the jukebox. No one recognized her.

"You're sure he's a good guy?" Holly whispered. "No chance he's a thug in disguise? Hurling stones through bridal shop windows, leaving nasty messages on walls and lawns?"

"I'd bet just about anything on it," Jake said. "He's the real deal."

"Then how could he like her?" Holly asked.

Jake smiled. "She's not 'her,' " Jake pointed out. "She's Suzy."

Holly glanced over at where Suzy and Dan were sharing a wing between their mouths. They each bit closer and closer until they were kissing.

The front door opened and in walked Dylan and Lizzie. Holly saw Pru freeze, then pretend great interest in the scarred tabletop.

Dylan waved at Jake and Holly, then stopped dead in his tracks. "Pru? Little early for Halloween, isn't it?"

Holly held her breath.

Pru said nothing. She slid the menu closer to her face.

341

"Pru?" Dylan said, tweaking the menu down with his finger.

"Who's Pru?" her date asked, an expression of confusion on his face.

"I'd know my baby sister anywhere," Dylan said, grinning.

Pru glared at her brother.

"Suzy, I didn't know you had a brother," Dan said. "Hi, it's nice to meet you. I'm Suzy's boyfriend, Dan Martin." Dan stood and shook Dylan's hand. "Aren't you Dylan Dunhill?"

"Guilty," Dylan said.

Dan looked from Pru to Dylan. "You're a Dunhill? I thought your last name was Morelli."

Pru let out a deep breath and took off her glasses. Then she took off the wig. Her blond hair was in a tight low bun at the nape of her neck.

"What the hell —" Dan began. "You're Pru Dunhill?"

She gnawed her lip, then nodded slowly. "I brought my car in when it was having trouble and you barely gave me the time of day. So I decided to become someone more your style, and you fell for me immediately."

Dylan, Lizzie, Jake and Holly all stared at Pru.

"Look, I'm not getting this at all," Dan said, visibly upset. "Are you playing some sort of game?"

Pru shook her head wildly. "Dan, when I saw you for the first time, I — I fell completely in love. That's never happened to me before. I've never had that kind of reaction to any man before. I saw you and then I watched you work for a little bit and it was like I had the wind knocked out of me. I tried to flirt with you, but you weren't interested."

"And I made that perfectly clear the night I ran into you at your high school reunion," Dan said. "I happened to be in the Troutville Plaza Hotel that night to have a drink in the bar with an old friend who was there for the reunion, and you came barging in, interrupting. 'Come talk to me, Dan. Come have a dance with me.' I told you I wasn't in your class and didn't feel comfortable crashing the party, and you thought I meant your class as in your *station* in life. That's how snobby you are, Pru. I meant your class in *school*."

"Dan, I —"

"But you wouldn't give it up. You made up a story about seeing someone passed out drunk in the woods to get me out there with you, and then you tried plastering yourself against me."

"I didn't think you'd be able to resist," Pru said, her eyes downcast.

"Pru, I admit you're a beautiful woman. But I found you and your style very resistible. Yet still, you wouldn't give up. You threw a little tantrum in the woods, throwing rocks to emphasize your point. You were like a child. *That's* Pru Dunhill."

Ah, the famous fight in the woods. Now that it all made sense, it was still hard to believe.

"No!" she cried. "It isn't! That isn't me. Oh, God, I don't know. Maybe that was me. But it's not me anymore. Since I met you —"

"Since you met me you've been lying, Pru," Dan said. "What about the next time you came to the shop? You made up a lie about your car dying near the railroad tracks so that I would come with you. You lied through your teeth!"

That must have been the day when Aunt Louise had seen Dan and Pru — not in disguise — walking down to the tracks.

"Oh, yeah, like lying would really make you appeal to me," he said, exasperated.

"Let me finish, please," Pru said. "I knew I'd blown it that day, and I didn't know how else to get you to give me a chance, so I came over to the shop looking a lot different to see how you'd react, and you asked me out right away."

"So you are a lie. One big lie."

"No!" Pru said. "I'm the same person! Just different clothes and hair!"

"But everything you've represented to me is a lie," he said, standing up. "What a dupe I am." He stalked out the door.

"Thanks a lot, Dylan!" Pru screamed. "Thanks for ruining the one good thing I had going!"

Before Dylan could utter a word, Pru had also stalked out the door. Dylan, Jake and Holly raced after her, but she'd peeled off in her Volvo, leaving skid marks.

"Okay, that was really weird," Dylan said. "My sister is in love with a Down Hill mechanic and has been pretending to be a Down Hill woman named Suzy? I thought I'd seen it all these past few weeks, but this is really crazy."

"Wow," Lizzie said, dropping into a chair.

Dylan, Jake and Holly joined Lizzie at the table, shaking their heads in wonder.

Holly and Lizzie were about to turn in for the night when the doorbell rang. Holly parted the living room curtain and glanced out to make sure the security car was still parked across the street. It was. She nodded at Lizzie.

"Who is it?" Lizzie said, shrugging at Holly.

"It's Pru."

Holly and Lizzie exchanged glances as Lizzie opened the door.

"I know it's late," Pru said, back to looking like herself. "But I'd like to talk to you if that's all right. The both of you."

Lizzie nodded. "Of course. Come in."

Pru declined offers of tea or soft drinks, but Holly made a pot of tea anyway. When she returned to the living room with a tray, Pru and Lizzie were seated at opposite ends of the sofa, their hands folded in their laps.

Holly wasn't sure who looked more nervous.

"I just wanted to drop by to ask a favor," Pru said. "I would appreciate it if you would keep what happened this afternoon to yourselves. It's worth a good deal of money to me, so" — she removed her checkbook from her wallet — "just tell me how much would be enough to guarantee no one hears about it — especially not the *Troutville Gazette*."

"Pru," Lizzie said. "Put your checkbook away. If you want us to keep mum about today, asking is all you need to do."

"Why would you keep quiet for nothing?" she asked. "What's in it for you?"

"Nothing," Lizzie said. "Holly, what's in it for you?"

"Nothing," Holly repeated.

"Why would you do me a favor?" Pru asked. "I've been nothing but mean to you. To both of you."

"How we treat people is a reflection of us, not other people," Lizzie said. "Just because someone is a jerk to us doesn't mean we have to be a jerk back. That's not who we are."

"Fine," Pru said. "So I have your silence. You swear."

Lizzie nodded. Pru looked at Holly, and she nodded as well.

"Fine, then," Pru said again. "That's all I came to say, then." She got up, slid her purse on her shoulder and walked to the door. But she simply stood there, facing the door, not moving, not saying a word. And all of a sudden she started crying.

"Pru?" Lizzie said softly.

"What am I going to do?" Pru said, covering her face with her hands. "What am I going to do?"

Lizzie and Holly exchanged glances.

"I love him," Pru said, still facing the door. "I love him so much."

"Pru, how about you come back over here, sit down and have that cup of tea," Lizzie said.

Pru turned around. "Maybe one cup. Do you have herbal?"

"I've got good old Lipton," Lizzie said.

"I guess that'll be fine," Pru said as she headed back to the couch. She sat down, eyed Holly at the other end of the couch and then Lizzie as she poured hot water into a mug. "Must seem crazy to you two, huh."

"That you fell in love with someone?" Holly asked. "Someone from a different walk of life?"

Pru nodded.

"Not so crazy," Holly said, smiling. "It happened not so long ago to someone very close to me. "It did seem crazy at first, un-believable, until I realized that love is love, no matter who you are, where you come from, what you do. Magic is magic. And sometimes what you have in common has nothing to do with outer trappings."

"Magic," Pru repeated. "That perfectly describes how it is between me and Dan. But now he hates me. He won't return my calls, he won't answer his door. I've lost him."

"Well, he's probably just in shock," Lizzie

said. "Once he has a night to digest it, he'll probably be willing to hear you out."

Pru nodded. "I hope so."

"Pru, I'd like to ask you something," Holly said. "If you've been in love with Dan these past few weeks, if you've learned yourself how love works, how your brother could have fallen in love with Lizzie, then why have you been so cruel?"

Pru looked down at her feet. "Part of it is wanting to keep up a front, protecting myself from how I feel, I guess. Maybe that's what it's always been about. Protecting myself from I don't even know what. It's why I've pretended to be so crazy about Jake. I mean, he's a great guy and sexy as hell, but I thought he was a safe cover for me. Especially because my mother likes him so much."

Wow, Holly thought. *That's a heck of a lot of trouble to go through.*

"Pru, I'm going to ask this just once and then never again," Lizzie said. "Has it been you who's been trying to sabotage my relationship with Dylan?"

She shook her head. "Not me. And it's not Arianna, either. I'm sure she's on the top of your list of suspects after me and my mother."

Lizzie nodded.

Pru stood. "Thanks for the tea."

"You don't have to rush off," Lizzie said. "We're pretty good listeners if you need to talk."

"I just feel like being alone," Pru said. "Maybe take a drive and think about what I'm going to say to Dan tomorrow."

"Sounds like a good idea," Holly said. "Good luck."

Pru offered a weak smile. "Thanks. I'll need it."

Lizzie walked Pru to the door. "Just out of curiosity, Pru, are you going to tell your mother about Dan?"

"A few days before he proposes," Pru said. She winked at Lizzie. "I think Dylan had the right idea there."

Lizzie smiled, they said their good nights, and as Lizzie closed the door behind her future sister-in-law, she shook her head in wonder. "A day ago, I wouldn't have thought there was even a possibility that Pru Dunhill and I could ever be civil, let alone friends."

Holly smiled. "There're a lot of strange happenings going on in this town."

Lizzie laughed. "That's the understatement of the year." She dropped down on the sofa and leaned her head back. "I'm beyond relieved that it's not Pru or Mrs.

Dunhill or Arianna who's been trying to ruin my life and my friends' lives. But then, who is? I'm out of guesses."

"I don't know, Lizzie," Holly said honestly. "But I do know Jake is working on the answer around the clock."

She nodded and let out a deep breath. "The wedding is set," Lizzie said, "and I don't have anything but a bridal party and a groom."

"That's pretty much all you need, honey," Holly said. "The reverend is still set, and you can wear one of the prettiest dresses in your closet."

"That's true," Lizzie said. "I guess it doesn't matter what I wear so long as the people I love are right there with me."

Holly squeezed her cousin's hand.

"And at least we're telling the psychopath that he or she hasn't won," Lizzie said. "Dylan and I are marrying despite their best efforts to keep us apart or drive me out of town. Maybe once we're married, the psycho will just admit defeat and leave us alone."

Holly nodded a hopeful smile, but she wasn't so sure that would happen.

The doorbell rang. Lizzie and Holly practically jumped out of their seats.

It was Pru Dunhill again.

"I'm sorry to barge in on you like this," Pru said, "but, um, well you said I could come by if I needed to talk, and . . ."

"And we're glad you did," Lizzie said, shooting Holly a perplexed look. "Were you able to talk to Dan?"

Pru nodded. "I reached him from my cell just sitting in the car. He wants to meet at Morrow's Pub tonight and he wants me to come as me." Pru suddenly burst into tears. "But I can't do that. When I'm with Dan I'm Suzy. I'm not Pru Dunhill. And it's fun being someone else. Someone who can do and say and be whatever she wants."

"Pru, you do say and do whatever you want," Holly pointed out.

Pru shook her head. "It might seem that way, and I'm not trying to come off as the poor little rich girl, but being so rich and beautiful and perfect and envied comes with a cost, too."

Holly tried not to burst into laughter. She exchanged a glance with Lizzie. "Pru, why don't you tell us what it is that you like so much about being 'Suzy.' "

Pru smiled. "I love being able to dress in rocker-babe clothes and have wild hair. I love being able to drink a beer. I love being able to be sweet and nice and lovey-dovey with Dan and his friends. I'm an entirely different person when I'm Suzy."

"Pru, why can't you just try to incorporate Suzy, the person you want to be, into who you are now. You can be whoever, whatever you want — you've seen that. So just *be* Suzy. Get some more fun clothes, play with your hair, be sweet and nice. That's all you have to do. You don't have to pretend to be someone completely different."

"I'm not sure I *can* change," Pru said. "I wouldn't know the first thing about changing."

"I would," Holly said. "And so would Lizzie. It's tough, but in the end, you just might get what you really want."

"So it's worth it?" Pru said.

Lizzie nodded. "Don't you think, Hol?"

Holly thought of Jake. She'd changed too late to get what she wanted.

"Yes," she said. "It's worth it even if you don't get what you want."

The wedding plans changed even more dramatically. Instead of the big church wedding that Lizzie had always dreamed of, the ceremony was now scheduled to take place under very tight security at Dunhill Mansion tomorrow, a day earlier than planned. Instead of two-hundred-and-twenty-five guests, all of whom had accepted the invitation, only family and close friends would attend. And instead of being warmly greeted by the bride and groom and their families, all guests — and the bride and groom — would be subject to intensive security checks of their persons and possessions before they would be allowed entry into the house.

Mrs. Dunhill had been surprisingly agreeable about hosting the wedding at her house; she'd made the arrangements with the reverend and hired a wedding planner to quickly turn her ballroom into a flower-and-gazebo "garden" and her kitchen into a makeshift catering center. She'd also personally called all the guests who were essentially being "uninvited" to inform them of the change.

Apparently, a grandchild with married parents meant a lot to Mrs. Dunhill.

As Jake made the last of the calls to ensure the security force would be in place, he swiveled around in his desk chair and stared out the window down onto Troutville Plaza.

In two days, Holly would be leaving.

Once again, he was Troutville and she was not. Ten years ago, it had been easy to let her go because of her dreams. He'd wanted her to realize them all, to be happy. To find the life and home that she'd always dreamed of.

But now, letting her go wasn't so simple. There was unfinished business. And there was the little matter of his feelings for her.

How do I feel? he asked himself. Part of him loved her like crazy. And part of him knew he'd never be what she was looking for because he *was* Troutville.

Then again, if Pru Dunhill could fall in love with a Down Hill mechanic and change her entire being for him, anything was possible.

CHAPTER FIFTEEN

The weather cooperated for Lizzie's wedding day. It was sunny and warm with a lovely breeze. A breeze that should have sent the aroma of Holly's chocolate chip muffins up the stairs to Lizzie's bedroom to wake her up.

Holly glanced at the clock on the kitchen wall. Nine o'clock. "Lizzie, honey, are you awake?" she called up the stairs. "It's nine o'clock. Come down for breakfast — I'm making my specialty."

Holly waited a moment for a response, then headed into the kitchen. Lizzie Morrow could sleep through a jackhammer outside her window, but she could never sleep through the knowledge that Holly's chocolate chip muffins were waiting for her.

Ingredients mixed, Holly slid the muffin tray into the oven, then brought the telephone over to the kitchen table and sat down. She'd forgotten to buy coffee yesterday, and since Flea lived closest and was addicted to the stuff, she thought Flea wouldn't mind bringing some by when she came over this morning to attend to Lizzie.

That's odd, Holly thought. There was no dial tone. She replaced the receiver in the cradle, then picked it up and put it to her ear again.

Nothing.

Ah, Lizzie, Holly remembered, heading over to the jack to make sure it was plugged in. Lizzie often unplugged the phone because their psycho enjoyed making threatening midnight calls — that of course, couldn't be traced.

The phone cord was plugged into the jack — but the phone cord wasn't plugged into the phone itself.

Because the cord had been cut.

Holly's stomach rolled over. "Lizzie!" She flew through the living room and up the stairs and barged into Lizzie's room.

It was empty.

"Lizzie!" Holly screamed.

There was a note on the bed. Holly grabbed it and read the words typed all uppercase on white paper:

TOO LATE, HOLLY. SHE'S DEAD.
AND SO IS HER CRIPPLED KEEPER!

Holly ran as fast as she could to Lizzie's

neighbor. Out of breath, she asked to borrow the woman's phone. The woman produced a cordless, and Holly punched in Jake's number as she paced frantically back and forth in the yard.

Please be home. Please be home. Please be home!

The phone was silent.

She shook it and pressed the off key, then pressed it back on. No dial tone.

Oh, my God.

Holly dropped the phone and ran in the direction of Flea's house, just two blocks away. *Flea, please be there and safe, she prayed. Please!*

She knocked frantically. No answer. She ran around to the back.

Voices! She could hear Flea's voice.

Thank God she's alive, Holly thought.

She put her hand on the doorknob, then pulled it back. Was their psycho in there now? With Flea and Lizzie? If Holly barged in, would he or she do something rash?

What should I do? What should I do? she screamed at herself. *Think!*

Okay, just calm down and listen. Listen. And look.

She peered through the small gap in the curtain covering the back door. This was the entrance to Flea's apartment, though Flea usually used the shop entrance around the house.

The house was silent. The only thing Holly could see was the door that led into the basement. A light flickered and waned, like a candle.

She heard a muffled sound and pressed her ear to the door.

Nothing.

She tried the door — it was open.

Oh, God. Oh, God. Oh, God.

Slowly, Holly opened the door and slid inside. She tiptoed to the basement door and pressed her ear against it, straining to listen. She heard muffled voices again.

Someone was down there! Were Flea and Lizzie bound down there, their mouths covered in duct tape?

Open the door very quietly, she told herself.

She opened it a crack, grateful it didn't make a sound. She could see Flea standing in the dark, a candle flickering on a table beside her. She was holding something.

Holly very gently opened the door a bit more, and it creaked.

Flea jumped. "Holly!" she called in a frantic whisper. "Is that you?"

"Yes, Flea. It's me! Are you OK? Is Lizzie OK?"

"Yes, we're fine! Hurry down here, Holly. I can't get Lizzie's rope untied!"

Holly threw open the door and rushed down the long, steep stairwell. She tripped, and landed on her ankle. She screamed.

"Poor Holly," Flea said. "Hope you're not crippled for life. Let me tell you, it's no fun."

Holly grabbed her ankle against the rush of pain and glanced up at Flea.

The woman held a butcher knife in her hand.

Oh, my God.

A movement in the dark corner caught Holly's attention. It was Lizzie.

"Lizzie!" Holly cried.

Her cousin was bound with rope in a chair. A piece of duct tape was across her lips. Holly could see the fear and panic in her eyes.

"Flea, what is going on here?"

"You stupid, stupid snotty slut!" Flea shouted, waving the knife. "Shut up right now!"

What?

Holly stared at Flea. And comprehension slowly entered her brain. No wonder security hadn't registered that Lizzie was in grave danger. She was with Flea — one of her best friends.

Oh, God, Holly thought, strangling on a sob.

Flea moved quickly over to Lizzie and stood next to her. She placed the knife's tip at Lizzie's throat.

"Flea!" Holly cried.

"My name is Felicia. Not Flea. *Felicia.* Say it with me now, Holly, since Lizzie can't speak at the moment."

Holly opened her mouth to speak, but no words came.

"I'll give you a moment to figure out how to talk, you stupid snotty slut," Flea said. She grabbed a fistful of Lizzie's hair and held it high above her head. She took a pair of scissors from the table and began cutting close to Lizzie's scalp.

Lizzie looked absolutely terrified. Holly's heart was hammering in her chest.

"If you so much as move, Holly the Whore," Flea said. "I will jam these scissors in her neck so fast she won't know what cut her. Get it? I made a funny."

Holly swallowed.

"And then I'll take this knife and jam it in her slutty chest!" Flea snapped.

"It's me he should have loved!" Flea screamed as she grabbed another fistful of Lizzie's long blond curls and cut within an inch of her scalp. "If I wasn't disfigured, if

I was pretty like *you* —"

"Flea, we're best friends," Holly said as evenly as she could. "I don't understand!"

"How could you, *snob?*" Flea yelled back. "You moved away. How could we be best friends if you haven't even lived here in ten years?"

"But —"

"But *nothing,* snob," Flea screamed. "And I told you. My name is *Felicia.* Your latest conquest knows my name. So why don't you? I thought we were *best friends.* You lying snobby slut!"

"Felicia," Holly said. *Think, girl. Reason with her. You know her. You've known Flea all your life. Do something!*

But she didn't know Flea. Felicia. She clearly didn't know her at all.

Flea continued cutting, her eyes on her handiwork. "It's your fault I'm disfigured," she snapped as clumps of Lizzie's hair fell to the floor. "You didn't save me in time!"

Oh, God.

"She tried, Felicia!" Holly said. "She tried. She was burned herself. She had to stay back!"

"And she let me burn. She saved her precious skin and let me burn!"

"No, Felicia!" Holly said. "It wasn't like that! They wouldn't let her back in! The firefighters held her back!"

"No boys ever liked me," Flea said. "No, they all went for you, Lizzie. Of course they did, since you slept with them all."

If Flea believed that, why would she single out Lizzie? Why not go after Holly or Gayle, who had equally undeserved reputations based on lies?

"And now you've hoodwinked the man of my dreams," Flea said. "I've loved Dylan Dunhill since my 'accident,'" Flea said. "Do you know why?"

"Why?" Holly asked softly. She looked at Lizzie. Tears rolled down her cousin's cheeks.

"Because I'd had a mad crush on him since seventh grade," Flea said. "I never told any of you because I thought you'd laugh at me for liking an Up Hill boy and the richest boy in town, at that. So I kept it to myself. And Dylan was nice to me. Always nodded at me as he passed me in the halls at school. Agreed with me a few times in a class discussion. And after — when my scars healed and I started going outside again, he was the only person who didn't stare. He was nice to me. Once, he even said my scarf was pretty and made me look like a movie star."

"Felicia," Holly began.

"I love him so much!" Flea cried. "And Lizzie got her hooks into him! Slutted onto him and got herself pregnant and now he's forced to marry her because he's so up-standing a person! Well, I won't stand for it. I won't let him sacrifice himself for you. The way you didn't sacrifice yourself for me!"

Flea transferred the scissors to her left hand and picked up the butcher knife with her right.

"Did you find my note?" Flea asked Holly, the knife perilously close to Lizzie's shoulder.

"Yes, I did."

"I said the 'cripple was dead too,' " Flea said. "And she is. From now on, I'm living. Once I get rid of Lizzie, I can live again. Be the person I was meant to be before she ruined my life."

Flea slowly lifted her arm, and the knife shone in the dim light.

"No!" Holly screamed.

"Don't waste your breath, Holly the Whore," Flea said. "No one can hear you. Thanks to Lizzie, no one ever comes around my little house."

The knife slashed down.

CHAPTER SIXTEEN

Inside job. Inside job. Inside job.

The words echoed in Jake's head. They'd been echoing all night long. Unless the psycho they were dealing with was Lizzie herself or Gayle or Felicia or Holly, Jake couldn't see how the person had managed half of what he or she had accomplished.

Had Holly attacked herself in the park? Had Flea struck herself with a brick-sized stone? Had Gayle —

Nothing terrible had happened to Gayle. Her car had been keyed weeks ago, and her boss had received that vile letter about her, but she could have done both herself to include herself among the victims.

Lizzie, Holly, and Felicia had all been viciously attacked.

Gayle was the only one who had not.

But Gayle was one of Lizzie's best friends. Granted, Jake didn't know her all that well, but his gut refused to believe what was going around in circles in his head.

She's not the one, his cop's instinct seemed to say.

Then who, dammit!

He got out of bed, took a fast shower and threw on clothes. He had to talk to Holly. Had to talk out this Gayle theory, no matter how distasteful.

Perhaps she was secretly in love with Dylan.

You've got it wrong, every fiber of his being screamed. *You're barking up the wrong tree.*

As he grabbed his keys and headed for the front door, he knew that there was something he wasn't thinking of, something he couldn't focus his thoughts on. The culprit was right under his nose, that much he knew for sure.

So if not Gayle, then who?

He unlocked the door, but it wouldn't open.

That's weird, he thought, yanking on the doorknob. The door wouldn't open.

He grabbed his telephone. It was dead. That was weird. His cell phone was also dead, despite the fact that he'd charged it last night.

What the hell?

Panic rose. Six flights up, there was no way out except through the door. And someone had made sure he couldn't get through it — or call anyone.

"Not too pretty now, are you?" Flea asked Lizzie, cutting another clump of her beautiful blond curls. "You are hideous. Now you're the kind of girl who'd get invited to a dance as a dare."

"Fle— Felicia," Holly said, her knees trembling. "You —"

"Holly," Flea said, holding a point of the scissors to Lizzie's throat. "If you keep talking, if you say one more word, in fact, I will jam this into your ugly cousin's throat."

Oh, God, Holly thought, her mind racing. *What can I do? I have to do something. Outthink her. Think, Holly, think!*

Lizzie looked absolutely terrified. She was crying and shaking.

"Poor, poor, ugly Lizzie," Flea said. "Too bad Dylan won't want to marry you now. Not when he sees you like this." Flea's eyes seemed to light with an idea. Then she began slowly unraveling the black scarf from her neck. Holly hadn't realized how long the scarf was — there seemed to be yards of material.

Flea's bare neck was just visible in the dim light. Holly had never before seen the scars on Flea's neck. They were large patches from skin grafts.

Lost in her own world, Flea put down the scissors and ran her fingers over the scarf. She moved behind Lizzie and wrapped the scarf around Lizzie's neck.

Oh, God, Flea, Holly thought. *Please don't let her hurt Lizzie. Please!*

Flea continued wrapping.

Now, Holly ordered herself. Now was the time. When Flea was lost in her own world. *Act now!*

Her eyes on the scissors and knife on the table, Holly realized she had this one opportunity to save Lizzie's — and her own — life.

She lunged.

But Flea was too fast. In the blink of an eye she had the knife in one hand and the scissors in the other. Flea raised the knife high in the air and turned in one motion to strike at Lizzie's neck.

"No!" Holly screamed.

The sound of gunfire split the air, and Flea fell to the ground.

Dazed, Holly looked up to the stairs, and there were Jake and Dylan behind two uniformed police officers, their guns drawn.

"Noooo!" Flea screamed. She coughed, blood sputtering out her mouth. "Don't let Dylan see me this way." She brought her hands up to her neck and tried to use her hair to shield her scars. "He'll never want me if he sees me like this! I'll be as ugly to him as ever! As ugly as Lizzie is now! I tried to stop the wedding, Dylan. I tried to stop her from ruining your life. I even hired some thug to hurl a stone at me through the bridal salon's window, but —" She stopped talking and gasped for air. The sounds of approaching sirens filled the silence of the room. "I can still get rid of her and we can be together —"

The cops rushed forward to assist her, to try to stop the bleeding, but Flea was already gone. One of the officers closed her eyes.

Dylan flew to Lizzie and untied her. And Holly, on the verge of collapse, fell seconds before Jake caught her in his arms.

"How did you know?" Holly managed to whisper.

"I just kept remembering what we spoke about — that it had to be an inside job. And when I let myself focus on Lizzie's side, I finally hit on Felicia and everything clicked — how she was able to accomplish her attacks. I wasn't sure, but I called Dylan and the police and rushed over here. I had to break down my door first, thanks to Felicia, but it's amazing what adrenaline does to a person. Felicia also managed to turn off my phone service."

"If you'd come a minute later —" Holly said. "Oh, Jake."

"I'm here now. And you're safe. Lizzie's safe. Everything is going to be okay now, Holly."

She closed her eyes and breathed in his scent, relaxed against his strong arms. *Don't let me go,* she said silently, but she wasn't sure if she'd said it aloud.

The police had found a duffel bag full of empty prescription medication bottles — antipsychotic drugs — hidden away in a closet in Flea's bedroom. Apparently, she had been under psychiatric care since the fire when she was fourteen.

"How could we not have known?" Holly asked.

Holly, Lizzie, Gayle, and Dylan were seated in Lizzie's living room. It had been five hours since that morning's ordeal. Lizzie, rejuvenated by the knowledge that it was over, truly over, was doing better than anyone expected.

Lizzie and Gayle shook their heads. Lizzie leaned back against her living room couch with a sigh; Gayle's eyes pooled with fresh tears.

According to the police, Felicia Harvey

had been seeing a psychiatrist in private practice an hour away from Troutville from the ages of fourteen to eighteen. When she became a legal adult, she switched doctors a few times.

"I don't even know how to process this," Lizzie said. "The attacks, Flea's death, the Dunhills — How am I supposed to go on with the wedding when nothing in my life makes any sense? One of my best friends has hated me for over a decade —"

A knock on the door interrupted Lizzie, and Holly went to answer it. Jake stood outside, his expression grim.

"I've just come from the precinct. Felicia is now at the morgue."

Lizzie swallowed. "Now that I know it was Flea all along it does make sense. She locked herself in the basement — even, or *especially* because she was always terrified of basements. She bashed *herself* in the forehead with the stone. Who would ever suspect her? She had complete access to me, my house, to Holly and Gayle."

"And during all our conversations about that — the access the culprit had — it never even occurred to me that it could be Flea," Holly said, shaking her head.

"That's not a bad thing, Holly," Jake said. "Why would you suspect your own friend? Your childhood friend?"

"But all the evidence — if I would have opened my eyes, I might have seen it."

"And I saw it almost too late," Jake said. "I'm trained to be objective — and I thought I was being objective. I learned a serious lesson on this case."

"I think we all did," Holly said.

CHAPTER SEVENTEEN

"Am I really expected to enter . . . a pub?" Mrs. Dunhill asked, her expression incredulous. Louis snug against her beige blazer, Mrs. Dunhill eyed the outside of Morrow's Pub as though it might attack her at any minute.

"Mrs. Dunhill," Jake said, "it's a very nice place. I think you'll be quite pleasantly surprised — if you ever go in."

She had been stalling since he'd picked her up an hour ago. First, she needed a "bracing cup of coffee." Then she needed some fruit. Then she needed to walk Louis in the gardens. When Dylan called her to say that if she didn't come immediately, he and Lizzie would elope to Las Vegas, Mrs. Dunhill announced that she was ready to go. Of course, she spent ten minutes arranging herself in the passenger seat of Jake's car, then another ten minutes getting out of the car in front of Morrow's Pub.

Mrs. Dunhill glanced sharply at Jake to chastise him for his impudence, then raised a gray eyebrow. "I've never been inside a common pub in all my life. Of course, I've been in some lovely, elegant hotel bars, but I'm sure the Morrows don't have the top-shelf liquor that I'm used to."

Jake mentally rolled his eyes. "Again, Mrs. Dunhill, I think you're going to be very surprised." He pulled open the door. "Shall we?" He hesitated. "Actually, before we go in, there's something I need to know. Why did you leave the engagement party — and where did you go?" Jake had been unable to pry this information from Victoria, but perhaps now she would explain.

"Oh, Jake, really! I simply *had* to escape, that's *all*. All right, let's go," she said, clutching Louis more tightly against her. "You'll protect me, won't you, Louis," she cooed to the dog — who didn't respond. "I still can't accept the idea of a pregnant girl in a bar. It's in such bad taste, smoking ban or not. It's the way it *looks*."

"Mrs. Dunhill, after you," Jake gritted out. And finally, the woman walked into the pub.

Inside the brightly lit room, Dylan, Lizzie, Pru, and Holly sat around a large round table, a pitcher of lemonade and a cheese platter in the center.

Everyone looked miserable. Dylan was

slumped in his chair, staring at the ceiling. Lizzie was biting her cuticles. Pru was looking around as though she might catch a disease from the walls. And Holly was staring at her clasped hands.

"Pru? Who is that man sitting next to you?" Mrs. Dunhill asked.

All eyes swung to Pru. Sitting next to her was Dan. They held hands atop the table.

"This is Dan Martin, Mom," Pru said. "He's a mechanic at the auto body shop. I met him when I brought in the Jag."

"Is it necessary to hold hands with your mechanic?" Mrs. Dunhill asked pointedly. "And I thought this was a *family* meeting."

"It is," Pru responded. "Which is why I asked him to come. I'm in love with this man. Madly, crazy in love. He *is* family to me."

Mrs. Dunhill looked as though she was going to pass out. "Jacob, dear, help me to a seat, will you? My legs may give way."

Jake helped Mrs. Dunhill into a chair next to Lizzie's mother. The queen of Troutville immediately slid the chair over a ways so that she wouldn't be contaminated by the "common folk."

Jake rolled his eyes and sat down across from Holly. She looked exhausted. Vulnerable.

"Okay, let's just get started," Lizzie said. "The wedding is being postponed indefinitely."

"That's unacceptable," Mrs. Dunhill boomed. She sat across from Dylan, slightly set back from the others as though she were a queen. "I will not have an illegitimate grandson!"

"Mother, wedding or no wedding," Dylan gritted out, "this baby will not be illegitimate. It is my child and Lizzie's child. And as you know, we have not determined the sex yet, so please stop referring to the baby as a boy."

"If you're not married, he's illegitimate, Dylan," Mrs. Dunhill retorted. "That's the definition."

"In your dictionary, Mother," Dylan said. "In mine and Lizzie's, our child is ours regardless of marriage, regardless of name, regardless of anything."

"It's because of the baby that we're postponing the wedding," Lizzie continued. "We can't imagine creating a family when our own families can't support us." Mrs. Dunhill opened her mouth to speak, but Lizzie cut her off. "For the baby's sake, Dylan and I ask all of you to please put aside whatever negative feelings you may have about us as a couple. For the baby, we all need to get along."

"Whoever isn't willing will be cut out of our lives," Dylan said. "It's that simple. "So, Mother, if you can't be civil, you *will* be denied your grandchild."

Mrs. Dunhill's jaw dropped. "How dare you!"

"I dare because I have to," Dylan said. "Same for you, Pru. If you cannot be civil to my future wife, I will keep you from your niece or nephew."

"Honey," Lizzie said, touching his arm, "Pru and I have already started working on a new relationship."

Mrs. Dunhill stared from Pru to Dylan. "Prudence Dunhill, what is going on! First, you're taking up with your mechanic and then you're suddenly making truces?"

"What about that upsets you, Mother?" Pru asked.

Mrs. Dunhill opened her mouth to speak but said nothing.

"I think it's the fear factor," Jake said. "Change is hard for people to accept. Especially those closest to you. Your family is changing, Mrs. Dunhill. The world is changing and your children are changing. Even Troutville is changing."

"Nonsense," Mrs. Dunhill said. "Phases are phases. They're not permanent."

"Mom, it's easy to believe what you need to feel safe and secure," Pru said. "It's a lot harder to accept what is and decide how you're going to deal with it, how you even feel about it. I'm in love with Dan and want to be with him. Dylan's in love with Lizzie and wants to be with her. That's all that should matter."

"But —" Mrs. Dunhill began.

"But what?" Dylan said gently. "I love you, Mom. A lot. I want you in my family's life."

"Mrs. Dunhill," Lizzie said, "You don't have to accept me. You don't have to love me. I'm willing to extend my hand and welcome you into my life. You don't have to take it, but I hope in time you will."

"Mom?" Dylan prompted. "Are you with us or against us?"

Mrs. Dunhill looked at her son, then at Lizzie, then back at her son. She put Louis down, then walked over to Dylan and bent down to hug him. "I love you, Dylan. And I already love my grandchild so much. I'm with you."

Lizzie let out a cry and jumped up, and Mrs. Dunhill embraced her.

"I suppose we both have to get used to each other," Mrs. Dunhill said to Lizzie. "I think we can do that."

"I think so, too," Lizzie said with a smile.

"Thanks for doing my hard work for me, brother dear," Pru said. "You've softened Mom up for me and my new relationship."

Mrs. Dunhill scowled. "I didn't say that. I'll deal with you two later."

The room erupted in laughter. Surprised, Mrs. Dunhill scowled again, then allowed herself a hint of a smile.

"Mrs. Morrow?" Dylan said, turning to Lizzie's mother. "How do you feel about all of this?"

"I'm feeling in the mood for some of my amazing macaroni and cheese," Mrs. Morrow said. "I've had some baking in the oven for the past hour — can I interest anyone?"

There was a chorus of yeses.

"I'm quite the cheese connoisseur," Mrs. Dunhill said. "I like a mix of three cheeses . . ."

Suddenly, Mrs. Dunhill and Mrs. Morrow were discussing cheese and recipes, Dylan and Lizzie were embracing, and Pru was playing with her boyfriend's hair.

"About the wedding," Mrs. Dunhill said. "There's a lovely square between Up Hill and Down Hill that would make a wonderful wedding locale."

Lizzie grinned. "Between Up Hill and Down Hill. That does sounds perfect."

"I agree. The in-between square, it is," Dylan said.

"Tomorrow?" Mrs. Dunhill asked. "The delicious food the caterer made will keep till then. Everyone is invited to my home for the reception."

Lizzie and Dylan smiled. "Tomorrow, it is," they said in unison.

Mrs. Dunhill beamed.

"I guess our work is officially done," Jake whispered to Holly.

She smiled, and his heart broke all over again.

CHAPTER EIGHTEEN

"I could wear this for the ceremony, I guess," Lizzie said, pulling a white sundress from her closet. "It's a bit casual, but it's pretty."

"It's very pretty," Holly said. "I think you'll make a beautiful bride in that dress."

Lizzie smiled, but it didn't reach her eyes. "Thanks, Hol. But with this hair," she added, touching her very short blond curls, I don't think beautiful is quite the right word."

"Lizzie, I really love how your hair looks," Gayle said. "The Cut and Chat salon did such a wonderful job."

Earlier today, Holly and Gayle had taken Lizzie to the hair salon in a neighboring town. When they'd walked in, all eyes went to Lizzie's crazily cut hair — cut within inches of her scalp, save a few long curls that Flea had missed. Lizzie had ignored the stares and asked for the stylist to work whatever magic she could.

"She's a bride tomorrow," Gayle had whispered.

"Don't you worry, honey," the stylist had

said. "You're in good hands. You're going to look like a young Meg Ryan meets Charlize Theron when I'm done with you."

The stylist hadn't been kidding. When Lizzie dared peek in the mirror, she had very short blond ringlets all over her head, shiny and bouncy. She looked fresh and trendy. Lizzie wasn't used to the new short look, but her hair did look fabulous.

"You'll get used to it, Lizzie," Holly assured her. "And besides, it'll grow. Your hair always did grow so fast."

"That's true," Lizzie said. "Anyway, it's just hair. I should remember that instead of complaining."

"Hey, Lizzie, you could wear your white espadrilles with the dress," Gayle suggested.

"The espadrilles will go great with the sundress," Holly agreed, dropping down on Lizzie's bed.

"You sound as excited as I do," Lizzie said, sitting down beside Holly. "Not! What's wrong, Holly?"

"Nothing, sweetie," Holly said, unable to look her cousin in the eye as she lied through her teeth.

Lizzie cupped Holly's chin and lifted her face. "Don't you 'nothing, sweetie' me, Holly-Molly. I've known you all my life and I know when something is wrong. Spill."

Holly flopped backward on the bed and stared up at the ceiling. "You're getting married tomorrow, and I couldn't be happier for you, Lizzie. But when you say 'I do,' I'll be saying good-bye, and I guess I'm not ready for that."

"Well, well," Gayle said with a smile. "Holly Morrow doesn't want to bid Troutville good-bye? I never thought I'd see the day!"

Holly and Lizzie laughed.

"Perhaps it's not so much Troutville she doesn't want to say good-bye to, but a particular Troutville resident."

"Residents," Holly corrected. "You two."

Lizzie wagged a finger. "Try again, Cousin. I'm talking about a certain tall, dark, handsome private investigator that you've been in love with your entire life."

Holly felt her cheeks warm. "I —" Oh, what was the use of trying to pretend she wasn't madly in love with Jake Boone when she was. Desperately, madly, happily in love.

"He hasn't exactly asked me to stick around," Holly said. "Once you and Dylan take off in your 'just married' car, it'll be time for me to go back home."

"You don't have to go home," Gayle said. "It's summer. You have the rest of the summer off from teaching school. Stay here!"

"But my life is somewhere else," Holly said. "I spent years building that life. I have friends there —"

That wasn't quite the truth. There was Miss Ellie and Herbert, who were more like family and would be with her always, no matter where she was, but she couldn't honestly say she had ever made any friends in Hoboken. She had some nice girlfriends at school, and enjoyed friendly conversations with neighbors, but she'd never made deep, long-lasting friendships like she had here in Troutville, the place she never wanted to step foot in again.

Flea aside, Gayle and Lizzie were her friends. True-blue friends who had stood the test of time, despite the distance. And there was Aunt Louise and Morrow's Pub, a place that had always felt like a second home to Holly.

And there was Jake. Jake Boone. With whom Holly was very much in love.

I'm home, a small voice whispered inside Holly. *But I can't stay. I can't stay and be so close to the man I love when he doesn't love me. When he doesn't want me in his life.*

Holly sighed. For so long, home hadn't been where her heart was. Her heart had been with Lizzie and Gayle and Aunt Louise and Jake, and even Flea, until very recently, but Holly had made a home elsewhere.

Isn't that odd, she thought. *My heart was in Troutville all these years. I didn't even realize it.*

"You know, Holly," Gayle said. "You could tell the man how you feel. Granted, telling my boss how I feel about him hasn't done me a lick of good, but hey, at least he knows how I feel."

"That's true," Lizzie said.

"But I know Jake doesn't feel the way I do," Holly said. "Why put myself through the misery of hearing him tell me that he's glad we became friends again, but that there's too much water under the bridge."

"Oh, Holly," Lizzie said. "That's just it — it's all water under the bridge. The past is the past and should be left there. What happened between you and Jake these past weeks happened *now.*"

"That still won't make Jake love me," Holly said, tears stinging her eyes.

"He does love you, Holly," Lizzie said. "I'd bet anything."

"I'm in, too," Gayle said.

Holly smiled. "Thanks, guys. But I think

I'd better pack my bags and prepare to go back to Hoboken before I end up with a broken heart."

Who am I kidding? Holly asked herself. *My heart is broken already.*

Lizzie gave Holly's shoulder a squeeze. "You really think I could get away with the sundress and my espadrilles?"

Holly nodded. "I think you'll be a beautiful bride in that outfit, Lizzie."

"You'd be beautiful in a potato sack and bunny slippers, and you know it, Lizzie Morrow."

"Lizzie Morrow Dunhill-to-be," Lizzie corrected with a wink.

"Yoo-hoo, Lizzie! Are you home?"

That was Mrs. Dunhill's voice. Lizzie shrugged at Holly and Gayle, then they all headed downstairs.

Mrs. Dunhill, Pru, and two women who looked a bit familiar flew in, laden with bags and packages and two step stools.

"Lizzie, dear," Mrs. Dunhill said, "direct us to your bedroom. You do have a full-length mirror, don't you? Preferably a three-sided one?"

Perplexed, Lizzie looked at Holly, then back at Mrs. Dunhill and her entourage. "Um, I have a full-length mirror in my room — upstairs."

"Fabulous," said Mrs. Dunhill. "All right, ladies, everyone upstairs."

"Mrs. Dunhill, I'm a little confused —" Lizzie began.

"Lizzie, dear, there's really no time for chitchat," Mrs. Dunhill said, ushering Lizzie toward the stairs. "If your gown is to be ready tomorrow by ten a.m., we really need to get you fitted immediately."

"My gown?"

"Hurry, hurry," Mrs. Dunhill scolded, shooing Lizzie forward. "Holly and Gayle, you two come on up in about five minutes."

Holly and Gayle couldn't wait five minutes. They waited two, then hurried up to Lizzie's room.

Lizzie stood on a step stool in front of her white wicker floor-length mirror wearing the wedding gown of her dreams, the dress she had seen in the window of Bettina's Bridal months ago, the dress that she had been about to try on when Flea had been hurt.

Correction: when Flea had hurt herself.

Tears rolled down Lizzie's cheeks. "It's my gown, guys. The gown of my dreams!"

"But how —" Gayle asked.

"Let's just say I had a little conversation with that pompous Tutweller," Mrs.

Dunhill said. "Come on, girls," she said to Holly and Gayle. "Your dresses are right over there. Ms. Tutweller sent along her seamstresses to fit you."

Inside the dress bags on the bed were the lovely pink silk dresses that she and Gayle and Flea had chosen.

As Mrs. Dunhill helped Lizzie affix her veil to her now short blond curls, Holly stared in the mirror at her cousin, her beautiful, sweet cousin. She had transformed into a bride, but she was Lizzie and always would be. And no one and nothing had ever been able to stop her from being Lizzie Morrow, even though quite a few people had tried.

You've taught me more than you'll ever know, sweet cousin, Holly thought before tears of joy overtook her.

Jake sat on a huge rock in Troutville Square, the little park between Down Hill and Up Hill, and the very setting for Dylan and Lizzie's wedding tomorrow. He leaned back, crossed his arms behind his head and stared up at the beautiful night sky, at the stars twinkling over Troutville.

How many nights had he sat in this very spot as a teenager, thinking about Holly, thinking about the division between Up

Hill and Down, the very division between him and the girl he loved. He would lean back on the rock as he was doing now, and think, try to figure out how to make Holly his when she had absolutely no interest in him. When leaving was the only thing on her mind.

Ten years later, how had he gotten himself in the same position? The woman he loved more than life itself would be leaving town tomorrow, leaving him.

Tell her how you feel.

Like last time?

Jake Boone is the last man on earth I'd marry.

Tell her how you feel, idiot.

From where he sat, he could see the top of the house where Holly had grown up. He could see the second-floor window of her bedroom and sometimes, he'd be able to make out her hazy figure walking past. So many nights he'd wait for Holly to turn off her light, and then he'd whisper, "Sweet dreams," into the air and be able to head on home himself.

Now, the house and the room and the light switch belonged to someone else.

Jake glanced over at Lizzie's house; he could just make out movements in her bedroom window, and if he wasn't mistaken, someone, probably Lizzie, was holding up a veil to her head.

He smiled. Lizzie had been through hell and back and had come shining through. They all had. Except for Flea.

Tell Holly how you feel, Jake ordered himself again. *Don't let her leave without saying the words.*

What words?

I love you, Holly. I love you with all my heart and always have.

But as he glanced up at Lizzie's window, at the figures he could just make out, he imagined a conversation.

Stay here in Troutville? Holly would be saying. *Marry Jake Boone? You must be kidding. I can't wait to get back to my life, my real life, far away from here. Far away from the last man I'd ever marry.*

Suddenly, the light went off in Lizzie's bedroom.

"Sweet dreams, Holly," Jake whispered into the night air. Then he got up and headed home.

Lizzie and Dylan's wedding day dawned warm and sunny. Mrs. Dunhill, who'd had to remind Lizzie seven times since yesterday to 'please call me Victoria, dear,' and Pru had come over at six a.m. to ask whether Lizzie preferred the pink or red roses to decorate the ceremony trellis, then set off for the Down Hill square where the wedding would take place so that they could boss around the fleet of volunteers who'd "signed up" in droves to help with the nuptials.

As Holly and Gayle helped Lizzie into her stunning gown, Holly realized that the dress, complete with puffs and high neck, was as much "Lizzie" as any of her clothes. Lizzie hadn't chosen the gown to fit in with the Dunhills; she'd chosen it because she'd fallen in love with it, just as she'd fallen in love with Dylan. Lizzie Morrow was her own woman and had been from the moment Holly met her, which was before they could even talk or walk.

"Oh, Lizzie," Holly breathed. "You look so beautiful!"

The three women promptly burst into tears.

"It's a good thing I haven't started my makeup yet," Gayle said, dabbing at her eyes. "I'd have racoon eyes, for sure."

"Not a good look for a wedding," Lizzie said. "I love you guys," she added. "So much. I might be getting married, but I'll always be your Lizzie."

"We know," Holly said, squeezing her hand.

For a few moments, Holly, Gayle and Lizzie just stared into the mirror at their reflections.

"Don't you dare make me cry again, Lizzie Morrow Dunhill-to-be," Gayle said. "Okay, that's it," she added, her eyes misting again. "I'm going into your bathroom to do my makeup. Though I'll probably start bawling in there anyway."

Holly and Lizzie laughed.

There was a knock at the front door downstairs. Lizzie headed out of the bedroom and called down, "Who is it, please?"

"It's your groom. Your chariot awaits, my bride."

Dylan had arranged for a horse and buggy to ferry them over to the square.

"Guess that's my cue," Lizzie said, hugging Holly one last time. "See you at the show!"

"I told you not to make me cry again!" Gayle called from behind the bathroom door.

And with her trademark beautiful, big smile, Lizzie dashed down the stairs.

As Holly and Gayle, in their pink dresses and strappy high-heeled sandals, crossed the square, Holly had to stop and gather a breath.

"Heels too high?" Gayle asked, concerned.

"No, it's not that," Holly said. "It's —" She pointed, literally unable to speak.

The center of the square had been turned into a fairy tale site for a wedding ceremony. At least two hundred chairs were set up on either side of an aisle strewn with pink rose petals, leading up to a trellis decorated with hundreds of pink roses and baby's breath. The surrounding trees were wrapped with sheer pink gauze paper, and everywhere people looked, there were flowers.

"I've never seen Down Hill quite so dressed up," Gayle said, smiling. "And speaking of dressed up, check out your man by the trellis."

Holly's cheeks pinkened. At the sight of Jake, standing under the flower-decked trellis next to Dylan and the minister, Holly almost lost her breath. She had never, ever seen him look quite that handsome.

Oh, Jake, she thought. *What I wouldn't give to be marrying you today.*

As Holly and Gayle crossed the square, another man headed over to greet them. "You look absolutely beautiful, Gayle," he said.

Gayle burst into a smile. "I didn't think you'd really come," she told the man.

"Greg, this is my dear friend, Holly. Greg is my boss," Gayle added, quite unnecessarily, from the look of pure love in her eyes.

"It's very nice to meet you," Holly said.

"You, as well," he replied.

Holly's heart was bursting with happiness for Gayle. The woman looked so happy, so dazzlingly happy, that Holly hoped this was the start of a new relationship for Greg and Gayle.

"You'll save me a dance at the reception, won't you?" he asked, and Holly could tell from his expression and tone that he had a thing for his receptionist. More than a thing.

"You've got them all," Gayle whispered, and he gently touched her cheek with his hand.

Holly slipped away to give them some privacy.

"Holly Morrow, just when I didn't think you could look more beautiful, you go and surprise me."

Jake.

Holly felt herself blush. "Thank you. And you're looking quite handsome yourself."

"Holly-girl, there you are!"

Holly whirled around. Standing not one

foot away from her were Miss Ellie and Herbert!

Holly rushed over to embrace her beloved neighbors. "I am so happy to see both of you!"

"We received a special invitation from the bride herself," Miss Ellie said. "She called us yesterday and said she'd heard all about us from a certain man in your life and that she would have invited us sooner but there'd been some wedding hoopla and for a while she wasn't sure if there'd even be a wedding. Sounds like quite the to-do!"

"Oh, it was," Holly said, blushing. "But everything's just fine now," she added, giving Jake's hand a squeeze. Oh, goodness, she thought. In her excitement and surprise at seeing Miss Ellie and Herbert, she completely forgot to introduce Jake!

"Holly has told me all about you two," Jake said with a wink. "I'm very pleased to meet you."

Miss Ellie grinned. "Oh, me too, dear." She winked back, and they all laughed. "Herbert, how about you dance me over to our seats. These heels are killing me!"

"You did practice —" Holly began.

"Just kidding!" Miss Ellie said, laughing. "I walked up and down the block in front of our houses. Herbert and I practiced our tango for this very occasion."

As Jake pointed out which side of the aisle was for the bride, Holly squeezed Miss Ellie into another hug, and the elderly woman whispered, "You come back to your old neighborhood and visit sometime, you hear? And bring that handsome man of yours with you."

Holly blinked back tears. As Herbert and Miss Ellie seemed to know way back when they escorted Holly to the train, Holly was going home to Troutville.

How she wished she *could* stay.

"You may now kiss your bride," the minister said, and Dylan dipped Lizzie for a Hollywood kiss to end all kisses.

Holly burst into tears of joy, and Jake handed her his handkerchief. "Thanks," she said. "Of course, I said I wasn't going to cry, and here I am."

Jake smiled. "Well, it's been quite an emotional time. I say you're owed a few tears."

Holly smiled back, and it was all she could do not to burst into a fresh round of tears again. But not tears of joy for Lizzie.

Tears of sorrow for her heart. Last night, she'd dreamed that she and Jake were getting married today. That it was the two of them standing before friends and family and saying "I do." Vowing to love, honor and cherish each other for all the days of their lives.

"All this lovey-dovey stuff is too much for me," said a voice behind Holly and Jake.

They turned around. Jimmy Morgan sat there in a suit and tie, his arm slung around his girlfriend, the girl of his dreams from school.

"For someone so lovey-dovey himself," the girl said, tapping Jimmy on the nose, "I'm surprised to hear you complaining!"

Jimmy blushed, defeating his attempt to appear cool, and Jake and Holly laughed and turned back around. Holly was so happy that everything had worked out between Jake and Dylan and Jimmy. The three men had spent several hours together reforming their friendship and offering Jimmy a new mentor role at the center. Jimmy had jumped at the chance.

Holly glanced around, spying Gayle and her boss staring into each other's eyes, Miss Ellie and Herbert indulging in yet another kiss, and Pru and Dan jumping in, hands entwined, to congratulate her brother and her new sister-in-law.

A bright future was in store for everyone. Holly had never felt so hopeful.

Tell him how you feel, Holly, she ordered herself. *Tell him.*

"Jake, do you know the big old yellow house at the end of this road?"

"The one right there?" Jake said, pointing to the storybook house with the white picket fence.

Holly nodded. "There was a 'for sale' sign posted yesterday. I took it as an omen."

Jake turned to her, eyebrow raised. "An omen for what?"

"That I was meant to buy it, meant to live in it. Between Up Hill and Down."

Jake took her hand. "You're sure?"

"I'm sure."

"I would like to live in a house like that," Jake said, smiling. "Between Up Hill and Down. With someone I love very much."

"Then perhaps you should live there, too," she said. "With me."

"I thought you'd never ask," he said.

"It took a long time, but you know what they say."

"You were worth ten years, Holly. You'd be worth a hundred, but thank God you didn't wait until we were both old and gray and unable to start a family of our own."

Tears came to her eyes and she blinked them back. "I love you, Jake."

"I love you, too, Holly. And if you'd marry me, I'd be the happiest man alive."

"Yes, yes, yes," she breathed. "Oh, Jake, yes!"

He leaned down to caress her lips with a kiss. "Sealed with a kiss."

She smiled. "Let's tell everyone tomorrow. I don't want to steal Lizzie's thunder."

"It'll be our secret for the night," Jake said. "And I know a great way to celebrate that secret."

She squeezed his hand.

He squeezed back, then reached inside his jacket pocket and took out a small manila envelope. "I did a little research last night. Just in case I needed some extra ammunition."

"For what?" Holly asked.

"For getting you to stay. To even consider staying. Here. Open it."

Holly pulled out several printouts from the Internet and some newspaper clippings, including several ads from the *Troutville Gazette*. "Eleventh grade English teacher needed at Troutville High," Holly read. "Twelfth grade English teacher needed at Riverton High. Eleventh grade teacher needed at Leesville High." Riverton and Leesville were neighboring towns.

Holly's heart moved in her chest and she thought she'd start crying all over again. "Oh, Jake."

"There's more," he said. "Keep reading."

She put the classified ads back in the envelope and read the clippings and Internet printouts. "Pastry chef wanted at family-style grill," Holly read. "Pastry chef courses at Troutville Community Center. Catering company seeks wedding cake baker. Become a Pastry Chef at Culler County's famous culinary institute. Pie contest at the Troutville Fair next Saturday — best pie wins two tickets to the Troutville Cinema."

"I've been in the mood for a movie," Jake said, winking. "Popcorn's on me."

"I've got to bake a winning pie first," she said, tears in her eyes.

"You'll win, Holly," he said. "I have no doubt."

"I've already won," she said.

He smiled and kissed her, a long, sweet kiss that she was sure she'd remember for the rest of her life.

"Ahem," said Gayle, laughing, in the row

behind her. "Isn't it the bride and groom who are supposed to be doing all the smooching?"

Holly couldn't suppress her laugh.

"Good thing I'd already planned to make an honest woman of you, smoocher," Jake whispered into Holly's ear.

"Jake Boone, I love you so much."

"I love you, too, Holly Morrow. I've loved you my entire life."

"Single gals, line up!" Lizzie shouted. "If you catch it, you're next!" She stood with her back to the crowd and threw her pink-and-white bouquet high in the air.

It landed in Holly's waiting hands. She locked gazes with Jake and grinned, certain that she would be the "next" bride in the crowd, and very soon.

EPILOGUE

Seven months later, a little miracle was born in Troutville. A baby girl, half Up Hill, half Down Hill, seven pounds, six ounces, a fuzzing of soft blond hair and slate blue eyes. Her parents, Lizzie and Dylan Dunhill, named her Dorothea Victoria after Lizzie's beloved grandmother and Dylan's mother. They called the baby Thea. Victoria Dunhill doted on her tiny granddaughter, spoiling her like crazy with frilly dresses that even Lizzie had to admit were adorable, if completely unwearable except for a few holidays. And Pru, with a modest engagement ring on her finger from her fiancé, Dan, had turned to complete mush the moment she laid eyes on her little niece. Lizzie's mom was so enamored with her new granddaughter that she'd hired a couple of extra waitresses at Morrow's Pub so that she could spend as much time with Thea as possible.

Six months after baby Thea was born, another little miracle joined the residents of Troutville. The eight pound, three ounce son of Holly and Jake Boone. They named the baby Jacob Jr.

Holly would never forget the look in Jake's eyes when he held his baby son, a carbon copy of himself, for the first time, just seconds after his birth.

Of course, the buzz had already started around Troutville. *Thea and Jake are going to marry,* everyone said. *Mark my words.*

The four parents rolled their eyes at the gossips, but couldn't help smiling.

Today, Lizzie and Holly were taking Thea and baby Jake for a walk around Down Hill, to show them the houses their mommies had grown up in.

"Look, Thea, there's Mommy's old house," Lizzie said, pointing to the yellow bungalow. "Now it's Mommy's photography studio."

Lizzie had transformed the downstairs of her house into the studio of her dreams, complete with darkrooms, Photoshop station, backdrops, lights — the works. She had decided to become a portrait photographer, and once people saw the photos she took of Thea and little Jake, they lined up with their children and pets for Lizzie's magic camera.

The upstairs had been converted into a nursery and playroom for Thea while Lizzie worked downstairs. Lizzie's mom offered to watch Thea whenever Lizzie wanted to work.

"And there's the shop that Mommy is going to buy for her bakery!" Holly told baby Jake, pointing to the old bakery that had been closed for over a year. The owner hadn't been able to find a buyer and had retired to Florida; he'd been thrilled when Holly had called to buy it.

Holly had decided to open her own bakery, her dream, and volunteer as a tutor at Troutville High for students needing help with English. She spent three days a week at the school, tutoring for three hours a day, and the schedule was perfect. She could help kids as she always wanted, and bake, having her own business. It was a dream come true.

"And there's where your mommy-to-be used to live before she finally convinced her stubborn boss to fall in love with her and marry her!" Gayle said, patting her rounded belly. She was five months pregnant and just starting to show.

Gayle and Greg had married in exactly the same square that Lizzie and Dylan, and Holly and Jake had married in.

Holly laughed. "Gayle, I think I'm having sympathy cravings. For a hot fudge sundae."

"Oooh, me too!" Lizzie said. "Oh, my back!" she mock-complained, rubbing an imaginary sore spot. "I need ice cream now!"

"Must. Have. Ice cream. Now," Gayle said, laughing.

"And what do you say we invite the daddies?" Lizzie suggested.

"Jake would never pass up an opportunity for a hot fudge sundae," Holly said. "How about you, little guy?" she added, bending down to trace a gentle finger down baby Jake's soft cheek. "Are you going to take after your daddy and be an ice-creamaholic?"

Holly would swear that at that exact moment, baby Jake smiled his first real smile.

ABOUT THE AUTHOR

JANELLE TAYLOR is an eight-time *New York Times* bestseller and multiple award-winning author of forty-six books and three novellas in many genres. Her contemporary and romantic suspense releases include *Anything for Love*, *In Too Deep*, *Night Moves* and *Don't Go Home*. Janelle resides in Georgia, and can be contacted via the Web site www.readersheart.com or by E-mail at readersheart@aol.com.

AUTHOR'S NOTE

If you would like to receive a current Janelle Taylor newsletter and list of all of her books, please send a self-addressed, stamped envelope (SASE) to the address listed below. A legal size/long envelope is needed for these materials. Or you can print them from the website, along with newsworthy updates.

Readers Heart
P.O. Box 285
Buford, GA 30515

To learn more about Janelle Taylor, her past works, future releases, and topics special to her, visit the Janelle Taylor website at: *www.readersheart.com*. It also contains a photo gallery. You can send her e-mail to readersheart@aol.com or to JnATaylor@aol.com.